WITH

WELCOME TO MY WORLD

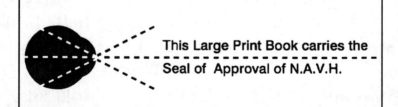

This Large Print Book carries the
Seal of Approval of N.A.V.H.

WELCOME TO MY WORLD

CURTIS BUNN

THORNDIKE PRESS
A part of Gale, a Cengage Company

Farmington Hills, Mich • San Francisco • New York • Waterville, Maine
Meriden, Conn • Mason, Ohio • Chicago

LIBRARY OF CONGRESS CIP DATA ON FILE.
CATALOGUING IN PUBLICATION FOR THIS BOOK
IS AVAILABLE FROM THE LIBRARY OF CONGRESS

ISBN-13: 978-1-4328-4606-0 (hardcover)
ISBN-10: 1-4328-4606-x (hardcover)

Published in 2018 by arrangement with Strebor Books, an imprint of Atria Books, a division of Simon & Schuster, Inc.

Printed in the United States of America
1 2 3 4 5 6 7 22 21 20 19 18

For America's homeless and depressed, hoping they are inspired to welcome into their worlds agents of change.

ACKNOWLEDGMENTS

God is real . . . and powerful . . . and ever-present. How else can I explain the blessings I have received all my life?

My blessings start with my family, including my late father, Edward Earl Bunn, Sr. and grandmother, Nettie Royster. I deeply miss them. I am blessed with my mother, Julia Bunn, the most caring and generous person I have ever known. My brothers, Billy and Eddie, and my sister, Tammy, have been blessings all my life.

Meanwhile, my children, Curtis Jr. and Gwendolyn (Bunny) exist as my inspiration. My chest protrudes with pride for who they are as people.

My wife, Felita, has been a blessing since the day we connected.

My nephew, Gordon, has always been like a second son who has grown into a fine young man. And my niece, Tamayah (Bink Bink), and nephew, Eddie Jr. are blessings that I love so much. My cousins, Greg Agnew and Warren Eggleston, are like my brothers. And I am grateful for my Uncle Al and aunts Thelma and Barbara and Ms. Brenda Brown, who has been like an aunt/ second mom much of my life, and cousin Carolyn Keener.

My extended family means the world to me: Blake Rascoe, Shirley and Larry Jordan, Ted and Cecilia Baker, Tony, Erika and Eric Sisco, Ashley and Darius and Billings, Avant Baker, Zoe, Channing, Rain and Bell Baker.

Again, Zane, Charmaine Roberts Parker and the entire Strebor Books/Atria/Simon & Schuster family have been great, and I am eternally grateful for you. I'm proud to be a part of the wonderful, talented Strebor family.

I enjoy listing by name the supporters because you all mean so much to me: My ace, Trevor Nigel Lawrence, Keith (Blind) and Delores Gibson, Kerry Muldrow, Randy and Flecia Brown, Sam and Maureen Myers, Ronnie and Tarita Bagley, Tony and Rae Starks, Darryl Washington, Darryl (DJ) Johnson, Wanda Newman-Johnson, Lyle Harris, Sheila and Dwight Wilson, Bob and LaDetra White, Monya Battle, Karen Turner, Star Rice, Tony (Kilroy) Hall, Marc

Davenport, Brad Corbin, Daphne Grissom, William Mitchell, J.B. Hill and Ericka Newsome-Hill, Clint Crawford, Earle Burke, Robert Diggs, Tony Hodge, Bob and La Detra White, Kent Davis, Wayne Ferguson, Tony & Erika Sisco, Betty Roby, Morechell and Bonita Pryer, Robin and Derrick Nottingham, Kathy Brown, Venus Chapman, Andre Johnson, Sheila Johnson Miller, Tara Ford, Kim Davis, Herman Atkins, Greg Willis, Al Whitney, Brian White, Ronnie Akers, Jacques Walden, Dennis Wade, Julian Jackson, Mark Webb, Kelvin Lloyd, Frank Nelson, Hayward Horton, Mark Bartlett, Marvin Burch, Derrick (Nick Lambert), Gerald Mason, Charles E. Johnson, Harry Sykes, Kim Mosley, Steve Nottingham, Rev. Hank Davis, Joi Edwards, Stacy Harden, Monica Cooper, Tim and Melanie Lewis, Linda Vestal, Christine Beatty, Ed (Bat) Lewis, Shelia Harrison, David A. Brown, Leslie LeGrande, Rev. Hank Davis, Shirley Mitchell Farrell, Kevin and Hope Jones, Susan Davis-Wigenton, Donna Richardson, Curtis West, Bruce Lee, Val Guilford, Natalie Crawford, Denise Brown Henderson, Nikki Adams, Cathy Migonet, Sherri Polite, Derek T. Dingle, Ramona Palmer, Melzetta Oliver, April Kidd, Warren Jones, Deberah (Sparkle) Williams,

9

Leon H. Carter, Zack Withers, Kevin Davis, Sybil & Leroy Savage, Avis Easley, Demetress Graves, Anna Burch, Najah Aziz, George Hughes, Monica Harris Wade, Nikita Germaine, Mary Knatt, Serena Harris Knight, Denise Taylor, Dian Rhodes-Williams, Diana Joseph, Derrick (Tinee) Muldrow, Rick Eley, Marty McNeal, D.L. Cummings, Rob Parker, Cliff Brown, D. Orlando Ledbetter, Garry Howard, Stephen A. Smith, Clifford Benton, Kevin Rodgers, Leonard Burnett, Lesley Hanesworth, Billy Robinson, Sherline Tavenier, Jeri Byrom, Hadley Evans, Angela Tuck, E. Franklin Dudley, Skip Grimes, Carla Griffin, Jeff Stevenson, Angela Davis, Ralph Howard, Paul Spencer, Jai Wilson, Garry Raines, Glen Robinson, Dwayne Gray, Jessica Ferguson, Carolyn Glover, David R. Squires, Kim Royster, Keela Starr, Mike Dean, Veda McNeal, Dexter Santos, John Hughes, Mark Lassiter, Tony Carter, Kimberly Frelow, Michele Ship, Michelle Lemon, Zane, Tammy Thompson, Karen Shepherd, Barbara Hopkins, Carmen Carter, Erin Sherrod, Carrie Sherrod, Tawana Turner-Green, Sheryl Williams-Jones, Danny Anderson, Keisha Hutchinson, Olivia Alston, John Hollis, Dorothy (Dot) Harrell, Aggie Nteta, Ursula Renee, Carrie Haley, Anita Wilson,

10

Tim Lewis, Sandra Velazquez, Angelle Owens, Patricia Hale, Pam Cooper, Regina Troy, Denise Thomas, Andre Aldridge, Brenda Charlie O'Bryant, Pargeet Wright, Laurie Hunt, Mike Christian, Sid Tutani, Barry Roosevelt, Tammy Grier, Roland Louis, April Tarver, Penny Payne, Cynthia Fields, Patricia Hale, LaToya Tokley, Dr. Yvonne Sanders-Butler, Anna Coleman, Alicia Guice, Alicia Walton, Clara LeRoy, Denise Bethea, Hadjii Hand, Kaira Akita, Petey Franklin, Shauna Tisdale and The Osagyefuo Amoatia Ofori Panin, King of Akyem Abuakwa Eastern Region of Ghana, West Africa.

Special thanks and love to my great alma mater, Norfolk State University (Class of 1983); the brothers of Alpha Phi Alpha (especially the Notorious E Pi of Norfolk State) and Omicron Phi Lambda of south Atlanta; Ballou High School (especially the Class of '79), ALL of Washington, D.C., especially Southeast.

I am also grateful to all the readers and book clubs that have supported my work and the National Book Club Conference over the years and to my literary many friends Nick Chiles, Denene Millner, Nathan McCall, Carol Mackey, Linda Duggins, Terrie Williams, Kimberla Lawson

11

Roby, Walter Mosley, Eric Jerome Dickey, Caesar Mason and Marcus Johnson.

I'm sure I left off some names; I ask your forgiveness. If you know me, you know it is an error of the head and perhaps aging, not the heart. J I appreciate and I am grateful for you.

Peace and blessings,
CURTIS

More than a half-million people in America are homeless, according to the Department of Housing and Urban Development. Cities like Los Angeles, Seattle, Portland and others have declared a state of emergency over homelessness.

The causes, besides not enough affordable housing in the U.S., are plenty: untreated mental illness, post-traumatic stress disorder, depression, and physical disabilities, to name a few.

Meanwhile, depression is a "silent killer" in the African-American community, mental health advocate Terrie Williams wrote in her best-selling book, *Black Pain: It Just Looks Like We're Not Hurting.* And that is true, the book points out, because too often the troubled do not seek help.

CHAPTER ONE:
ME
BRENDA

I used to think the world owed me something, you know? I mean, *seriously.* If there really was something to that karma thing, then something good was due to come my way. And I was not talking about money. And I *damn* sure was not talking about a man. I could have used both — I wasn't stupid — but for the first time in my life, I realized neither of them could have saved me.

I had been in a place of . . . dissatisfaction and discontent and . . . displeasure. Very little pleased me. I received satisfaction in . . . well, very little. Except eating. I ate because my heart was discontent, and had been that way for far too long.

Worst of all, I never saw that for myself. As a kid, I was fun and lively and laughed all the time and made people laugh. My sister often used to say, "Brenda, you're so silly" in her high-pitched voice that I used to believe could break glass if she tried.

Last time I remembered her saying *anything* was several months ago. It was the last time I saw my dear big sister Theresa awake and able. We were at a cookout at Stone Mountain Park outside of Atlanta with family and friends celebrating her son's graduation from college. My nephew, Donnie, was a disappointment. A small, young man with small dreams, as it sadly turned out.

Anyway, Theresa was carrying a cake from the car to the area we had sectioned off near the foot of the mountain. The go-go music — that's a Washington, D.C. thing, where I'm from — played from somebody's device. She bobbed her head to the beat, and I came up from behind her and tickled her.

She dropped the cake — and I burst into laughter as it splattered onto the grass. Theresa couldn't be mad. Doing something like that brought us back to our youth, which, truth be told, was the best time of our lives.

Not too long after that, her son was busted for conspiracy to commit murder of his girlfriend's husband. Yes, that's what I said. Broke Theresa's heart. She'd put so much into this kid — the best schools, ultimate devotion, relentless love. Seeing him in jail took something out of her. She wasn't the same. And I believe that's what caused the

16

stroke she suffered a little while later that rendered her lifeless in the hospital.

I visited her on most days. But I wondered if I should continue going. I couldn't bring her any cheer. I didn't have anything inspiring to talk about because nothing good was happening in my life. But I went and I talked about our upbringing in Southeast D.C. We were a family then, kids who only cared about the next opportunity to play.

It was sad, though, to reminisce about those times when I was living in a personal dungeon. It was dark inside me, empty. I needed something to brighten my life, to feed me the nourishment that I knew came with a fulfilling life.

I tried the church. Couldn't go wrong with the church, right? Well, at my church, the pastor was caught dating women *and* men. I had never put my faith in man, but, boy, did that turn me away from church. And it disappointed me so much because if so-called anointed men of God couldn't do right, what chance did the rest of us have?

It added to my broken spirit and helped accelerate my descent into this emotional abyss. I liked words, and sometimes I would humor myself — if you can call it that — with literary flights of fancy like "descent

17

into this emotional abyss." It was sad that it became a way for me to generate fun in my life.

Besides my sister falling into a coma, my nephew getting arrested and my pastor cheating with *both* sexes . . . my best and only *real* friend took a job in London, my job of sixteen years laid me off, I gained so much weight that I did not resemble the "super fine" Brenda of my younger days . . . *and* my husband left me.

Stacked on top of one another, with all that occurring over about eighteen months, and it was an avalanche of a mess.

And then it happened. I met the most unlikely life-changing people. I stopped at McDonald's on Ponce de Leon Avenue, near downtown Atlanta. I stopped there almost every day on my way to work and on my way home to pick up one miserable thing or another — it was sort of my meal after breakfast and before dinner. That's how I gained weight; I tried to feed my depression.

For some reason, though, today the homeless man who always asked me for money accepted my counteroffer of a sandwich. He never had in the past. He'd just look at me. So, I almost didn't hear him when he said, "Quarter Pounder with Cheese."

Made me feel good when I delivered it to him. I waited for him to say "thank you." He didn't.

"Do something different," he said.

"I beg your pardon."

"Your life is shit," he went on.

"Excuse me," I said, stunned.

"The doctors say I'm bipolar, have some other paranoia disassociation something or other . . . and they might be right," the man said. "But I ain't crazy. I'd have to be crazy to look at you go in there and eat that garbage every single day and not know your life is shit."

I was so . . . so . . . shocked and appalled that I couldn't even move, much less respond.

"I'm not trying to be mean," he added. "I'm just trying to make a point so you won't leave here and say, 'That bum didn't know what he was talking about.' You don't ever blush. I saw a man tell you that you looked nice and you didn't even blush.

"Don't you know that blushing is healthy?"

I didn't know what the hell he was talking about.

"You mean smiling?" I asked. "*Smiling* is healthy?"

"Did I say 'smiling'?" the man snapped.

19

"I'm talking about blushing. When you blush, that means you care about what others think of you. And when you care about what others think of you, you believe you matter. And if you believe you matter, then you feel like you're alive . . . You don't think you matter. That's why you don't blush. And that means you don't feel alive. And if you don't feel alive, then your life is shit."

I was shaken by his words. I was shaken because he was right — I didn't feel like I mattered. I didn't feel anything about myself. But he made me think. This bipolar, homeless man saw something in me that I didn't see in myself, couldn't see in myself . . . didn't want to see in myself. Processing it made me believe I was wrong. The world didn't owe me anything. I owed it to myself to save myself. I wanted to leave my personal dungeon. I wanted to matter. I wanted to blush.

But I didn't see a need to stay there and debate with a homeless man, so we stared at each other for a few seconds before I walked off. On the way to the car, I decided I would dismiss what he had said to me. He didn't know me. He'd only seen me. Why should what he said matter anyway?

I pulled out my two cheeseburgers and ate them as I drove down Ponce to my downtown Decatur apartment, pausing only to sip on my vanilla shake. I turned on the radio, but was disgusted as some conservative talk show host spewed lies and venom about how the Obama administration ruined the country. I quickly turned and found some nonsensical rap music that was silly but distracting.

Finally, I turned off the radio and focused on my food. I was done before I was halfway home. And as much as I tried to ignore that homeless man, his words stayed with me.

As I prepared dinner — fried pork chops, rice and corn — the image of him and the sharpness of his words resounded in my head. I was stumped as to why his words seemed to matter so much.

But my mom used to say, "A hit dog will holla," meaning if something was true, it would impact you.

I woofed down my dinner and watched a little CNN. Nothing interested me, so I crawled into bed and I lay on my back in total darkness wondering about this man. Who was he? How did he end up on the streets? Why did what he said about me matter? It was true, but so what? He was the least significant person I had encountered.

And yet, I was curious about him. I could

not shake him from my mind. Worse, I was not sure how I could face him, what I would say, what I wouldn't say, if I would say anything at all . . . if I saw him again.

But I wanted that moment to happen. I needed to tell him about himself and about me, and maybe I could get some sleep.

My mother was once so mad at me that she told me, "Shut up and don't call me until you get your attitude together."

That really bothered me. But I slept with no problems. And yet after this stranger insulted me, I had to turn on the light and pull out a book to read myself to sleep — all because of the harsh words of some bum I didn't know?

The reading worked. After about forty minutes, the words began to run together and I got drowsy. My last thoughts before I fell asleep were about that man and how I knew I had to say something to him in the morning.

CHAPTER TWO:
THE STREETS
RODNEY

The world didn't owe me anything. If karma really was karma, I'd be dead. Instead, I was living on the streets, afraid to die and not deserving to live.

That lady looked at me with an expression I couldn't figure out. It was like I insulted her, hurt her feelings and made her angry at the same time. I wasn't trying for any of that. I was just telling her the truth. People don't like the truth.

You lived on the streets long enough, you learned people. I knew who was going to give me money before I asked. I knew based on their body language, how they walked, how they made or didn't make eye contact.

I didn't think people who said no or ignored me were mean or uncaring people. Most just didn't like the homeless. They'd rather not be bothered. They thought we're the scum of the earth. They thought we were lazy. They thought we were crazy. They thought we had wasted our lives. They thought if we could ask for money, then we could ask for a job. They thought we were filthy and didn't want to be close to us. They thought we stunk, that we smelled of the streets, and they didn't want their noses insulted.

They thought we were dumb or ill or both. They thought we had given up on life and had no purpose. They thought we were a waste of taxpayers' dollars. They thought we thought we were owed something.

They were right.

And they were wrong.

There was no simple answer to the homeless issue in America. In my nearly two years living on the streets, I had met peers who fit all those impressions people had of us. And I had met peers who fit none of them.

Me? I was an example of life flipping upside down so hard that right-side-up made no sense. I earned a bachelor's degree in English and an MBA. I had seen the inside of the Sistine Chapel, enjoyed plays on Broadway, frequented the High and Fernbank Museums, shopped on Rodeo Drive, parasailed in Barbados, swam with stingrays in the Cayman Islands, danced salsa in Cuba — *before* President Obama lifted the embargo.

And I had slept on the ground beneath the skyscrapers of Atlanta and the steps of churches.

How could I have experienced so much, but had so little? That was the thing that people didn't get: I had everything I experienced, which means I had more than most. I just didn't need more of anything. I'd had enough.

I didn't deserve anything else.

I asked people for money, so I could buy enough to live. I asked that lady almost every day for months, and she always answered with this idea that she'd be doing me a favor to buy me food. Fast-food restaurants were the death of healthy lifestyles, so I always refused her offers for food instead of money by just looking at her.

This time, though, I was so hungry that I had to take her up on her offer. I hadn't eaten fast-food in four years. Still, the memory of the taste of a Quarter Pounder with Cheese was strong — and I gave in to my hunger.

Others offered me food, but I considered them just token gestures. I didn't feel any warmth from them. You would think a guy who had nothing would not care where something came from. And most of my . . . my peers, my street comrades, didn't care.

But I did. I needed to feel good about the people who help me.

It was a personality quirk, one of the few parts of my being that I retained over the years. I appreciated the lady because I could see she was troubled. Her life was a routine. Get into a routine and it was an easy indicator of someone lacking in self-esteem and living a boring life.

But also I could see the compassion in her eyes as easily as I could see emptiness in her life.

"How do you think you could say something like that to me? *You?* Where do you get off?"

The lady was more transparent than I ever had been. When I was troubled — which was every day, all day — it did not show in my face or words. Well, not often. But when she said that to me, it was clear I had upset her.

"I know I live on the streets," I told her, "but that doesn't mean I can't see. And it doesn't mean I won't speak up. You don't have to listen. But I'm gonna speak when I want."

"But I've seen you almost every day for months. I have always been nice to you, offering you food. But when you finally say something to me, you curse at me? You're mean to me? I don't get it and I don't like it."

"It wasn't for you to like, but it was for you to get," I told her. "And you will."

She walked away shaking her head. I knew she wanted an apology, but I hadn't been big on apologies because if you had to give one, that meant you'd already done something wrong, and nothing could take away what you'd already done. An apology was just bullshit.

I decided that *if* I saw her again, I would tell her that. If I saw her again. I also hung near the Starbucks in Midtown, near Georgia Tech or the Waffle House downtown by Georgia State University or the Popeyes in the West End, near Morehouse College. The main reason I went there was because I liked to see the kids working on making something of themselves in a world that was against them. They were young and enthusiastic and eager. Their enthusiasm about the future kept me from going insane. Well, *totally* insane.

You'd have to be insane to sleep in shelters or on the streets, right? That's what most people thought. I would say the majority of the homeless suffered from some sort of mental illness. Another percentage had their lives collapse, fell on bad times, and had no other recourse. And then there was me.

I saw many others, too, who were drunks or drug addicts. But I was one of a few whose life collapsing brought out other issues. It was hard for me to call myself "mentally disturbed" because I didn't feel that way . . . most of the time.

My thoughts were clear. I looked at those students and engaged them because they reminded me of a better time in my life, when I was in college and looking at the world as a place of potential. But as excited as I was for these young students, I was just as scared for them. The world was not fair. Obstacles were everywhere. I read the paper. Sometimes. Racism was alive and thriving. It was going to hurt so many of these kids who wouldn't be ready for it. I hoped they would be tough enough to survive it. Tougher than me.

Not only that, but they would learn that things happened, horrible things, that prevented sleep, things that made could make life unbearable. I knew.

If I were not such a coward, I would have killed myself. But I didn't have the guts, if that's what it took to end my life. Or I was not crazy enough. Either way, the reality was that suicide would have been too good for me. I deserved to suffer.

The doctors said the fact that I took that position proved that I had mental problems. When I told them I wanted to punish myself they said I was crazy. Not in those words; they had more tact than that. But I could read between the mumbo jumbo. But I wasn't crazy. I was sick — sick of the nightmares, sick of the daydreams, sick of the pain, sick of feeling worthless and sick of a life of filth.

But I didn't have the strength and courage — the *whatever* it took — to get off the streets and to check out of the shelter and to resume the life I had that seemed like a long time ago.

Time passed slower when you live on the streets. A day was interminable. A night was longer than a day. I used to complain that there was not enough time in twenty-four hours to do all that needed to be done. That was before my life flipped.

That was before I killed my family. After that, time slowed down.

Chapter Three:
My Name Is . . .
Brenda

I didn't understand why I primped in the mirror or why I picked out my best suit or why I spent so much time on my hair. I was going to see a homeless man. Why did I feel a need to look my best for *him*?

I had no answers. For some reason, I felt compelled to impress him. I had guessed I didn't want to look like my life was shit, as he had so eloquently put it.

The closer I got to McDonald's, the more anxious I felt. I hadn't expected that. I was glad there was traffic on Ponce. It gave me more time to compose myself.

But the traffic eased and there he was — in the same spot, wearing the same clothes with the same attitude. I stopped myself before I checked my lipstick. But I was nervous. *He* was the one who should have been nervous. *I* was the one who was insulted and I was going to let him have it.

But our encounter was nothing like I expected.

I drove to work afterward feeling like I needed to see him again. Not romantically. *God, no.* But I felt something inside him that was interesting and, strangely enough, alive. But it was buried deep.

He was smart. When I walked up to him, kind of passively, he said, "Good morning, young lady."

I had forgotten how his voice sounded; it was strong and confident, surprisingly so. He took away the power I thought I had in the way he said those four words. It was so pleasant, as if we were old friends. But he didn't take away my sarcasm.

"You're speaking to me today like you have some sense?" I said.

"You think I spoke to you like I didn't have any sense yesterday? I have plenty of sense."

"That doesn't mean you say anything to someone, especially someone like me, who has tried to help you."

"Oh, you're special?"

"Everyone's special. That's how we should look at people. I have always been nice to you."

"You think it's being nice to assume I'm a drug addict or an alcoholic. That's the only

31

reason you don't give me a dollar and keep it moving."

He was right . . . again. I had no idea what was up with the homeless. I figured drugs and alcohol had to be a major part of the problem. I could never drink enough or do enough drugs to not want to sleep in my own bed. But I figured something significant, something bad, had to have happened, starting with drinking or drugs, to end up on the streets.

But once he said that, I recalled that he always seemed clear in his thoughts. His eyes were never bloodshot and he never had the physical traits of someone who was addicted. And I thought maybe it was reasonable for him to think I should at least try to understand his frustration without stereotyping him.

Then the other side of my brain said: *Stop trippin'. He's homeless, for goodness sake. What else were you to think?*

"You're an interesting man," I said. I noticed people looking at me with strange expressions, looks that translated into: *Why is she talking to this bum?*

I ignored them.

"I didn't give you money because I thought you needed food. Yeah, it may be fast-food, but it's food. I wasn't trying to insult you."

What was I saying? *He* insulted *me*. And there I was offering him a quasi-apology?

"I wasn't trying to insult you, when I said your life was shit."

"Oh, you remember that?"

"I told you I ain't crazy. And it ain't so much going on in my life that I forgot what I said yesterday."

"You're a wise ass, I see."

"I speak truth. Period. I have no reason to not be straight-up honest. For instance, you're depressed."

"How can you say that?"

"OK. Name the things that you love."

"I love my sister, food and movies, reading, traveling. I love good wine. Why?"

"See that. Asked you to name things you loved and you never said yourself."

He got me. I actually was not that happy with myself at that point. I ignored his valid point.

"Well, I'll be honest when I say I was really bothered by what you said to me. I didn't sleep well thinking about it. You don't know me. You don't know what's going on in my life. And because you don't, you shouldn't speak on it. Especially being nasty like that."

"I spoke the truth. If it's not true, why

does it bother you?"

"It bothers me because you don't have a right and you shouldn't feel comfortable saying something so mean to someone — especially someone who has only been nice to you."

"You're going to be late for work."

"There you go, assuming. Who said I was going to work today?"

"Your shoes say it. Your suit says it. Why else would you be here? You come here every day at the same time, morning and evening. I could set my watch to you . . . if I had one."

It was exhausting talking to him. He was a classic oxymoron: a keen homeless man.

"What's your name?"

"Why? You're not going to remember it tomorrow."

"Why do you think you know what I'm going to do? What's your name?"

"Rodney."

"I'm Brenda, Rodney. Brenda Lowry. And you're wrong: I won't forget your name."

"Rodney Bridges. I was once called R.B. It meant more than my name. It also meant 'Rhythm and Blues' because I loved music and was a smooth dancer."

"Don't you still love music? Why would you say, 'loved'?"

"I haven't really heard or focused on music in two years. It is what it is."

"Don't you miss it? Don't you want to dance and tap your feet and party and have a good time?"

"A good time? I'm not in the market for that. I'm good."

"You're a good dancer? I can't see it."

"That's not very astute. You can't see anything in me — I'm homeless, living on the streets most nights, asking strangers like you for money."

"But why?"

"What's the question?"

"Why is this your life? You obviously have a lot of common sense and intelligence."

"This could all be an act. You don't know."

"Exactly. And you don't know what's going on in my life. So please don't talk about it. My life is none of your business."

Then I turned as he pondered or didn't ponder that and went inside the restaurant and ordered hot cakes and sausage. Because I had talked to the man longer than I expected and wanted, I was running behind time.

When I exited McDonald's, he was still there, in the same area, but talking to a second homeless man.

"That's her," he said to the guy as I moved

from the threshold of the restaurant toward the car.

I stopped in my tracks. "Why are you talking about me?"

"This is Chester. I was telling him about how nice you are, that's all."

Chester was light-skinned and thin. He was solemn and withdrawn, far less loquacious than Rodney.

"Hi, Chester."

He waved a hand and lowered his head. He mumbled something about space missions being fake. I turned to Rodney.

"Is he OK?"

"No. But he will be. Or he won't. I don't know. He has lots of issues. And drinking is one of them. Still, he's a good man. Strong man."

"Where are your other friends, friends who could help you?"

"Who said I needed help? I'm fine. Friends I had are gone. It's just me now."

"Are you going to answer my question?"

"Just did."

"About why you're out here."

"Why you want to know? You don't care about me."

"Well, maybe I want to care about you."

"Why would you want to care about a homeless man?"

"Because I care about people."

Rodney looked at me intently, as if he were trying to see into my psyche or my heart. Or both.

"You'd better get to work."

I glanced at my watch. I was behind schedule. But I wanted an apology.

"If I say 'I'm sorry,' it does not get you the sleep back that you said you missed last night. And it doesn't take away from the truth."

I shook my head.

"I'll see you this evening. Right?" he said. The way it came out, though, was if he *wanted* to see me. At least that was the way I took it.

"God willing," I told him, turning and heading for my car.

I wanted to know more about Rodney. Unless he was a great actor, he had the brains to be a productive citizen. If nothing else, he could provide for himself.

I went through the rest of the day on the temp job I had as an executive secretary at a law firm in the Bank of America building in somewhat of a fog. I became virtually obsessed with learning Rodney's story.

Instead of going to lunch, I stayed at my desk and did searches on homelessness in America. For me to miss a meal, that was rare — or more like unheard of. But I was engrossed in this subject. I found a website called makethemvisible.com. It showed videos of people and families posing as homeless — and how the public reacted to them. They either did not notice them or they were so used to seeing homeless people that they deftly ignored them.

I sat there at my computer and tears flowed from my eyes. It hurt me to see how cold people could be to another human. It hurt so much because I saw myself. I was like those people who walked by without batting an eye. I pretended I was busy. I went so far as to act as if I were on my cell phone when I saw a homeless person approaching to feign being occupied.

I offered Rodney food because we were in an open area where others were always around. I did not feel threatened. But in other cases, times I felt vulnerable, I walked right on by, as if I didn't see them.

After browsing that website, I was embarrassed. I was ashamed of myself.

"Are you OK?" Mr. Washington asked. He was one of the partners in the firm.

"Yes, sir. I was just watching something on the Internet and it upset me."

"Really? What is it?"

I wasn't sure if I should share with my

boss something so personal, but it was a temporary job and I needed to explain why I was bawling.

"I met this homeless man; I see him every day. Today, we talked for the first time and he's so smart. So I looked up this website about the homeless and it showed how most of us walk past them without noticing — or we act like we don't see them. And I've been guilty of that a lot, and it just made me feel bad."

"Well, it's a tough thing, Brenda. I've done it, too. I have given and I have ignored, and after each case, I didn't feel good. Even when I have given, I wanted to give more. When I didn't give, I felt guilty about it. It's an issue bigger than us."

"But we've got to find a way to help. It makes no sense that people are living on the streets. In America? With all its boasting of 'life, liberty and the pursuit of happiness.' It should not be like this, Mr. Washington."

"It's a problem around the world," he said. "We were in Rome — my wife and I — last summer and little old ladies who looked so much like a grandmother or your favorite aunt, hounded you for money at certain tourist spots. My wife said, 'I thought I got away from this by coming to Italy.' I told her: 'Honey, it's a problem here, but worse in the U.S., which is sad because of who we're supposed to be.' "

Before I could say something, he was called away, which was fine because he didn't have the words to comfort me anyway. Nothing would — unless I did something. And in that moment, Rodney Bridges became my project.

CHAPTER FOUR:
PARAGON OF PARANOIA
RODNEY

I was glad to see the lady, Brenda. I figured she had a basic name, a traditional name. Her name matched her personality. But she also carried herself like she was carrying the weight of something buried deep inside. It was subtle, but in the few years I was on the streets, I had watched people more than I had in all my life.

I was six months from turning forty-six. For my forty-third birthday, my wife, Darlene, insisted on throwing me a small birthday party. We didn't celebrate my fortieth because she had bronchitis and I spent the week tending to her. She felt bad about that, but I didn't care about a party over her health. She was that type of person, though — always putting herself second.

So she threw me the party at the Live Edge Restaurant in Southwest Atlanta. It was a wonderful night of enjoying friends. I remembered so clearly Darlene, saying,

"Your life is just beginning, baby. The whole world is in front of you."

It was one of the best evenings of my life. I believed her. It all seemed so in front of me. We had two daughters: Diana was seventeen and Joy was fifteen at the time. We had been married since we were twenty-two. We battled through the shit that comes with marriage, especially when you say "I do" so young. But we stuck it out and made a great family. A *great* family . . .

Long before that party, I started feeling different and seeing things and people differently. Strangely. It was like this other world popped up — or this other way to look at the world — and no one could see or understand it but me.

With all I had in my life, I became unhappy. And because I wasn't happy, I became depressed, meaning every so often, I wasn't the most pleasant person to be around. I didn't trust anyone. I didn't know why. Somehow, the kids were kept unaware of my issues. But my wife took it all.

At times, nothing she did or said was good enough. Once she made my favorite: baked salmon with this lemon butter sauce, Brussels sprouts and these mashed potatoes that she mashed herself. Halfway through the meal, I picked up the plate and slammed it on the floor.

I told her: "There's poison in that food. I can smell it. You're trying to kill me." Then I calmly came over to her and put my hands around her throat. I choked as I screamed: "Who are you? Are you a spy? Are you a plant? Who sent you?"

Tears streamed down her face and onto my hands. Something inside me made me stop before I choked her to death. I let her go and she gasped for air. And when she caught her breath, she ran upstairs into our bedroom and locked the door.

I crumbled to the floor and cried. I had lost control of who I was, and I realized it.

An hour or so later, Darlene came downstairs to find me on the floor, weeping. She came over and put her arms around me. "Honey, baby, we have to get you help. You have to find out what's going on with you."

I nodded my head. I felt like a child in my wife's arms. Her words and love comforted me.

"I'm . . . I'm sorry," I managed to get out.

Darlene hugged me tighter. "I know you are, baby. I know."

At the doctor's office, a psychiatrist named Dr. Kaminski saw me. I was nervous but aware that I needed his help. He was a patient man. Guess he had to be in his line of work.

"Mr. Bridges," he said, "you have what we call a paranoid personality disorder. You've heard of bipolar disorder, I'm sure. This is a version of it. It's among a group of conditions we call 'Cluster A,' which are about, let's say, eccentric ways of thinking. Part of what comes with PPD is paranoia, a strong distrust of people, a strong suspicion of people — although there is no reason for that suspicion."

I wasn't sure what to think. Was he trippin'? Was he really talking about me? Did he just call me crazy?

"You calling me crazy?" I asked. I had hostility and fear in my voice.

"No, sir. Not at all. PPD is very common, and it's common in men more than women, and it reveals itself generally in adulthood. We don't know why it happens, but research on several fronts indicates it could be something from a traumatic childhood experience that festers and is triggered later in life."

My wife was teary-eyed. "How do we treat this, doctor?"

"Mrs. Bridges, that's the good news. Treatment for PPD can be very successful. A lot will depend on your husband, however. I must say that most individuals with this condition have issues accepting treatment. You see, someone with PPD often does not see or believe his symptoms. If an individual is willing to accept treatment, which includes medication and psychotherapy, it makes success much easier."

I sat there as if I was not in the room. It made no sense to me. I'M CRAZY? That's all I could think.

"What will the therapy do?" my wife asked.

"It will help your husband learn how to accept the disorder and cope with it so he learns how to exist in social situations. It will minimize the feelings of paranoia that you've discussed, Mr. Bridges. Now, there also are medications that can serve as part of his treatment."

"Like what?" Darlene wanted to know.

"Antidepressants, antipsychotics, benzodiazepines. And when you combine the medication with the therapy, you can really see strong results."

As I sat there listening to all that talk about me, I remembered seeing Mike Tyson sit on the couch as Robin Givens told Barbara Walters and the television world that he was a "monster" and that living with him was "hell."

That thought made me cry. Dr. Kaminski

asked what was wrong. "I don't want my wife to be Robin Givens."

"Who?" Darlene asked.

"The actress who was married to Mike Tyson," the doctor said.

She remembered. "Oh, honey, no. No. I love you. You're going to be fine. We're going to be fine."

"The fact that you care how your wife feels is significant, Mr. Bridges. You love her and you're able to express that. That's very encouraging."

It wasn't encouraging to me. That was normal. I left there feeling like something was seriously wrong with me — and it was. But I also was determined to not let it rule my life. I was going to go to counseling and take the meds and do whatever it took to feel like myself again and not have my wife scared of me.

I repeatedly apologized for strangling her. She said she forgave me, but I didn't think she ever looked at me the same. That's what I meant when I said apologizing doesn't matter — the damage had already been done. There would be no reversing it.

Later, I told my therapist, Dr. Hindsman, that and she said: "Could it be that you haven't forgiven yourself? That could lead to all kinds of thoughts you *think* Darlene is having. If you've forgiven yourself and she said she's forgiven you, then you have to accept that. Also accept that she's still there with you. Don't you think she would have gone if she was afraid of you?"

"Is this the paranoid part of what's going on with me?"

"Exactly. All any of us can do is accept what people say at face value — especially someone we're as close to as you and your wife are. You know her. You should know or have a real instinct about what she's expressing to you."

The doctor made sense. And after about four months of therapy and taking Citalopram, an antidepressant that heightened energy and good feelings, I felt like myself and my life was back on track.

A few years later, we had a great summer with our daughters, who were looking ahead to college. We went to the Cayman Islands and laughed and enjoyed each other so much. My wife and I had agreed to not tell Diana and Joy about my condition. We believed it would serve no good purpose to have them worrying while they should have been focusing on their studies.

Besides, we had found the solution to the problem. I didn't want them looking at me differently and neither did Darlene. So I took my medication when they weren't around and we had our best family vacation — swimming in the Atlantic, dining at Camana Bay and swimming with the stingrays.

I cried one night when Darlene was asleep. They were tears of relief. When I got the diagnosis, I put up a brave front, but inside I was terrified. My family meant everything. I would never put my hands on my wife. But I had choked her and therefore put my family at risk. I was lucky Darlene loved me and knew that was not me — not the *real* me. It was a version of me that came from some disturbed place.

So, our last night, as she slept, I put one hand on her hip and cried. Despite my "condition," I felt super lucky because my wife did not leave me. She stayed and fought for her family. Fought for me. I felt like I had a new life, and that vacation solidified that I had defeated the demons.

When our daughters went back to school about a month later, I became overconfident, though. I believed I was good. I was myself. It was me that brought me back, not the meds. Not the doctor. I didn't need therapy anymore; we talked about all we could talk about. The medication helped me to see that I could return to who I was, but it didn't actually do it. It was a path to me finding myself.

Darlene came home from work one evening with that look on her face that I had not seen in some time. She looked anxious, worried.

"What's wrong?"

"Dr. Hindsman called me. She said you didn't show up for your appointment today. Or last week. What's going on, Rodney? We agreed this was the way to go — and it has been working."

I immediately got volatile. "It hasn't been doing shit. I've gotten back to myself on my own. The drugs only pointed me in the right direction. The therapist helped me talk it through. I'm back on track."

"But honey, why stop what has been working?"

"I can be doing something for you or for us instead of going to those sessions."

"No. That's not what we agreed to. Next thing is you'll be putting aside the medication."

"I have. I haven't taken it in a week and look at me. I'm fine. I told you, those things just helped me get back on track. I'm good now, baby."

"Rodney, you're scaring me. You know — you have to know — that the meds and therapy *have* helped you. They didn't help you get to see the light. They are the light."

"You don't trust me. You think I don't know anything, like I'm some dumb kid who needs people telling me what to do to be OK. Well, those days are over. I know myself. And those meds kept me up at night. I didn't tell you this because I didn't want you to worry, but I would get headaches during the day — and you know I never got headaches before. Also, I would almost every day get this jolt, like an electrical shock. Those side effects are tiring."

Darlene stared at me. "Rodney, listen to me. I have read up on Citalopram. And it says you should continue to take it even if you feel good. And it says as big as day that if you suddenly stop taking it, your conditions will worsen. We can't have that, honey. I know you don't want that."

"I haven't taken a pill since last Wednesday. Today is Wednesday. That's a week. And I haven't had any issues. And I don't have any more headaches or that electrical shock feeling."

"I can't take this. If you won't start taking your meds again, I'm not staying here. You choked me. Do you remember that? That's how we found out what's going on with you. There's no cure for PDD, honey. There's only the treatment."

Darlene then turned and ran upstairs. I didn't follow her. I believe she ran because she saw someone looking at us through the window. So, I closed all the blinds in the house. I made sure the front door was locked and then I wedged a chair up against it. I went into the garage, to a box I had on a high shelf under a blanket. In it was my gun. A Glock 9. I made sure it had bullets in it and I turned off the lights in the house. I sat on the floor with my back up against the wall facing the front door.

I was ready for him to come in. I felt like someone had followed me home and was ready to come in and take our stuff or kidnap my wife. I wasn't going for that. I was ready. The first person I saw, that person was going to get a bullet right in the head.

CHAPTER FIVE:
BAIL OUT
BRENDA

Six o'clock came and my desk was neat and I was ready to head out of the office. Usually, I would stay at least an extra thirty minutes, tidying up or making sure I wasn't needed to do something last minute for one of the partners. Not that day, though.

After reading up on the homeless, I was anxious to see Rodney. I wasn't sure what I was going to say to him. But I would say *something.* I would let him know I was willing to do all I could to get him back on track with his life.

The thick rush-hour traffic frustrated me. Sometimes I stayed at the office until seven or later — to let the traffic die down. Leaving on time only put me in this bumper-to-bumper that drove me crazy.

It was only about three miles to McDonald's from my job, but it took me about fifteen minutes to get there. I was hungry, too, since I had passed on lunch — a first.

But my desire to talk to Rodney was more intense than the hunger.

But I didn't see him. I saw that man every day during the week for about three months, and the one time I *needed* to see him, he wasn't there. My disappointment was so strong — but not enough to spoil my appetite.

So I placed an order of a Quarter Pounder with Cheese, two large fries and a vanilla milkshake, with the extra order of large fries to make up for the lunch I missed. I figured that would hold me until I finished cooking dinner about an hour later.

I saw Chester, the strange homeless guy I met with Rodney earlier that morning, on my way out. I was not sure about talking to that man, but I felt compelled to try.

"Hi, Chester. Remember me from this morning? I know Rodney."

He looked at me, waved and lowered his head.

"Do you know where Rodney is?"

"Jail."

"Jail? Did you say *jail?"*

"Cops took him. Said he stole something, I think. Then they said he had no respect. I told them to stop. But the cop pushed me down."

I didn't know if the guy knew what he was

talking about or if he'd made it up in his head.

"When did this happen? Where?"

"This afternoon. Southwest Atlanta."

I asked myself if I was crazy and not Rodney as I headed back into traffic to the Atlanta City Jail on Garnett Street to see if I could get Rodney out. I couldn't trust Chester's interpretation of what had happened, but I was going to find out.

I ate my food as I drove. I wanted to get it down, knowing I could see something at the police station that could spoil my appetite. But mainly I was starving. The jail was downtown, near the courthouse and no more than five miles from the McDonald's.

So when I finally got there, why were all the people I saw in handcuffs black? It shouldn't have surprised me, but it angered me. Still, I knew I had to be calm as I dealt with the cops.

After a thirty-minute wait, the desk sergeant was polite and helpful. "Yes, Rodney Bridges is in for disorderly conduct. He was caught urinating outside and when confronted, got ugly with the officers. Resisting arrest. His bail is set at one thousand dollars."

"Which means I can get him out with a bond for one hundred dollars, right?"

"That's right. But let me ask you something," the officer said. "Is this your family or friend? I ask because he needs help. He's homeless. He stays sometimes at the Peachtree-Pine shelter. But he's been in here more than once. Believe it or not, being in here is better than being on the streets."

"You think that's why he got arrested. He wanted to?"

"I asked him that. He told me he'd have to be a fool to prefer being confined over free on the streets. But to my way of thinking, sleeping on the ground is not better than sleeping in jail. Neither are ideal. I know that. I'm just saying."

"Well, I agree. But I want to help him get back to freedom. So I will get the bond paid."

I dealt with the creepy bail bondsman and got back to find that the officer I had been dealing with was gone. But I had secured the bond. Even at that, it took another ninety minutes before Rodney was released.

"It's a process, ma'am," an officer told me. He was not as nice or patient as the other guy. "It doesn't happen quickly. We have protocols."

Finally, when Rodney emerged from the prison, I could see the confused look on his face. He turned to the desk sergeant.

"How did I get out of here? Who bailed me out?"

The officer pointed to me. I expected to see a smile on Rodney's face. I didn't get one.

"You bailed me out? Why would you do that? How did you know I was in here?"

"I saw Chester at McDonald's. He told me."

"And you came? I'm thankful, but why? What are you doing?"

"I'm trying to be nice to you."

"But why?"

"Why can't you accept kind gestures?"

"This doesn't make sense. You don't know me. Why would you do this?"

"I want to help you. Simple as that."

Rodney yawned and his breath smelled, as my nephew would have said, like hot garbage. His clothes didn't smell that fresh, either. But I offered him a ride. It was instinct.

"The officer said you sometimes stay at the shelter near downtown. I can take you there."

"He talks too much. And I'm not getting into your car. I can smell myself. I'd rather just say thank you and move on."

"What? That's it? I come down here to

make you a free man, and you're ready to go?"

"Oh, you think you deserve more because you bailed me out? You think you own me now? Well, forget that thought. I'm my own man."

"Yeah, and that's really served you well," I said. It just came out.

"Your life is shit, remember?" he responded. "You're the one who complained about not being able to sleep. I get my rest. And I have more adventure in my life than you have in yours. I'm sure of that."

"Because you say it, doesn't make it true."

"Actually, it does."

"The truth doesn't give a damn about your opinion."

I got mad then. I could have been at home eating dinner. Instead I argued with this guy who didn't give a damn about me or that I was trying to help him.

"You know what? Fine. You win. I'm going home. Have a nice night."

But something wouldn't allow me to leave. I'd never felt like that, like I was stuck. So instead of leaving, I just looked at him.

"What happened to you?" I asked.

"You're just dying to know why the homeless man is homeless."

"No, I want to know why this smart man

is such an asshole."

"Because I killed my family."

He looked at me to see my expression, and it was one of shock and fear, no matter how hard I tried to conceal it.

"Look at you now," he said. "Scared."

"I'm not scared. I'm confused. Are you serious?"

"You asked me a question. I gave you an answer."

I was scared. Here I was, trying to save someone who killed his family. I didn't want to be there anymore. I wanted to get into my car and go. But I couldn't let him know I was scared.

"When you want to talk about it, I will listen."

"I will talk the same time that you tell me why you're so depressed."

"You don't want to know about me. You just want to say shocking and mean things to me. I don't know why, but that's all that's going on here."

I walked from the passenger side of my car to the driver's side, never turning my back to Rodney.

"See you in the morning," he said.

I nodded my head, but I didn't know if he would see me or not. I felt like I needed a new routine, one that did not include coming face-to-face with a man who said he'd killed his family. He had to be serious. No one — no matter how sick he may have been — would joke about something so horrifying.

CHAPTER SIX:
REVELATIONS
RODNEY

I didn't have any feelings anymore. Well, anger . . . I had that. I could get angry and express it, and was angry about a lot. I couldn't express sorrow or kindness or sympathy, though. I had cut off those emotions.

I didn't feel sorry for myself. Whatever bad thing that happened to me — getting thrown in jail, beaten up by stupid teenagers, cursed at by strangers, marginalized by society — I deserved it.

That wasn't my so-called illness talking, either. This wasn't the meds talking. This wasn't the lack of meds talking. This was the life I had chosen for myself.

That was the life I deserved. I was clear about that. I knew some people would say that was proof I was crazy.

Brenda was trying to help me, which was something I was not used to and didn't know how to receive. What did she really want? I thought: Were there people who *really* cared about strangers, a stranger who lived on the streets? I'd been at shelters where people came and donated clothes and food and then they would be gone. Did the donation mean they cared? Or did it mean they had clothes they decided to not throw away? Or did they feel guilty about having more than some?

At the same time, what more could I have asked of them? I had been fighting with myself on all that stuff. I didn't believe I was bipolar. I didn't want to believe it. I had conflicts in my mind that canceled out each other and left me . . . nowhere. Other people had the same issues. Why was I bipolar and they weren't?

Most of the time, I wandered the streets of Atlanta with no real destination. I just walked. I could walk ten, twelve miles at a time, carrying my backpack full of my burdens, with no problem. I took my time, saw the people, felt the neighborhoods.

I made my walk to the shelter slowly most of the time because I hated going there. It was somewhat of a haven when it was cold, but in the summer, it was hot and stinky. And I didn't like the mentality of the people there. Too many had some twisted idea that someone owed them something.

But I could get a shower there. I could get fresh clothes there sometimes. I knew I stunk a lot of the time, but I didn't like to stink. And then I would leave and find a comfortable place — a bench, a small park, a building front — and sleep. Couldn't sleep in jail. It was always too much to see. Too much sad stuff to see, like young African-American men with no interest in doing right. Troubled at a young age. A system of injustice and harassment got them all out of whack. They'd just as soon die before letting bad cops and racist laws hold them down.

They were not like me. They were young and could have been anything positive. Institutional racism got 'em. Well, it got a lot of them. Something else got the rest. But for sure there was a system that had been designed to kill them and undereducate them and make it harder for them, in some cases *impossible* for them. But some of them were just bad seeds. I couldn't deny that.

The system did not get me, somehow. My brown skin worked against me, but I made it through. Still, I blew my chance at a "normal" life; my *chances,* actually. No one did it to me but me. And Brenda came along and wanted to save me? If I couldn't save myself, how could anyone else?

But I had to confess to myself: The fact that she wanted to do something for me meant something. Sometimes I thought she wanted to research the homeless life. Sometimes I thought she was pure and nice — and curious.

"Don't leave," I told her as she opened the door to her car. She said she was not scared, but she had to be. But I didn't want her to be scared.

"You should stay — if you can."

"Stay? Why?"

"You made me want to answer your question. I don't know how, but you did."

Her curiosity was too strong for her to leave. She looked into my eyes as she closed the car door.

"As soon as you are mean to me, I'm leaving."

I nodded my head.

"Don't you want something to eat? I'm hungry." Brenda told me to stay while she went to a seafood spot not that far from the jail, on Peter Street. After about twenty minutes, she returned with meals for both of us. We sat on the hood of her car and ate.

"I want to say grace," she said. "Don't you bless your food before you eat?"

I didn't respond — I didn't want to get

into my views on God with her.

"Please, Lord, thank you for the food we are about to receive for the nourishment of our bodies. Thank you for us meeting, and we pray that through discussion, we will become friends. Amen."

I didn't say, "Amen." Praying and all that didn't mean that much to me.

"OK, you can start," Brenda said.

"I killed my family."

"You already said that part."

"That's what happened to me."

"That's not something that *happened* to you. That's something you *did.* And when you say 'family,' what do you mean?"

"I killed my family — my wife and two wonderful daughters."

Brenda stopped eating. She put down her plastic fork.

"Then why aren't you in jail?" she asked. I ignored the question.

"It was a couple of years ago. Everything was fine, great, wonderful. My daughters were home from the summer from vacation up north."

I hadn't talked about it in so long that I had forgotten how difficult it was to share. That surprised me. I had control of my emotions because I had rid myself of everything but anger. But I could feel something rising in me.

"Go on. What happened?"

I ate more of the shrimp and salad and sipped on the water. It felt good to have a decent meal.

"Listen, Rodney, if you don't want to tell me, you don't have to. We can talk about something else."

"Something else? What else is there?"

"Like, where you're from and what did you do before you, you know . . ."

"Ended up on the streets? Well, I'm from here. I grew up here. I'm full-fledged from Atlanta. There aren't many of us around anymore. People come here in droves and don't go back. Spent most of my childhood in Southwest Atlanta. It was a good upbringing. Just me and my cousin and my parents. We took vacations to Savannah. When I was a kid, it felt like we drove forever, like we went to this magical, far-off place. It shocked me when I realized as I got older that it was just four hours away."

"But those trips meant something to you."

"How do you know?"

"Because you brought it up. You could have talked about anything — or nothing. But you brought that up. And you probably didn't mean to, but you almost smiled when you did."

"I hadn't thought about that in so long."

"So what do you think about? If you're not remembering important moments of your life, what are you thinking?"

"I think about not being here, about being put out of my misery. I think about the hypocrisy in the world. I think about how so many men that I have been around or seen in shelters or on the street were driven there by society."

"What do you mean?"

"Someone like you, who have never been on the streets, believes it's always the homeless man's fault. He's lazy and prefers to just do nothing over doing something. Well, that's true in some cases, a small percentage of the cases. Many of these men have been damaged by drug abuse, which was a killer in the black community by design. No one can tell me different.

"We can get men on the moon in the sixties, but forty years later, we can't keep heroin and cocaine and crack and meth and PCP off the streets of the inner city? Call me a conspiracy theorist if you like, but evidence is everywhere that certain people wanted to wipe us out."

"Actually, I don't disagree with you. And you know why? It wasn't until white kids started dying from meth and heroin and other stuff that the government has taken notice. But in our neighborhoods, what we got was our men locked up for possession of even the smallest amounts of crack. So, at the time when our neighborhoods were infested with drugs the most, the laws on drug possession were the harshest. And we lost a lot of our men."

I was impressed that she was aware and didn't just blame black people's problems on black people. I understood we make our own decisions and choices and do harm to ourselves. But to just lay it at our feet was a simplistic way to look at it.

"I had you for one of those right-wing people who thought all our troubles were our doing. I lay a lot of our issues on us because we're strong enough to overcome the evil in people. But we can't let them get a pass on how their evil and violence and corruption and immoral values created a system with all that evil and violence, corruption and immoral values and worked only against us. And, yes, I'm going back to slavery."

"Rodney, listen, I talk to you and listen to you, and you're clearly an intelligent man. *Very* intelligent. The question won't leave me."

"I know. What happened to me? I killed

67

my family."

"Rodney . . ."

"The family vacations we went on to Savannah were so great that I made sure I included them when I got my own family. My wife — her name was Darlene — and I had gotten over some things, including me being diagnosed as bipolar. But I kept a gun in the house and on me at all times because I had to protect my family.

"So, anyway, we took our usual trip and it was not the same because the girls got older and they didn't really want to go. They had parties and friends to catch up with. But we hardly saw them anymore, so I was insistent on them going on this trip. I overruled my wife, who had said, 'It's OK, honey. As long as they are home.'

"But I couldn't let it go. Those trips meant everything to me as a child. I never wanted them to end. I wanted my girls to feel the same about our trips as I did about the ones I took as a kid. Anyway, I fell asleep. I fell asleep on Interstate 75 South, just past this little town called Cordele. I was awake, I felt alert . . . but I fell asleep."

"Oh, no," Brenda said.

"We crashed. I broke my clavicle, fractured my wrist and broke an ankle. We flipped, people say, at least twice. I don't remember any of it. Last I remember, a Michael Jackson song was playing, 'Another Part of Me,' and Diana and Joy, my daughters, were in the back singing it.

"Next thing I know, I'm upside down in the car, which was smoking. I was in a state of shock. I managed to look to my right and Darlene was there, bloodied, lifeless. It took me a few seconds to process that and I was spinning. I called out the girls' names. No response.

"I used all my might to turn my body so I could look to the backseat. My girls weren't there. Both had been ejected from the car.

"I looked outside the front window and I could see Diana. She was sprawled on the ground. My heart sank. To the left was her sister. Both were dead. I was pinned in the car and forced to look at my dead wife next to me and my dead daughters outside the window for about twenty minutes before help came. That's when my life ended. That's when I knew I didn't deserve to live."

"Oh, Rodney, I'm so sorry. I cannot even imagine the pain of losing your family.

"I can't even imagine what you went through. But I know this: It wasn't your fault. You have what's called 'survivor's remorse.' I'm sure you asked why you were the one to survive and wished that you would have been the only one to not make it. You're carrying a burden not many people can understand.

"But you've got to believe that God has you here for a reason. He —"

"God? God? I ain't got no love for God. I mean, this is the God that let my family die. My kids are dead. The only woman I have ever loved is dead. But I'm alive. That's the cruel part. That's my problem with Him, more than even having my family die. Why let me live through this?

"My family was my life. My family is gone because I fell asleep while driving. And your God allowed it to happen. And He kept me here to live with this constant nightmare."

"I'm so sorry, Rodney. I can't say it enough. But I wouldn't be honest with you if I didn't say that we don't always understand God and what He does. But you're here for a reason. I'm sure God does not want you to be in a living nightmare. I'm sure He wants you to honor your family by living."

"I'm here. I'm living."

"On the streets, though. I don't think that was His plan for you. You have so much to offer. Let me ask you something: Did you believe in God before the accident?"

"Sure. We went to church as a family.

Some Sundays. *Most* Sundays. But what He allowed to happen? No, I don't have faith in Him anymore."

"I don't want to sound like some religious freak, because I'm not. But do you know that God has protected you on the streets? So many bad things could have happened to you."

"Who said bad things haven't happened to me on the streets?"

"I don't doubt it. The thing is, there was stuff bound to happen to you that He prevented from happening, stuff you will never know about. He's protecting you. That's why you're still here. As long as you're here, why not make the most of it?"

"I am."

Brenda was exasperated.

"So why has God allowed you to have your troubles? I mean, if He's so merciful and all that jazz, why do you have so much pain in your life? And you're a believer. I can see it in you. You have a light in you. But it's flickering, not blazing.

"What happened to you? Since we're being all open and shit."

Brenda was caught off guard.

"Me? Well, a lot."

I waited for her to continue. I had worked in corporate America for decades. I knew how to deal with people. She needed me to not push her.

"I used to be fine, as they say. I used to wear a six or an eight. I couldn't maintain it as life started kicking me in the ass. I was married for about six years. My husband left me. I can't even say why. He never gave a true reason. He said, 'We grew apart.' That's code for something else. He probably grew closer to another woman.

"That hurt me. I never expected to be divorced. I never saw it coming, so it was a knife wound to the stomach. I actually felt like I didn't want to live anymore. Eventually, though, maybe it was a voice or maybe it was a dream, but I remember distinctly that I heard a voice that said, 'Get up.'

"And I got up, you know? I was depressed, but I started to live again. And eat. And eat. It seemed the food eased the depression. And look at me now — twice as big as I was at my best.

"So, guess what: I was depressed over my weight, and the only thing that helped it was eating. Then, my sister's son went to prison for conspiring to kill his girlfriend's husband. It was hard to accept that, but my sister, who has always been fragile, just broke down.

"Our parents had died a little before then,

and that crushed all of us. My sister took it the hardest. But her son going to prison, that broke her. She had a stroke and is in Piedmont Hospital. It's me and Theresa now. We're all we have left.

"Other stuff happened, too, including losing my job. So I've been doing temp jobs until something that fits my talent and experience comes along . . . So, nothing but food offers me comfort. I just eat and go to work and watch TV and repeat the cycle."

"You might as well be on the streets."

"Excuse me?"

"It's true. You'd have more excitement and you'd lose weight because you wouldn't eat as much and you'd be walking."

"Uh, I believe there has to be a way to lose weight other than walking the streets, living on the streets. That's not for me."

"I didn't think it was for me, either. But I have no one to answer to. I'm free. For me, that's important."

"I don't understand that. You mean because you don't owe a landlord or a car dealership or a boss, you're free?"

"It's more than that. I don't owe society. I've given all I can, all I love — my family — and got nothing in return. Uncle Sam can't say I owe him. No supervisor can say I owe him. No bill collector can say I owe him. I'm free."

"So why not live as a free man? You need help. You're more depressed than me . . . Don't look at me like that. You have to be to live on the streets. I don't mean to demean you. But how do you go from having a home and family to living on the streets?"

"And I don't how you go from being a small woman with a life and hopes to a big woman with no hopes and depressed."

"Yeah, well, we're quite a pair, aren't we?"

CHAPTER SEVEN:
SLEEPLESS NIGHTS
BRENDA

I couldn't sleep. Again. The talk with Rodney haunted me. It scared me. But, in some kind of twisted way, inspired me.

I couldn't sleep because Rodney was heavy on my mind — his look, his mind, his pain. It was obvious he did not share his story often. But he welcomed me into his world. And I was haunted, scared and inspired by that.

Pain could break or empower. Rodney was broken in one sense, devastated and saddled with guilt. But he had so much on his brain. And it was needlessly going to waste. I felt so bad for him.

And I felt bad the next morning when I went to McDonald's and Rodney was not there. Chester was, however, and he said: "I don't know" when I asked about his friend.

"He said somebody was following him," Chester added. "He was scared. Said it was the FBI. Or the CIA. I don't know. Never seen him like that. He just ran."

That made me scared. Chester had mental issues, so it was hard to determine if what he said was true. But he was right about Rodney having been arrested.

Rodney had seemed fine the night before. Clear. I was no expert on bipolar disorder, but I knew the effects of it could rise at any time.

I was amazed that I had cared so much. I cared when he was in jail when I didn't know him at all. And, after speaking at length with him, I cared more. Not knowing where he was bothered me.

I had no way of contacting Rodney. I had to trust that he would be at McDonald's when I got off work. And the uncertainty made my day go slowly.

I was distracted by thoughts of what could have happened to him. The only place I knew he seemed comfortable was at that McDonald's on Ponce. So, instead of eating lunch, I drove over there, hoping to see him.

I didn't.

Neither Chester nor any other homeless I had seen lingering were there, either. I went back to work and functioned OK, but my mind floated to Rodney every free moment I had.

I headed to the elevator at six o'clock; I

was anxious to see if he had returned to McDonald's. My third time of the day there brought anxiety. I needed him to be there.

He was not. I was so caught up that I did not eat — a major feat. I just sat there, looked at every person who came near the restaurant. Before I realized it, it was seven o'clock. I finally drove home in silence — except for the questions that rattled around in my head.

Was he OK?

Where could he be?

How could I find him?

Why did this bother me so much?

I spent another Friday night at home alone and bored — the thirty-second weekend in a row. I contemplated if I should look for him. But I knew it was a silly thought: There was no telling where he would be.

Saturday morning, instead of sleeping until I couldn't sleep any longer, I woke up before seven. Rodney was on my mind. The possibility rose that I might not see him again, and that kept me up.

Finally, around eleven, I got up, made something to eat, dressed and made my way to Piedmont Hospital to see my sister. It was part of my routine.

The family members who visited her when she first slipped into the coma many months earlier had long since stopped coming. The nurses told me I was her only visitor.

I couldn't blame them. It was hard to see Theresa like she was — limp and unconscious. And with the prognosis not bright, it almost seemed pointless to come. But I needed to.

I had nothing else in my life.

Theresa and I had a conversation once. She said, "If someone says I committed suicide, don't believe them. I would never do that. If I'm on life support, don't pull the plug on me too soon. I could just be resting."

We laughed about it, but I told her I felt the same way about both cases. So I was not eager to pull the plug — no matter how grave the situation looked. People had come out of comas after years. I was giving her time to rest, just as she said she might need.

It was quiet in her hospital room, but not peaceful. It was eerie, actually. The sounds of the machine that breathed for her and the other that monitored her brainwaves broke the silence and created an air of death.

So I always prayed with Theresa before I sat down.

"Dear Lord, this is my sister, Your child. I ask that You wake her up and let her live out her life praising Your name. She has so much to offer, God. She has so much to do. Bless me with the gift of her life. I ask this knowing You are capable, only You, of opening her eyes and freeing her from this deep, deep sleep. And I believe in Your time You will bring her back to the world. That is my prayer. In Jesus' precious name, I pray . . . Amen."

Sometimes I struggled with what to speak to Theresa about or whether to just sit there with my mouth shut. But something in me told me she could hear me. So I talked. And, of course, on that morning, Rodney was on my mind.

"So, Rodney, the homeless guy, is missing. Well, I can't say he's missing because he doesn't have an address. He's homeless. But, you know, he's becoming my friend. He opened up to me two nights ago, telling me about his past, his horrible past.

"He is devastated by the death of his family — two girls and a wife — from a car accident when he fell asleep while driving. What a horrible burden to carry.

"Then, Theresa, there's the fact that he is bipolar and likely schizophrenic. I have no idea how that plays out, but I was told he ran from another homeless guy saying he was followed by the FBI or CIA. So, that sounds like something not normal. You know what I mean?

"But I listened to him really closely, Theresa. Really closely. And in almost every word, I could hear the pain and suffering in his heart. He doesn't know how to deal with it. And I ain't no damned psychiatrist, but I want to help him. I can help him. If only I could find him.

"I know what you're thinking, sis: I need to work on myself and not focus on saving someone else. And I understand that view. But here's the thing: Helping him would be helping me. I don't know how I have linked his getting better to my feeling better, but they are linked.

"I need to save him to save myself. And the reason I think I can do it is because he talked to me Thursday night. He talked. Said he hadn't talked about his accident in the two years since it happened. But he told me. He told me. That means something.

"And I take it to mean he wants to be helped. He wants my help. I can sense it. I can read people, and I can read this man.

"But I can't find him. I don't know if he's in jail or dead or just decided to hang somewhere else . . . Maybe he doesn't want to be my friend. Maybe he opened up to me knowing he would never see me again. Or maybe he opened up and had time to look back on it and figured he didn't want me to know that much about him. I just don't know."

It would have been great, amazing if Theresa responded to me. But she couldn't.

"I'm going to take a walk," I told Theresa. "The doctors are due to come in here any minute. I'm going to stretch my legs and think."

Not sure why I wanted to do that because I always considered hospitals the second-saddest place on earth. Graveyards were the saddest. And usually, if you were in the hospital long enough, the cemetery was your next stop.

But I really needed to walk. When I told Rodney about my life, I started by recalling how I used to look. I did that because I wanted him to know I wasn't always obese and I wanted him to know that I was aware of my issues. Being aware was the first step to doing something about it. That was the only step I had taken, however.

It was hard for me to not glance into the hospital rooms as I walked the halls. It may have been morbid and sad, but it confirmed that as bad as my life was, it could have been worse. I hated that I used other people's troubles to feel slightly better about myself. But that's how down I was; I needed something, someone, anything, to pull me up.

What the hospital should have done was inspire me to stop eating. I needed to get my jaws wired, have liposuction done and do Weight Watchers — all at once. I was so sick of myself. Looking into the mirror below my neck was something I stopped doing.

And yet there I was — standing outside the cafeteria. Eating was the last thing I should have been doing. But it was habit. A bad habit. I tried to turn around and go back up to Theresa's room. But it was too hard. I was not starving, but I was in need of fulfilling the habit of eating. Using all the willpower I could muster, I left without getting so much as a candy bar. That small feat was an accomplishment.

I headed back upstairs to read and talk to my sister. At the elevator, though, I could see a patient in a wheelchair out of the corner of my eye. A nurse pushed him. I didn't want to make him uncomfortable, so I didn't stare. But then I heard a voice.

"I know you."

I turned, and to my amazement, I saw him.

"Rodney? Rodney, oh my God. What are you doing here?"

He just looked at me. No expression. I looked at the nurse.

"You know him?"

"Yes, he's my friend."

"Friend?" Rodney said.

"Yes, *friend*. What happened?"

"Appendectomy," Rodney said.

"Emergency appendectomy," the nurse chimed in.

"Oh, my. Are you OK?"

"Unfortunately, yes."

"Unfortunately?" the nurse asked.

"Don't mind him," I jumped in. "He's always peddling doom and gloom."

"The truth doesn't give a shit about your opinion," Rodney said. "I heard someone say that."

The elevator opened and we all entered.

"Why you want to be mean and nasty?"

"We are who we are?"

"Really? You think you're mean and nasty?" the nurse said.

"No, he doesn't. He just doesn't want to be happy. He doesn't know how to be happy."

"What do you know?" Rodney wanted to know.

"I know what you told me."

"Well, this is our floor," the nurse said as she wheeled him out of the elevator.

"What's his room number? Can I visit him?"

I held the elevator door open as she spun the wheelchair around, so he could see me. She motioned to Rodney. "It's up to him." "Rodney, I looked for you the last few days. I was so worried. To see you here is a miracle. I wasn't sure if I would ever see you again."

"How can you be mean to someone who wants to be friends with you?" the nurse asked. "You're better than that. I can tell."

I looked into Rodney's dark eyes for a few seconds. "Room 306," he said. I smiled. He didn't. The nurse turned and wheeled him away.

The emotions that came over me were many. I was stunned to see Rodney. I was relieved to see him. I was happy to see him. I knew from all that the man had become important to me. Was not sure how it happened, but it did.

I got back to Theresa's room in a daze.

"Sis, you're not going to believe this. I almost don't believe it myself. What are the odds? I saw Rodney. He's here. He had appendicitis. How crazy is that? Not that he was sick, but that he is here. And we ran right into each other. What are the odds? It has to be meant to be that I find him."

84

I had almost forgotten that Theresa could not respond. I was looking forward to her saying, "Girl, there are no coincidences, only realities." That was one of her responses when I would point out the irony in something.

Making sense of seeing Rodney there was something I could only chalk up to "it was meant to be." I wondered how he got there. How was he going to pay for the surgery? He didn't have an address to have them send the bill.

I had a bunch of questions for him. It was just a matter of deciding the best time to go to his room.

It took all the discipline I had — and some I didn't know I had — to not get up right then and head to Room 306. "Should I go now?" I asked Theresa.

It was a game I played with myself sometimes when I visited her. I pretended she responded based on what I knew of her personality, views on people, relationships, politics, religion, life.

In that case, I thought Theresa would ask, "What's the point of waiting? Go for it. It can't hurt."

That could have been me rationalizing leaving then; I couldn't be sure. But I waited another thirty minutes, reading *Up-*

town magazine about a wine-tasting event it was having in Napa Valley. "This would be something we could do together," I told Theresa.

I shared about a feature on Seattle Seahawks' Russell Wilson and his new wife, Ciara — Theresa loved sports and music. I shared other news and information with her until I finally succumbed to my desires to visit Rodney.

I was not sure what to say to him. I was not sure how he would receive me. I was not sure if I should have actually gone down there.

But my feet moved toward the door, despite the questions and doubts that floated in my head. My need to see him dominated any concerns.

The door was slightly open to Room 306. I wondered why my heart pounded? Rodney could sense someone was at the door.

"Who is it? Come in."

That was enough for me. As I slowly opened the door, my throat dried and I sounded like a mouse. "It's me, Brenda."

He didn't answer, but I walked in to a sight I didn't expect: Rodney was lying on the floor.

"What are you doing?"

"Never seen a man sleep on the floor

before?"

"Not in a hospital room, no."

"I don't deserve a bed."

"But you need to be in one. That can't be good for you."

"As long as I'm resting, it doesn't make a difference. I'm about to get out of here anyway."

"They are releasing you already?"

"I can leave when I want. This is a sad place. I don't need to be here."

"Actually, you do need to be here until the doctors say you can leave. I'm going to talk to the doctor. I know they rush people out of hospitals these days, but you should wait until they tell you to go."

"You need to worry about yourself. I don't see you losing any weight."

"So you're going to be mean to me, when I'm here out of concern for you? I thought we were beyond the insults. I don't insult you and, believe me, I could."

"You insult me by being here, like you have a stake in my life."

"You just have to be mean, don't you? You have no control of yourself."

"I do."

"No, you don't. If you did, you would thank me for caring. I don't see anyone else here visiting you. If you had control, you'd get into that bed and let your body heal. But you're totally undisciplined, like a child."

"That sounds like an insult to me."

"Well, good. I have several more to catch up to you."

I was not playing nice anymore with Rodney. I didn't know why, but I felt a strong need to be there for him and to be honest with him. Maybe it was to give me something meaningful to do. Maybe it was my heart that my sister always talked about. Whatever it was, I couldn't let go and didn't want to let go. He made it difficult, though.

"Listen, Rodney. I'm not going anywhere. I'm going to be your friend, going to try to be your friend. I'm going to help you as much as I can, in any way I can. That's just who I am. Accept it. Embrace it. I will only make your life better."

I believed every word I shared. I had to be strong to be a positive force in his life. I had to stand up to him.

Rodney pulled himself off the floor and got into the bed.

"Why?"

"Because I care about you. I genuinely care about you. I didn't care that much before we had that talk that night. You welcomed me into your world, which I took to mean something big. I have welcomed you into mine. After all that sharing, how can we go back to just people we see and move on? It can't be like that. It won't be like that. I won't let it.

"And here's the thing: You don't want it to be that way, either. You just have so much pain built up in you that you can't figure out how to release it."

Rodney closed his eyes and curled into a fetal position, his butt exposed from the open back of his hospital attire. I was not sure if he went to sleep that quickly or if he was faking to get me to leave. Either way, he clearly didn't understand my resolve.

I was the woman who was caught off guard when I was downsized out of my human resources manager position at AT&T. I was devastated that my livelihood could be snatched from me without any regard to how I would eat or pay my bills. It wasn't just business to me. I took it personally.

But instead of crying about it, I'd gathered my belongings, dumped them in a box, and went to my car in the parking lot. I'd pulled out my cell phone and I'd placed calls to all the job leads I could think of. Some of them were cold calls. Some were strategic calls made to people I knew or people of people I knew. I'd attacked the situation and by the time I'd left, I'd believed I had done all I could do to change my plight. I was in my car for ninety minutes.

That was my resolve. Rodney going to sleep or faking sleep was not going to discourage me from being there for him. He wouldn't tell me that he needed me, but I felt it. The man lost his family at his hands. His wife's family made him persona non grata. *His* family was nowhere around. And he left any friends he had behind, destroyed by grief.

There were many people who had just a few people in their lives . . . including me. Rodney was the first person I had come in touch with who had *no one.*

I had to change that. I sat there and watched him sleep for several minutes before I dozed. I wouldn't leave him.

"Oh, damn. You scared me," I said to the nurse who walked into the room. "But I'm glad you're here. Do you know he had been sleeping on the floor?"

"What did you do to get him into the bed? He started in the bed, then was on the floor. He's been here three days; I think most of the time he was on the floor. He's homeless, right? So sad."

"Looks like you all have cleaned him up a little."

"We did. And we have some donated clothes for him hanging in the closet. What's your relationship to him?"

"We're friends, new friends. I still can't believe I ran into him here. I didn't know he was here. My sister is upstairs and I was visiting her."

Rodney turned over and opened his eyes. His look was one of confusion.

"Who is she?" he said, looking at the nurse. "Who do you work for?"

The nurse was confused, but I wasn't. This bipolar thing was serious, and he told me he often got paranoid when it set on.

"It's OK; she's the nurse."

"Yes. You know that," the nurse said.

"I don't know shit," Rodney snapped as he sat up. "I don't trust anybody in a goddam uniform. Who you working for?"

"Uh, I'm going to leave now," she said on her way out.

"What *you* doing here?"

I felt like I was looking at a person I hadn't met before. It was freaky and a bit scary, too.

"You don't know me?"

"I know you. Don't know why you're here, though. Who you working for?"

"What? Rodney, you may not want to call me your friend, but that's what we're working toward. You don't think so?"

"What I think is that you need to get out of my room. And take your hidden cameras and microphones with you."

This definitely was not the Rodney I'd spoken to for hours a few nights before. This Rodney was scary.

"I'm leaving. Here. This is my cell phone number. Call me at any time. I'm going back to my sister's room upstairs. But I will come back in a few hours. Maybe you'll be feeling better."

"Don't bother. Spy."

I could only shake my head as I left his room. I had never experienced someone switch personalities. I had seen men act one way, and after sex, act another. I had seen former girlfriends turn mean and abrasive during their cycle. I'd never seen a man just flip into what I had seen with Rodney.

It made me think. What if he flips when we are alone and gets violent? What could I do? He was a big man — about six feet three inches and lean and strong. And why wouldn't he turn violent if he felt threatened by me, if he thought I was a spy or someone after him?

It made me rethink everything. I couldn't put myself in a position for that guy to flip and potentially hurt me.

My stable mind told me I should stay away from any man who chose to live on the street instead of in a shelter. At the same time, my heart empathized with his story and his pain.

Additionally, he was a smart man who had something to offer society. At the same time, he was sick and needed to be under a doctor's care. I had told all this to Theresa, who I was sure would think I was crazy to be involved with Rodney on any level.

I could hear her in my mind: "This is just like you. Remember that stray dog you kept out back for about two months before Mom and Dad found out what you were doing? And the men in your life — all of them had issues. Now you're telling me you want to help a homeless man who doesn't want your help? Girl, bye."

As I folded into the chair next to her hospital bed, I took those thoughts of my sister into my sleep. Then something strange happened: I dreamed about Rodney — and Theresa. I was sitting on a bench at the Piedmont Park, near the swimming pool and playground. Along came Theresa from one direction, wearing all black. And Rodney came from the other direction, looking worse than I'd ever seen him — and he'd never looked great.

"This is Rodney. I was telling you about him," I said to Theresa.

"This is the guy? I understand why you are committed to helping him. I can see it deep in his eyes — he's hurting. He needs you. You're doing the right thing."

The dream felt so real. I woke up to tears streaming down my face. I hadn't seen my sister up and moving and talking in so long. It made my heart feel good to see her talking and walking.

It also made up my mind about Rodney: I was going to do what I could to help him. There was no turning back. Theresa had told me to, and I didn't care if it was in a dream. It meant something to me. It meant everything to have my sister speak to me again. It was the first dream I had had with her speaking to me in it.

So I held her hand and talked to her and told her about my dream and my ambition. I cried as I did it. The reality of her condition and the purpose of my life combined to bring tears.

After a few hours sitting and sharing with Theresa, Dr. Teasley entered.

"I was going to come in earlier, but I heard you talking to her, so I didn't want to disturb you."

"How is she doing? Any change?"

"Not for the better, I'm sorry to say. Her heart rate is weakening."

Those words scared me. After seven months, I clung to a miracle happening.

The truth was, I had lost Theresa a long time ago, though not officially, which probably explained why Rodney was so important to me. I needed someone in my life. I needed to matter to someone.

Rodney had to be it, but I wanted to do or say something to make him comfortable with me. Theresa used to say, "People don't write anymore. The person who takes the time to actually put pen to paper is a person who really cares."

A nurse honored my request and got me a pad and pen, and I began, not knowing what I was going to write. I just pulled every honest and raw emotion out of my body.

"Rodney," I began, *"I'm in my sister's room here at the hospital, Room 706. From here, as I look at my lifeless sister, who would do anything to come out of her coma, I think of you and what struggles you have. We all have struggles — some are just more serious and hard to overcome than others.*

"I see so much in you, and it bothers me that I can't help you. You won't let me help you. If you think it's because I feel sorry for you, you're wrong. Trust me: I don't feel sorry

for you. I feel badly for you.

"*That difference makes all the difference in the world. And this is important too: I need you to help me. Your outlook on life has impacted my outlook on life. I want to do better. Let's help each other. The fact that you're still here means you're a strong man. My sister is not in a position to do anything about her situation. You are. And as hard as it is for you to realize it, you deserve more.*"

I gathered my mind and my heart and went back to his room to deliver the note and let him marinade on it.

It was alarming, though, that his door was slightly open. I'd thought the nurse would practically lock him in there after what she saw. But I was not scared. Not anymore. I was committed.

My knocks on the door went unanswered, however, so I slowly pushed it open. The bed was empty, which didn't surprise me. But Rodney was not lying on the floor, either. His backpack, which was in a chair, was not there. He was gone.

Worse, my card that I gave him with my cell phone number was on the bed, where I had left it. I turned to find a nurse to see about his discharge. She was at the station, filling out paperwork.

"What happened to Rodney Bridges? You

all discharged him already?"

"What do you mean?"

"He's not in his room and his belongings are gone."

I followed behind the nurse back to the room. There was panic in her steps.

"I can't believe it? Where did he go? I saw him in here, on the floor sleeping, about fifteen minutes ago. Isn't he homeless?"

"Yes, he is homeless."

"He shouldn't be out there this soon after surgery. What's he gonna do, sleep in the streets? This is crazy."

I was stumped. Didn't know what to do or what to say. I put the note to Rodney that I had into my purse, turned and left the room.

Chapter Eight:
Street Life
Rodney

I hated hospitals . . . especially that one.
Piedmont Hospital was the same place I was
taken after the accident. My family was
taken to Grady, the city's trauma center,
although their fate had already been determined. My trauma was mental. It would
have been better if they had taken me to a
psych ward.

At Piedmont the first time, I couldn't
really feel the physical pain, despite my
many injuries. The depth of my anguish was
all in my heart. It was smashed.

Returning there two years later made all
that pain overflow. I couldn't sleep or rest.
All I could do was replay my two days there
two years earlier, and how it was in that
place that I realized my world was over.

So, I had to get out of there. I was weak
and in pain, but I would have preferred to
die in the streets than in that hospital.

I did not stay around to get the prescription for the painkillers, but I didn't care. I had to go. Being there ate me up. It was too much to bear.

So, when no one was looking, I had pulled myself off the floor, gotten dressed into the clothes they had given me and had walked out of my room. Just like on the streets, I was invisible; the nurses did not take notice of me as I strolled past them at the desk to the elevator.

My mental pain offset my physical issue enough for me to walk about a mile to the Amtrak station in lower Buckhead. I found a corner on the backside of a building, placed my backpack on the ground, laid my head on it and went to sleep.

It was the kind of sleep I hated because it was a deep sleep, and I remembered my dreams. For two years, every dream I'd had was about the night my loved ones died, which was more than horrible. It was unfair.

Before I slept, I thought about being home with my family, the four of us around the dinner table, playing Trouble, the old board game where each player had to push down on a clear bubble that housed a small block that determined how many times you'd move your man around the board.

We played loudly and seriously, with the winners earning a second portion of dessert or deciding where we would eat out. Then I fell asleep and dreamed about the night of their death.

That made me angry because my thoughts are always about how much I loved my family, always about beautiful memories we created. But my dreams were about that horrible night.

It was sad because the reality of what my life was before the accident and what it had become after it was so dramatically different.

Because of the drugs I had been administered at the hospital and plain ole fatigue, I drifted back to sleep after maybe ten minutes. At some point, I dreamed of the accident. It was not exactly as it had occurred; we were all in the car and I was so sleepy that I could not keep my eyes open. In the dream, we fell off a cliff and tumbled down for what seemed like several minutes.

I could hear them screaming and I turned around to tell them, "it's going to be all right" — as the car dropped toward the ground. But before it crashed, I woke myself up out of the dream. The damage had been done, though. I was panicked, heart racing and, after realizing it was a dream, again saddened by the reality.

No way I could have fallen back to sleep.

I was too shaken — again. I'd had that dream or a variation of it countless times. And like the previous times, my head was jumbled with horrifying images, so much so that physical discomfort from the surgery was minimized.

It was dark — I could not tell what time it was, but I sensed it was late, after eleven and close to midnight. I could tell by the car flow on Interstates 85 and 75 and the pedestrian flow on Peachtree Street. Living on the streets, with nowhere to be, time for me was determined by the patterns of the day. I had given away my watch. I refused to get a cell phone.

From 1 a.m. until 5:45 a.m., it was virtually still in the city. It was what most people would call peaceful, but for me it was haunting. The quiet made it noisy in my head. I could see my family. I could hear their voices. I could feel their pain. And sometimes I could hear other voices or feel other emotions. That was the disease in me.

It all made me resent nightfall. The days were filled with activity, traffic, people. Noise. The nights were too quiet, causing me agony.

I stopped at a CVS and stole some Advil. I grabbed the box, pulled the bottle out and dropped it in my jacket pocket and walked out of the store. The box with the sensor was on the shelf where I'd left it.

Truth was, I could have paid for the pills. I had twenty-seven dollars in my pocket from money I had earned. It was earned because I had worked for it, either by helping women leaving Publix with their groceries, pumping gas for people at the BP gas station or asking for it. At that time, I considered asking for money a job.

I reasoned that I had put in the time, as people did on their jobs, and got rewarded for it. The pay was lousy. But on a good day, I could "make" about fifty dollars.

Every few hours, I took five of the Advil I had stolen and for the next three days rested, either on a cardboard box on the steps in front of St. Paul's Presbyterian on Ponce de Leon Avenue or in its back parking lot.

Other than the rats that came out from the sewers late at night, it was comfortable — relatively speaking. It took me about six months to get used to the ground as a mattress and the madness that came with staying at the shelter. I had given up my right to be comfortable. And when my body got used to sleeping on concrete or grass or wherever, it was no problem.

Most days I stayed up from sunup until

after midnight. I tried to wear my body down, so I would be exhausted and I could easily sleep. That way, I wouldn't have the burden of the quiet. So I would walk and walk when it was not too cold.

I was left with my thoughts as I walked, which could be painful, but I also had so much activity to take me away from it. Walking Atlanta's streets, I had seen much.

For instance, I saw a man making love to a woman at 2:30 in the afternoon, behind the Publix on Peachtree Road in Buckhead. They were in the back of the grocery store, near the loading dock. She was bent over into the passenger side of the car and he, with his pants down by his ankles, did his thing.

A few cars passed by, but I noticed that none of the drivers looked to their left or right to see them. That told me they had been there before and knew they were in a space no one would suspect them to be.

I solved a burglary once. These two guys pulled up in a Honda on Seventh Street in Midtown. One guy rang the doorbell and this unsuspecting white guy, who did not bother to ask who it was or look through the peephole, opened the door. Both the robbers rushed the house.

I took my time and came from behind the

lamppost, where I had been peeing, and memorized the car's license plate. After about ten minutes, the fools came running out. They jumped into the car and sped off. No one else was on the street.

The victim did not come out of the house until the police arrived about five minutes later. The man was shaken. He had nothing to offer the cops. I jumped in.

"Can I say something?"

The officer looked me up and down and dismissed me as a know-nothing bum.

"Listen, mind your business and keep moving. And take a bath."

I looked at the victim. "Mister, since he doesn't want it, maybe you'd like the license plate number of the car of those guys who robbed you."

Of course, he — and the cop — did. The officer put out a radio notice on the light-green Honda Accord with the license plate number, and, in a wild case of irony, the cops had caught the criminals several minutes later along my path down Tenth Street to Piedmont Park.

The cop I had given the license plate number to was on the scene. He saw me walking by and came over. "I just want to thank you for your help. We got the guys."

I nodded my head and kept walking.

Another time, over by the Kroger on Monroe Drive, I saw a young girl — could not have been more than fourteen — get picked up by this creepy-looking guy. It was after midnight, so it caught my attention that this kid would be out by herself at that hour.

The man talked to her for about fifteen minutes. I sat by the sidewalk and watched as the girl resisted at first. Then the man pulled out a wad of cash. The girl stopped retreating. The man motioned for someone driving an Escalade to come over. The girl got into the car.

I could only believe I had witnessed the beginning of a life of sex trafficking for the teenager. I eventually told the cops and gave him as much information as I could, but I never knew if they located the girl.

Those were a few of the countless bad acts I had witnessed — without anyone noticing or caring I was there.

I also had witnessed acts of kindness that made me see the good in people. Once, a stray dog wandered into the street in Inman Park, near Highland Bakery. I was about to set up a makeshift bed just off the sidewalk when a car came careening around the corner and hit the dog, knocking it into the air and off the side of Highland Avenue.

The driver kept going.

But four people — two who were jogging, one who was sitting outside at Highland Bakery and a man who was driving by — had hurried to the dog's aid. They had held the distressed and wailing dog down and had comforted it until a veterinarian had arrived. The vet had told them they had saved the dog's life, and they had hugged each other after the animal was taken away, relieved they had bonded to help the animal.

I also had seen an African-American kid get yelled at by a white man and woman for no reason once in a residential area on Ralph McGill.

"Get out of here. You don't belong here."

He had kept his poise and had walked on. Just ahead of him, a white kid, zooming down the hill on a skateboard, had lost control, hit the curb and gone crashing into the street, headfirst.

Blood was everywhere. But that same black kid had rushed to the hurt child, taken off the shirt he'd worn over a T-shirt and had wiped blood from the kid's face as he'd called 9-1-1 with his other hand.

The man and woman who had yelled at him had come running to the scene; the hurt boy was their son. And the same kid they had wanted out of their neighborhood was the kid who had helped their child. When they saw the black young man they had harassed, they had apologized.

And to his credit, the kid did not say a word. He'd looked down at the bleeding teenager and said, "I hope you keep riding the skateboard when you get better. I saw you. You're dope."

That bleeding young man, stretched out on the ground, had extended his hand. I did not know how, but he knew that his parents had chastised the young man. The teenagers shook hands, and he had told the black kid: "I'm sorry about my parents."

The black kid had responded, after looking at the two adults: "Yeah, me, too." And then he had walked away.

It took everything in me to not say to the adults: *He could have let your child bleed out right there in the street. But he didn't. You wanted him out of your neighborhood, but being in your neighborhood likely saved his life — or prevented severe damage.*

Those examples were reasons I walked and walked. There was no predicting what I would see by people who would not see me. And it all kept my mind off my pain.

After I recovered from surgery, I went to the shelter to take a shower for the first time in four days. But when you smell so bad so often, you become immune to your body odor. At least I did. I didn't smell myself. But I knew I stunk. I had to, even though I was "cleaned up" while in the hospital.

I dreaded going to the shelter. It bothered me to see so many men, especially, black men, so down about life, so hopeless. Many of them did not believe there was anything better for them in the world. Many of them had been homeless so long, it was a way of life and they were not looking to get out and live. They were just surviving. Walking dead.

Many still were devastated by their plight. Those were the ones I gave my attention or conversation. They were the ones who came across hard times. Lost a job. Lost a loved one. Income was drained. No family or friends to turn to. And ended up on the streets or in the shelter.

I engaged them because they were like me, in a sense: Something traumatic happened that destroyed their world. And they listened and they believed when I shared some of my life's experiences because they had done some things in their life. They knew life presented infinite possibilities and that their troubles would eventually be reversed.

The homeless who were lazy or underexposed and hopeless essentially believed people only lived a good life in the movies or on television. They could not see beyond their plight. I already was depressed. Hanging with them would have only made me *more* depressed.

I had to escape Brenda because she actually made me feel good, which I did not believe I was entitled to feel. I gave up that right that night I killed my family.

Brenda's optimism, kindness and insistence to help me made her dangerous. I felt good about who she was as a person, which was too much for me to take.

I needed to feel nothing about her as I had about everyone else I had encountered over the previous two years . . . and that was a lot of people. No one seemed to *really* care about me. Not that I wanted them to, but I could feel their disconnection. Often they gave a dollar to me to just keep away from them.

I had seen people pull up on Courtland Street by the shelter with all kinds of food and clothing to donate. But I didn't see caring. I saw that they were trying to make themselves feel good about their lives by "helping" *our* lives. We were the pawns in that game.

But in Brenda, I saw something different. I did not want to feel for her or to feel something *from* her. But her heart was pure; I was sure of it. Her goodness did not need to be around my lack of interest in anything good. So I left the hospital without letting her know.

When I did so, I was honest with myself. The idea that I was making a mistake came to mind. *Why not embrace someone who truly wanted to embrace me?*

I was too sick, too hurt and too prideful to accept her help. Leaving the hospital assured I would not taint her life. She did not deserve that. Having that concern about someone was something I had not felt since before I'd killed my family. And I was not sure how I felt about it.

CHAPTER NINE:
THE FUNERAL
BRENDA

The night before my sister died, I talked to her about life.

"Sis, don't worry about anything. I'm not happy you're going to your final resting place, but I understand you're tired. You love your son the way God intended us to love our family. Your heart was broken and it could never be fixed.

"I just want you to know — and I believe you can hear me — that your love in Donnie will sustain him. It will protect him and it will inspire him to be the man you birthed him to be. I believe that. Your love is powerful and it runs through my heart. Get your good rest. Go home to God. You've done your work here with me and your son."

It was hard to believe I could speak so calmly with a broken, smashed, crushed, imploded heart. After almost eight months of being with her, absorbing her, I could see she was slipping away. It ached. It stung. It drained me.

"You were the best sister," my cousin Sean said after the service. "I'm sorry I wasn't there for her like you were. It was just hard for me to see her like that."

It was the wrong thing to say to me at that moment. The pain removed my filter.

"You think it was easy for me? That's my sister over there, the person I was closest to on earth. So think about how hard it was for me. I spent almost eight months talking to her and crying at her bedside. I never got used to seeing her lying there. So, I really don't want to hear about how hard it was for you to see her like that. I *saw* her like that."

Usually, I was more diplomatic. I always tried to make others feel comfortable. But at that moment, I did not care what Sean felt. He was my first cousin and I loved him, grew up with him. But he wasn't there for Theresa, and that shit pissed me off.

I was, in fact, pissed off at every person at her funeral. No one came to see her more than a couple of times. Most never came. They wrote her off. They didn't see the need to visit her. That pissed me off. And I knew Theresa was, too.

She treated Sean like he was her son. She skipped work when she didn't have any paid leave to attend his high school graduation. She and I put our money together to get his son a nice suit for a graduation present. Come to think of it, we contributed to Sean's high school class trip. And Sean couldn't come to sit with Theresa for an hour?

This is what I didn't like about people. They disappointed you. They were quick to take, hesitant to give. Quick to offer an opinion on what should happen, but wouldn't contribute to make it a reality. That's why I did Theresa's funeral the way I wanted it done — and the way I believed she would be honored and content.

Why wasn't the casket open? Why wasn't there any family allowed to speak? Who chose the poem? Why not wait to have the funeral on a weekend?

The questions came flying at me from people who might have cared about my sister, but did not show they cared in her time of need. So I answered all the questions at the repast with one simple sentence:

"Since I was the only one there for Theresa during her time in the hospital, when she needed to feel love the most, since I paid for this repast and any extras needed for the service, since I met with the funeral director and the printer and the musicians and did not get a single offer to help — all while I was grieving my sister — I did what the hell I wanted to do."

I liked the silence. It empowered me. They had nothing to say because they knew I spoke the truth. They hadn't heard me so mean or direct. And in a way, I credited Rodney for that. He could be mean and he could be strange, but he was direct. And through him, I learned you got your point across with no ambiguity that way.

I couldn't take my so-called family anymore, so I left the repast. The caterer had been paid and I didn't need to be around those people anymore.

I went home, got in bed, thought about my sister and cried myself to sleep.

I felt as empty about my life as I ever had. It was sad to visit Theresa in the hospital, but it gave me something to do and hope. With her gone, I felt lost.

Two weeks had passed since I had last seen Rodney in the hospital. I stopped every day at McDonald's, to and from work, hoping to see him. I didn't. I didn't see Chester, either. I was sad about it.

Finally, I decided to forget about Rodney and to forget about feeling sorry for myself and get out of the house.

So one Saturday, I got dressed up and

searched Yelp for a restaurant in downtown Atlanta to have a nice meal. I thought if I were around people, I could feel energized and alive.

I chose a place called White Oak because its menu was laden with fresh, healthy choices. The other thing I became adamant about was my health. I had to lose weight. My doctor had put me on blood pressure medicine and implored me to stop with the fast-foods.

At White Oak, I was proud that I passed on the rolls I was offered and dessert. I had a table by the window facing Baker Street, and I watched people walk by as I enjoyed my meal.

It was refreshing to be out, among people, and away from my apartment eating too much food I would prepare for myself. I needed to have someone serve me. Being there made me realize how much I missed socializing. I had not done much since my husband left — and not all that much when he was there.

I should not have been surprised he walked. We weren't getting along so well. He had troubles on his job and eventually lost it. I was frustrated with his attitude that he was wronged as opposed to working toward bouncing back. He worked at Coca-

Cola and he was dejected when the supervisor he considered a friend fired him instead of sharing his concerns or protecting him.

Financial issues for us came to the surface and he considered it crazy and demeaning that I insisted he drive for Uber or Lyft until he found a job worthy of his talent and experience.

"*You* go drive Uber," Troy had told me.

Eventually, it became too much for him. I came home from work and he was gone. Just gone. I knew it because his clothes were gone . . . and his golf clubs.

Because my self-esteem was newspaper thin and fragile, not having him there beat me down. I believed I had driven him away and that I couldn't exist alone.

"It's nobody's fault," he had said when he'd called me a few days later. "We grew apart. I'm sorry. I really am."

I wanted to resent him and hate him, even. But I couldn't. That's how low my self-esteem was — I couldn't blame him for leaving. I wanted to tell him that, but I never got the shot. I also wanted to tell him I wished he would have stayed.

Until that night at White Oak, I hadn't thought about a man. But doing so woke me up. I loved having a man around, to feel protected and cared for. I missed the passion Troy and I had. I hadn't until that moment.

I treated myself to a glass of Sauvignon Blanc. The more I sipped, the more I became unhappy with myself. I could see my reflection in the window, and it showed cheeks so chubby that I turned away. How did I get to be about fifty pounds overweight?

Eating did it, of course. But it really was about being depressed, and trying to feel better by stuffing my face with food. I kept going up a size in my clothes, vowing the next upsize would be the last. But it wasn't.

Looking at myself in the mirror disgusted me. And the more I sipped, the more disappointed I became with myself. Here I was looking to save Rodney, and I needed to save myself.

It was 8:30 and the wine gave me a buzz. One glass. That's all it took. I liked wine — loved it, in fact — but seldom treated myself to it. I was afraid to drive home feeling as I did, so I pulled out my flat pair of shoes I had in my oversized purse and switched out of the heels that I could only tolerate for about two hours. I decided to walk.

I seldom spent much time in downtown Atlanta, which was not as lively as Midtown or Buckhead. But if there were large conventions in town at the Hyatt Regency, Marriott Marquis or the Westin, people would flood the streets seeking something to do outside of the hotels.

There did not seem to be a convention on this day, based on the number of people walking. I went right out of the restaurant with the idea of walking up four blocks to Sweet Georgia Juke Joint, crossing the street and walking back.

I had no idea I would encounter so many people along the way — homeless people. Every fifty feet, I was either hounded or gently approached by someone seeking money. Other than Rodney outside McDonald's, I'd had limited interaction with the homeless. But this short walk was an adventure. And having established something with Rodney opened me up to engaging them.

Before I could get to the first corner, a woman wanted to know if I could help her get food. At first, I was comfortable. But then I looked her over and she was actually a man. It startled me. He was dressed as a woman, in a halter top, grungy skirt and a blonde wig. His skin was as dark as black ink. He was so skinny it jolted me.

I couldn't respond. He asked again.

"Hey, can you give me eighty-seven cents

so I can get something to eat?"

Finally, I came out of my momentary stupor and processed the request. *Eighty-seven cents? Who asks for such an obscure amount?*

It had to be part of a con. No one would stand there and count out eighty-seven cents. Rather, someone would give a dollar and move on. But asking for eighty-seven cents was sort of disarming because it was less than a dollar. Definitely, it was a psychological thing, the way commercials would say a car costs less than $20,000 at $19,995.

One thing I did not like was for someone to get over on me or to think they could. So I reached into my bag, pulled out my wallet and carefully went through the change compartment and counted out eighty-seven cents.

As I did, I asked, "Please don't take this the wrong way, but what happened to you? Why are you out here like this?"

"Out here like what?"

"Like this."

"What else you want me to do? Got nowhere else to go."

"No family? No friends?"

"No one."

"I was just asking. I'm sorry. I don't mean

to offend you. I'm just, you know, curious."

"Yeah, well curiosity killed the cat."

This person was thin but taller than me and so strange-looking that he was frightening. But I learned from my ex-husband to never show fear, especially when scared.

So I postured. "Well, I ain't no cat," I said. But I wasn't crazy. I did not want to incite this person. I handed over eighty-seven cents.

"Here you go. Nice to meet you."

"What's this?"

"You asked for eighty-seven cents."

I received a stare so intense that I could not fake it: I was scared. I didn't wait around for a "thank you" or anything else. I just walked away. When I got a safe distance, I turned back to see the man standing there staring at me. Then he took my money I had given him and threw it on the ground.

At that point, I didn't care. I was just glad to be gone. But not a minute later, I was approached again.

"Hey, sister," the pleasant voice came. The man was around my age, it seemed. He was boisterous and cheery, even, smiling and talkative. "You having a beautiful evening, sister?"

"It's fine."

"No, *you're* fine. Matter of fact, why is

your man letting you walk around this city by yourself? You should have a bodyguard."

Before I could catch myself, I blushed. That was more than Rodney said I had done the day I'd met him. I considered that progress. And he was right: It felt good to acknowledge a compliment, even if it came from a homeless guy on the street.

"I need to get this body right, not a bodyguard."

"Shoot, no. If you don't mind me saying, you look — what's that word — voluptuous. And don't let nobody tell you different."

I smiled. "You're a charmer, I see."

As he smiled, I looked around and noticed the strange looks I received from people who wondered why I dedicated time to this man, whose clothes were tattered and who reeked of the streets and pushed a shopping cart.

"Don't deny it, sister. Your beauty is lighting up this street."

"OK, what's your name?"

"Bobby. You can call me Bob. Or Rob. Or Robby. Or Robert."

"You're so funny. How can I help you tonight?"

"It's like this: I'm in a situation. Lost my job. Got caught up in something and got incarcerated. Now that I'm out, I can't get a job. So, I'm trying to put together some money to save so I can, you know, provide for myself. I'm not proud to be out here asking you for money, but it's a desperate situation."

"How long ago did you get out?"

"About nine months."

"And you haven't been able to find work in all that time?"

"I'll be honest: I didn't look for a job the entire time. I had some family business to take care of. But in the last four, five months, it's been a struggle. When you have a record, well, it's not like the doors are open for you."

The need to know more was superseded by not prying too much into the man's business. So I let it go and dug back into my purse. I could not afford the five-dollar bill I handed over, but I figured God would bless me for blessing Bob.

"Sister, you're all right with me. I thank you for your generosity. God will bless you."

I gave him a wry smile. "I wish I could do more," I said before walking away. Bob could have been lying or he could have been running a con on me. But I didn't care. It felt right to give.

But I learned that night that one person could not save the homeless world. Shoot, one person could not save every person in need he encountered. It would be too costly — financially and emotionally.

A minute or so after meeting Rob, there was Micah, at the corner of Peachtree and Ellis. He wore an Army jacket buttoned to the top, although it was around eighty degrees. I could smell alcohol. I knew to not judge him, though. It was not my place.

Before he could get started, I told him, "I wish I could help, but I do not have anything to give tonight." He accepted my words, but followed me as I crossed Peachtree Street toward the Ritz-Carlton.

"If you had some extra cash on you, how much would you give me?" he asked. That was a new one.

"How much would you need?"

"All of it, as you can see. But I wouldn't expect you to give me your all."

"Why don't you work? I'm not being mean. I'm just asking. You seem like your mind is sharp and you're healthy."

"You got a job for me to do? I'll do it."

"There are jobs out here. Are you trying to get one?"

"I work — sometimes. I may help some-one move or do some handiwork around someone's house. It just depends."

We walked back toward my car.

"Depends on what?"

"I don't know. How I feel, I guess."

"You can't like how things are for you right now. Why —"

"Don't say, 'Why don't I do something about it?' I've heard that before. Too often."

"I don't mean any harm, Micah. It's Micah, right? I just want to know, since we're talking and all."

"If I tell ya, I have to kill ya."

That didn't go over the way he planned it. It was not funny. I stopped and stared into his eyes, trying hard to not show the fear that ran through my body.

In looking at him, *really* looking at him, I saw a man with pain covering his being. There was something dark that had happened to him, something deep and lasting. I had seen it before in my Uncle Charles. He was a Vietnam War veteran. I had eavesdropped as a child when he'd told my daddy about the horrors he'd witnessed in battle: Friends blown up not ten feet away; comrades losing limbs; charred bodies after explosions. It scared me and made me cry years later when my cousin said he would enter the Army. I feared for him.

"That's not something you say to anyone, especially a woman you just met," I told Micah.

"You're right. I'm sorry. I was in the war . . ."

A chill came over my body.

"You were in the war? What war?"

"Desert Storm. Lot of stuff happened over there. I seen too much. Too much death. Too much hurt. I think I'm the same person, but everyone says I'm different. And, well, I guess I am because I'm out here."

"I'm so sorry. I have heard that America doesn't do enough for the vets. How can you fight for this country and then not get the care you need?"

"You asking the wrong person."

"I wish I could help you. I really do. I just don't have any money."

"It's OK. You helped me by talking to me. Wait. Hold on a minute."

Micah turned to another homeless guy who was saying something to me from his seat up against a building wall. He began to yell.

"Don't make me crack your head open, nigga. You see me here with this woman. Don't disrespect me and don't disrespect her. I'm surprised you're alive. You the type of nigga who will get killed, acting like some kinda damned fool. Mess around again and I'll be the one who does it."

The man said, "You better go on. You ain't

killing nobody."

Micah took a step toward him, his fists balled up.

"*Micah,*" I said. There was desperation in my voice. "Please, don't. Let's just go. *Please.*"

How was I caught up in that street mess? I just wanted to go for a walk. And yet there I was, in the middle of an argument between two homeless men. It was crazy.

Micah took one more step toward the man and stopped. He turned to me. The man scrambled to his feet.

"You'd better go on," Micah said to me. "I don't want you to see what's about to happen to this guy."

Part of me wanted to run. But I had seen my Uncle Charles in Micah. I wanted to help him. At least, he could end up in jail. Worse, he could kill the man — or get hurt.

"No, let's go, Micah," I said. I tried to sound stern, as if I had some power over him. I wanted to grab his arm, but I wasn't sure the last time that jacket had been washed or where it had been.

"Let's *go.*"

Finally, Micah turned and we resumed our walk. But he was not quite done with the man. "You'd better not be here when I get back."

I had no idea if my words would register with him. "You don't need to be fighting that man or any man. Please tell me you won't go back there and beat that man up. It's not worth it. Nothing happened to warrant a fight."

"The man has a problem. This isn't the first time I had to get on his ass. He sees me with you; he needs to keep his mouth shut."

"That's true, but you shouldn't let him get you so upset. We were talking nice and calm. Now you're yelling."

And I thought: Jekyll and Hyde. I also thought: I need to get the hell away from this man.

Micah would not look at me. He walked looking straight ahead. But I noticed he was sweating. And the look on his face dramatically changed. It was tight and tense.

"Can I buy you a soda?" I asked. "Or anything cold. I think it would help you calm down."

I said that as much for me as I did for him. I wanted to get away from him without enraging him.

"You don't have the money to buy me a soda," he said. "You feeling sorry for me? Please don't."

"I have a card I can use. Please, let me get

you something. It's not about feeling sorry for you. It's hot. I just thought you'd like a soda or water. We both can use something."

Micah didn't speak. "Stay here. I'll be right back."

It took me about five minutes to purchase two Pepsis and a bottled water. I had the cashier give me cash with my purchase also. When I got back outside, Micah not only had not moved, but seemed frozen in the same position I had left him: standing with his left hand in his jacket pocket, staring straight ahead.

"Here you go," I said tentatively. I held out the bag with a soda and water for him. He didn't move. After several seconds, I got frustrated. "You want this?" I asked with an edge.

"Now you yelling at me?" Micah said.

"What was that? You stood there like a mannequin."

"I was recalling a battle situation. The enemy closing in, you know? That happens and you're in a bad position, you have to be still. Can't let them know you're there."

"You know we're in downtown Atlanta, right? You're safe."

He finally looked at me. He had a confused expression on his face. He looked down at the bag.

"What's this?"

"I went into the CVS and bought you a soda and water."

"When?"

"Just now. A few minutes ago."

He took the bag and looked inside. "You bought this for me?"

"You don't remember?"

He didn't respond. "Here," I said, handing over a five-dollar bill. "I got some cash inside. I wish I could do more."

"Thank you. Thank you."

He stared at the money and I started to walk away. "I wish you the best, Micah. I will pray for you."

"Yes, pray for me, please. Thank you."

I walked to my car as fast as I could, ignoring another man who sat wrapped in a blanket on a slate of cardboard. I'd had my fill of feeling uncomfortable. And yet I felt so bad, so sorrowful for the men I encountered and so inadequate that I could not do more.

My few dollars would help them for a short time, a very short time. Then what?

CHAPTER TEN:
HISTORY
RODNEY

I slept in front of the church many times because my faith had been tested. It was hard for me to believe in God when I had lost my whole family. If there were a God, He would not allow me to live through this. He would have just taken me, too. But I wanted to believe in Him.

What I saw in the streets in almost two years, though, was evidence of the devil's works more than God's. That's how I felt.

I wasn't always that way. I grew up in the church. I didn't want to be there, but my parents insisted on it — even though they didn't go. They made me go, and I had to report back to them what I learned in Sunday School and the message from the sermon.

It became part of my routine as a child, all the way through high school. None of my friends went to church. *None* of them. Growing up in Southwest Atlanta was more about survival than anything else. And survival did not mean calling on God. It meant staying out of the wrong situations and being able to defend yourself if you were in the wrong place at the wrong time.

When I got to college, the idea of church faded away like a childhood memory. For the first time in my life, I had freedom to go to bed when I liked, to come and go as I pleased. It was liberating. It was fun.

I worked in the financial aid office, so I could have a little money to eat outside of the campus cafeteria from time to time. College was learning, but it was more interesting for me because I always had been a people-watcher. I didn't realize it at the time, but living on the streets gave me time to think about everything, and that's one of many things I discovered about myself.

I could see in certain classmates that they would not make it out of college. There was something in their DNA or background — or both — that prevented them from maxing out their potential.

Some just were not bright enough. Some were not committed enough. Some were destined for underachievement.

And I was the one who ended up on the streets.

It was hard for me to admit something about myself: I was sick. I was fine for a long time, until I was twenty-eight. I was so determined to be the best, to make my way, to succeed, that I worked long hours and rarely took off. Most days I would be the first to arrive at 6 a.m. and the last to leave at 9 p.m. After three days of working pretty much around the clock on a project I believed would take my career to another level, something happened.

I didn't know it at the time, but I later learned that sleeplessness was one of the triggers of bipolar disorder. And stress was a factor, which I certainly felt leading that project.

Not everyone who can't sleep or feels stress will get it. I was predisposed to it. I didn't learn it until years later, through family screening, but grandfather had it. I never knew him, but studies showed that if someone in your immediate family had bipolar disorder, you were prone to getting it, too.

No one else in my family was diagnosed with the condition that I knew of. But those three days, when I couldn't sleep because I was so hyped up and stressed about work, set off whatever gets set off to make the bipolar disorder kick in.

And so, instead of going to work that day,

I shut down. I felt sad, depressed, like my world was over. It scared me because I had never felt that way. I couldn't get out of bed. I had no confidence in all the work I had done. I was frozen in fear.

All day I stayed home in bed. Did not call my office. Would not answer the phone. Finally, that evening, out of concern, my boss sent someone to my apartment and the property manager let him in to find me in the dark, covered in bedding. They thought I was dead.

Thing was, I was alive — but I would never be the same.

It took more than a year before I was properly diagnosed. First, doctors figured I had given in to the stress of the job, and the combination of no sleep messed me up. They considered it a sort of stage fright.

Finally, when the other end of the bipolar spectrum hit — sudden and extended euphoria — my family took me back to the doctor. I had an episode during the funeral of a cousin. Instead of mourning, I was happy, singing and laughing, talking to anyone in my path.

It was embarrassing, but I could not control it. That was the disease — it took over and I could do nothing about it. There were extremes that went both ways. It was then that I had to learn about the disorder and how to handle it. Or *try* to handle it.

First, I had to believe something was wrong with me. I could not understand it. I was fine, perfect . . . and then I wasn't. It was confusing to hear doctors tell me, essentially, I was out of my mind, that I needed medication and therapy to "control" myself.

That news alone was depressing. And scary. And unbelievable. What was wrong with me? I heard all the technical stuff from the experts, but it didn't make sense. I had all my senses. How could I be bipolar or PPD or whatever they called it?

So I learned all I could about the disorder. But the more I learned, the scarier I became. Research said most of us bipolar could have attacks — manic episode or bouts with depression — nearly every day.

I took it all in and was almost manic about learning the medications that could help. But they were called "antipsychotics," and that was a jolt: olanzapine, quetiapine, risperidone, ariprazole, ziprasidone, clozapine.

For years, I was on a combination of olanzapine and fluoxetine, an antidepressant, and it kept me on an even keel, for the most part. But I didn't feel like myself. I felt programmed, restricted, trapped. Sometimes it was suffocating or stifling.

Like I was in a glass box at times, a glass box that could shatter at any time.

I also did therapy, which was helpful at times. Other times it was somewhat of a joke. The idea was to talk about my anxieties. I wanted to forget about them, especially the things I saw that I was told were not there.

That part had been really troubling — seeing things or people that others say did not exist. It felt so real to me.

That's why I ran from Chester at Mc-Donald's several weeks ago. I looked up and saw the men in black suits and hats coming for me. I didn't know what the hell they wanted, but I could tell they weren't friendly. They came around every month or so. And each time I ran and hid until I lost them.

One time, before I had killed my family, when times were great, I had sat alone at the dining room table. I had looked out the window and seen four Indians with arrows on fire, their bows cocked and pointed at our home. I had ducked under the table, just as my wife had entered the room.

"What are you doing down there?" she'd asked. I could hear the confusion in her voice.

"You don't see Indians out there, with bows and arrows?"

"If you don't stop playing around, Rodney. You know good and well there are no Indians outside."

I had played it off. "Was just trying to see if you would look before reacting."

I had looked back out of the window and the Indians were gone. I was scared. I knew what I had seen. But I also saw fear in my wife's eyes.

"I was just playing."

I'd had another episode years later after I had been diagnosed — I'd scared my daughters when I'd covered my head as we'd watched television. Looked as if the roof was caving in. Darlene was firm.

"Rodney, you're going to scare us to death. You have to take your medication. I know it makes you feel strange sometimes. But you can't do this to us anymore. You've got to do what the doctors have prescribed. Now be honest with me: Are you going to do what you're supposed to do? If you can't tell me that, we're going to have to leave. You know we love you so much. But, honey, please: I don't want to leave. But I have to protect our children."

That scared me more than my illusions. My girls had come to be my life, my pulse.

I knew I could not live without them. And once they were gone, I didn't die. But all that was inside me did. I was not alive.

CHAPTER ELEVEN:
IT'S A (HOMELESS)
MAN'S WORLD
BRENDA

What was it about me that I had come in contact with more homeless men in the previous several months than men with a job and home? Was I attracting them? And if I was, what did that say about me?

As much as I believed I didn't need a man, I sure missed the presence of one. Not just for the sex, which I needed too. I mean, two years without feeling a man's loving was the longest I had gone since William Brunson popped my cherry when I was sixteen.

I used to feel sorry for some of the members of the book club I used to belong to when they complained about not having a man. I was three years into my marriage at that time, and things were going well with Troy and me.

He was a strong man who, without trying, imparted wisdom and philosophies that stuck with me. We met online — a dating site. He said he was tired of meeting "women of no substance," and I was tired of meeting men who didn't know what substance meant. But we hit it off and less than two years later, we were married.

He had left me on a Saturday. We had sat at our kitchen table and had lunch that day. Nothing prepared me for his announcement. We had some issues, but nothing that was catastrophic . . . I thought.

When he'd called me, he said: "I didn't want to leave. I *had* to leave. You deserve more of an explanation, but I can't give you one. I just don't want to be married anymore."

I was mad at myself for a long time because I let him walk without saying much more. I was so dumbfounded that my mind was numb.

The idea that I would only hear from him again one time did not cross my mind.

I called him. I texted him. I left him messages. I got no response.

Once I stopped being mad at myself, I felt sorry for myself. I questioned who I was as a woman and wife. I could not stop thinking about what I could have done to run away a good man. It ate at me.

Worse, it made me feel less than a woman, like I didn't deserve a man. For a long time,

I was intimidated to talk to a man. I had no confidence.

Meeting Rodney changed that. We did not have romantic conversations by any stretch. But talking and debating with him, challenging and being challenged by him resurrected something in me.

My confidence in my thoughts grew. Over time, I became self-assured again. And with my appearance, while I still could lose some pounds, I knew I could attract a man. Rodney was homeless, yes, but he was a man, and that came through in how he sometimes looked at me. I was not trying to interest him, but I took notice that he took notice in me.

It was pretty remarkable that he had such an impact on me in such a brief time. Him leaving the hospital before I could see him reminded me of my husband leaving me.

At one point, I missed my husband and Rodney — for different reasons, but I missed them nonetheless.

I missed the passion that came with being married. Many nights, after I got over my anger and hurt, I needed to feel a man's hands on me. I missed the physical nature of a relationship, the romance, the *sex*.

With Rodney, I missed the conversations. I missed the banter — minus the insults.

Talking to Rodney and learning about him was like energy to my mind. And I missed the opportunity to help him.

I wanted and needed to see him. And then it came to me one evening as I watched *Atlanta* on TV: Rodney had told me the other places he liked to spend time were near colleges, so he could be around young people trying to better themselves.

Specifically, he mentioned a Popeyes Chicken and Biscuits near the Morehouse College campus. And right then, I got up, got dressed and drove over to the West End.

It was not a nervous ride for me, though. It was an anxious ride. I used to feel that way when I was in high school before a volleyball game or on the first day of a new job.

When I got there, it was close to 11:30 p.m., and only the drive-thru was open. I saw a man sitting in front of the building, facing Lee Street. My heart raced at the thought of it being Rodney. But when I turned into the parking lot, I could see it was not him; the man was older and a few complexions lighter.

I drove around the drive-thru line and circled the building. No Rodney. I saw two men hanging near the entrance of the Church's Chicken across the street — argu-

141

ing about what sounded like bus fare. Neither was Rodney.

I was disappointed. Before I got back on Interstate 20 East to head home, I noticed I needed gas. Conveniently, there was a gas station on a side street across from Popeyes. I was not comfortable going to it at that hour; it was not the best neighborhood.

In fact, I had read in the *Cascade Patch* about a rash of carjackings in that area. But that needle made me fear running out of gas on the highway, and so I took a deep breath, said a quick prayer and drove to the gas station.

Many identify theft sites and experts encouraged consumers to not swipe their credit or debit cards at local gas stations. But I was too scared to leave my car and go to the cashier. So I took a chance and swiped my card.

As fate would have it, as soon as I began to pump the gas, two men appeared that I might not have considered "suspicious" if it were not going on midnight in an area of town recently in the news for crimes against motorists. But under the circumstances, I viewed them as a potential threat.

"Can you help me get a two-piece?" one of the men said as he approached.

My heart pumped faster than the gas.

"Not tonight. I have no money," I said. I was firm, not scared. Well, at least my voice didn't crack.

"You got something," he said. "Gimme something."

The way he said it scared me. It was like, if I didn't give him something, he was going to *take* anything. Troy's words — "Fight crazy with crazy" — came to me.

"I can't give you what I don't have. Now leave me alone."

I spoke with no ambiguity or fear.

"We bothering you?"

"You need to go on."

"Now you telling me what to do? You getting way out of hand. You must don't know who I am."

In my fear, I looked at the man hard. He was light-skinned with light eyes, but they were set back in his head. He had bushy eyebrows and curly hair protruding under his hoodie. He would have been cute if he weren't so grungy.

"I'm gonna scream if you don't get away from me." I raised my voice.

"So, what? Who can hear you? Ain't no heroes around."

I became petrified then. I had no gun — was scared of guns. Had no pepper spray. Nothing.

He came closer, to within a few feet of me. I stopped pumping the gas and pulled the pump out of the tank. All I had as a sort of weapon was to douse the guy with gasoline if it came to that.

The other man came closer and then took a couple steps back.

"This gas will burn you," I told the first man, holding the pump up as I would a knife.

"I ain't afraid to burn. But you will die."

"Hold on, man," the second guy said. "Leave her alone."

"Why?"

"Leave her alone."

I was scared to look away from the threatening man, but my desire to see the other one took over. And so, I glanced to see Rodney staring at me as if we were old friends.

"Rodney?" I said. There was too much excitement in my voice, and not because he was saving me from trouble. I was so happy to see him that I forgot about what had gone on seconds before.

"You know this one?" the first guy asked.

Rodney's eyes locked with mine. After a few seconds, he finally answered.

"Yeah. That's my friend, Brenda."

The guy backed off. And they turned to walk away.

"Rodney?" I said. "Wait a second."

He stopped and told the other guy, "Go ahead. I'll catch up with you."

"Why are you hanging with that . . . that criminal?"

"We're all criminals in one way or another."

"I'm not a criminal."

"What are you doing here? And you should thank me, too."

"Thank you. What was that guy going to do to me?"

"Nothing."

"Nothing?"

"He gets off on scaring women. That makes him a coward."

"So why are you with him?"

"Why are you here?"

"Getting gas."

It was true. I did not feel compelled to tell the entire truth. I first wanted to see if he was happy to see me.

"Over here? What you doing over here?"

"So now you're my daddy?"

Rodney slowly nodded his head and turned to walk away.

"I came to find you," I blurted out.

And like in the movies, he stopped in his tracks. A few seconds passed before he turned back toward me.

"You miss me, huh?" he said.

I smiled broadly.

"I did . . . but just a little."

I smiled.

"Why?"

I was not sure why, but he forced me to think of a reason.

"Because . . . you're my friend."

It was like the sun came out. Rodney tilted his head and a smile almost creased his face.

"Everyone you meet is not your friend."

"Yeah, but you are. And you know it. Don't fight it when someone really likes or cares about you. I consider it a blessing that we met."

Rodney looked away for several seconds.

"I had a dream about you. I only dream bad dreams about that horrible night. If I dream about anything else, I don't remember. But I remember a dream about you."

"What was it about?"

The other guy yelled at Rodney. "Yo, come on. Let's go."

"You go ahead. I ain't going."

"What? You ain't going? Why?"

"Man, go on now."

He turned back to me.

"What happened in the dream?"

"We were sitting at Centennial Olympic Park talking and eating ice cream. Ice cream. I haven't had ice cream in two years. You dared me to run under the water fountain. I had you hold my cone and then I ran under the water with all the kids. We laughed so hard because I was soaking wet."

He literally smiled at the telling of the dream. I didn't think he realized it.

I didn't know what to say. But I was flattered.

"I laughed in the dream. I hardly laughed — real or otherwise — since that night. I . . . I felt so good. I felt normal — whatever that means. And then I woke up."

"What do you think that means?" I asked.

"I don't know. But it has to mean something that you were in my dream. Right?"

"I would think so, but I don't know if dreams have meanings or what? I'm glad I was, though."

Rodney didn't speak.

"Let me look on my phone and Google what dreams mean."

"There are no meanings to dreams," he said.

"Wait. Let me look it up . . . OK, here. This is what one website says: 'The question (of whether dreams mean anything) is so broad. The answer is no: Dreams don't mean something; dreams mean *everything.* Dreams are a mesh of memories, desires

and/or visions. Sometimes they mean something (to you) and sometimes they are
pointless.'

"So maybe the dream meant something."

"I know it meant something — it had to. I
don't know what, but for two years, I
dreamed of nothing but one thing — and
then I have a dream with you in it. I don't
understand why."

"Maybe it's because you felt what I felt."

"Which was what?"

"That we made a connection. That we're
friends."

"I don't have friends."

"I'm sure you had friends before, you
know, the accident."

"I did. Well . . . yeah, I did."

"What happened to them? I'm sure they
were there for you. Don't you miss them?"

"Missing them would mean I would have
to care, and I don't. Not that they weren't
good people. It's just that they couldn't help
me. And I had nothing to offer them. So
what would be the point?"

"Maybe they could have helped. You could
have tried. Why didn't you try?"

"Because . . ."

"That's a child's answer."

"Because I didn't want any help. I thought
I told you that."

"I think you do. Well, maybe you didn't then, but you do now."

"Why would you think that?"

"Because you're here talking to me. You dreamed about me because we made a connection and that connection was made because I want to help you — and you want to help me."

Rodney, who had been looking down, raised his head. There was an expression on his face I had not seen. I read it to be confusion. "You think I can help you?"

"You already have."

"Explain that."

I hadn't given it much thought, but I knew what I felt, so I just started talking.

"Meeting you awakened the woman in me, Rodney. By that, I mean parts of me that I had either lost or lost touch with began to come back to me. I didn't want to be around a man after my husband left me. I had no confidence to even hold a conversation. I hated how rude you were to me, but it forced me to fight back, to show some pride, which I had lost.

"My heart had been broken, and part of that brutality was that I lost my compassion for people. Meeting you helped me to find that caring heart that always had been a big part of me — and every woman. I don't know how you did it, but you made me care for you when you weren't even trying. And it felt good to care about you, to care about your well-being.

"So, all this time after seeing you in the hospital, I've been hoping to see you again. I looked for you at McDonald's every day for a while. Finally, I called myself giving up. But here I am tonight. I remembered that you said you liked being around young people getting their education.

"And here you are."

"Here we are," Rodney said. It was encouraging. He had not made any hint in the past of being open to me.

"Where are you going?" I asked.

"It's the same answer every time you ask me that: Anywhere. And no place."

"That's not a good state of mind, Rodney. We have to do something about that."

He looked at me with a curious expression, the same one I saw when he had told me he did not want my help.

"When I say, 'do something about that,' I don't mean to get you off the streets. I mean, I wish you would, but you seem to think you're supposed to be here."

"So what do you mean by help then?" he asked.

"I mean to help you remember all that life

has to offer and what you can offer to the world and people. When we understand we can help others, we realize we have a purpose. And that's all many people need to keep moving forward."

"Sounds like you were reading some self-help book."

"That doesn't mean it's not true."

I was becoming good at firing back at Rodney. Our banter made my mind sharper. And it built my confidence.

He always had a comeback, and so I waited. It only took a few seconds.

"Sometimes what's true isn't always right."

"We can go on and on, Rodney. The bottom line is we don't have to call it 'helping you.' We don't have to call it anything. I just want to be your friend and spend some time with you. And don't ask me why. I just do."

Rodney nodded his head. He wiggled out of the backpack that he carried and placed it on the ground.

"If I wasn't dirty, I would hug you," he said.

I knew him feeling that way was one thing, and saying it to me was a bigger thing.

"Thank you for saying that."

CHAPTER TWELVE:
BOSOM BUDDIES
RODNEY

For the next month, I spent time with Brenda almost every day. I felt good about it and I felt bad about it. I felt good because being with her, talking while walking the streets of Atlanta kept my mind off my pain. I also felt good because I could see that having someone to spend time with and talk to meant a lot to her. On top of that, I noticed that she stopped eating McDonald's and other fast-food. That, combined with all the walking we did, she had dropped about ten pounds.

"You getting skinny," I'd told her one day as we walked down Piedmont Avenue, past Georgia State University toward Auburn Avenue.

"Yeah, right. I'm a long way from skinny. But I definitely have lost some weight. My clothes fit differently. Actually, they *don't* fit. I haven't been on a scale, but the looseness in my dresses and pants tells me everything. I guess I should thank you, huh?"

"Don't thank me. You're the one walking and not eating garbage anymore."

"It's funny, but I feel better about myself. Not because I'm losing weight — well, not totally. Mostly because I feel better. I feel inspired. I love our conversations. I've learned a lot about you and myself. My outlook on life is more positive."

I was glad to hear Brenda speak so positively about her life. She had inspired me to be mindful of how I looked and especially smelled around her. In the beginning, she got the full me — if I was filthy and smelly, so it was. I did not care.

But the more I got to know her and to really see the person she was, I wanted to respect her. One way to do that was to shower at the shelter and change into donated clean clothes, to look and smell respectable. For someone who had no respect for himself, that was huge.

But I still had concerns about Brenda. Not about her sincerity — I had read her correctly. She was true blue. She did not have any friends, though. I began to believe I was the only person in her life. Her cell phone never rang or chimed while we were together . . . and we spent a lot of time together.

Whether it was from seven o'clock at night to midnight during the week or noon to six in the afternoon on the weekends, no one called her. No one sent text messages to her — unless she kept her cell phone ringer on silent.

I could not hold back asking her about it.

"Why don't you get any calls? Where are your friends?"

"I have friends and family," she said. "I just have chosen to not deal with them much."

Before I could ask, she answered.

"My family pissed me off when my sister got sick and none of them came around to check on her or to see if they could help in any way. I had a big problem with that. After the funeral, I decided I would give them a break for a few years to —"

"A few years?"

"Yeah. I don't want to deal with disingenuous people. I'd rather be alone. And my so-called friends, well, they were not much better. You really don't ever have that many friends anyway. You have associates. People you know. My father used to call them 'potential friends.' He said, 'And you watch: Most of them will never advance past P.F. — potential friend. If you understand that going in, you won't be disappointed.'

"He told me that when I was fourteen, I was upset that this girl I thought was my friend liked the same guy I did and told him lies about me. And he believed her. I was so hurt. Not about him believing her. About her telling the lies on me.

"Ever since then, I sort of kept most people as a potential friend just to avoid being disappointed."

I was fascinated by her life because it was somewhat similar to mine in that she distanced herself from people once close to her. And her thinking was similar, too. She had lost her parents and sister. Her husband left her and her best friend moved out of the country. Deep down, through talking to her, I realized she was as troubled as me.

That's why I felt bad about the friendship we formed. It felt like I was using her to build up my life.

We walked down historic Auburn Avenue, past the original Ebenezer Baptist Church on our right and the newer version of Martin Luther King Jr.'s church on our left, toward the home the Civil Rights icon lived as a child.

"Do you see how we are similar?" I asked. I talked to a lot of people in the two years I was on the streets. But Brenda was the only person I encountered who *related* to me . . . and I related to her.

"Hmmm. Well, maybe in some instances. Like, we lost our families and the loss has damaged us."

"How do we get over it? I think about my wife all the time. She was a good-looking woman. Not glamorous, but attractive. Sweet. Kind. Supportive. There's a hole in my heart for her. Don't you feel that for your husband?"

"I do. Sometimes. Troy was a good man. I just wish I knew what happened to him. One of my old book club members told me of her sister's husband one day deciding that he wanted to leave. No explanation. Just gone. I thought that was horrible. And then — what? — four years later, it hap-pened to me."

"Are you mad at him? I'd be pissed."

"I was furious for a long time. And I was sad. And I felt sorry for myself. Now, I feel sorry for him."

"What?"

"I know this man. *Knew* this man. For him to leave like that made no sense. I'm a good woman. I questioned that for a long time. But I know I am. And he walked away from me."

"Does he have mental illness in his family?"

"What? I don't know. Why?"

"Because mental illness in the black community is more widespread than we want to acknowledge. We don't get the help we need, so it goes undiagnosed. What I learned is that it passes down from generations. My father was bipolar. My grandfather was, too. And paranoid schizophrenic. But no one told me anything.

"It wasn't until my second episode that my Aunt Claire told me about her brother, who was my father. I would check your husband's family history if I were you."

"At this point, what good is learning about it? He's gone."

"If you wanted to help me, you damn sure would want to help him, if you could. Right?"

"That's true, but he probably ran off with another woman. And that ain't got nothing to do with being bipolar. But it's kinda ironic you telling me all this. How are you doing with managing your thing?"

"Hahaha. My thing? That's a nice way to put it. I'm doing all right. I have had my moments, though, that you haven't seen — I hope you never see."

"Like what?"

I was hesitant to tell Brenda because I had finally come to accept her as a potential friend. I didn't want to run her off. Hearing about my issues could have turned her away. But I took the risk because she asked and also because it would serve as a test to see how committed she was.

"Two or three nights ago, about an hour after you went home, I had this feeling of paranoia come over me. It seemed so real that dogs were after me. They came from everywhere. I was sleeping over near the Civic Center. I woke up scared and all I could see were dogs coming at me from all angles. I got up and ran.

"I ran about two miles, down past Krispy Kreme and up Ponce toward Boulevard before the dogs disappeared — just when I got too tired to run anymore. Something in me knew it wasn't real. But it felt too real to not run."

"Oh, my God, Rodney. I'm so sorry to hear this. How often does this happen?"

"No telling. Every few days, once a week."

"OK, I'm your friend, right? And you're mine?"

"Yeah."

"Then let me take you to a doctor to get you some medication."

"I don't know about that."

"Why?"

"I told you that medication makes me feel different and trapped. I don't feel like myself. It's like I'm a zombie or not in control."

"But the medication keeps away the drama, right? It helps you function more stably, right?"

"Overall, it does. Yes. But. . . ."

"But I'd like to see you one hundred percent healthy."

"That's never going to happen."

"Well, the best you can be. That's all any of us can ask of ourselves. Shit, even on our best days, we fall short of being a hundred percent. It has to be about being the best we can be.

"And if you will allow me to say this: You're not at your best living on the streets and in a shelter."

"That's your opinion. And opinions are like assholes — everyone has one."

"But Rodney, if you get consistent with your thoughts and not have the stretches of paranoia and hallucinations and stuff, you will settle in and realize you need to pick yourself all the way up, get a job and a place . . . and live. Your wife and daughters would want that."

She had some nerve telling me what my

family would want. I was able to talk to her because she seemed careful about not overstepping her boundaries or assuming to know what my life was like or what was best for me.

"You ever seen my wife? Ever talked to my daughters?"

"No."

"So how in the hell you gonna tell me what they would want?"

"You're right. I'm sorry. I'm just guessing."

"Don't speak on them. They are looking at me and glad I'm living like I'm living. Why would they want the best for me after I killed them?"

"It was an accident, Rodney. You didn't kill them. They died, but you didn't kill them."

"That shit makes no sense. This conversation makes no sense. I know what went on and what's going on in my life and in my head and you can't change it. You ain't God. You ain't a hypnotist. What's in my head is in my head. And it ain't never going anywhere."

"So this is it? This is the life you're going to live for the next twenty, thirty years?"

"Hopefully long before then, I will die. Pneumonia. Hit by a train. A stray bullet.

Cancer. Brain tumor. Something. Maybe then I can see my family again with smiles on their faces. All I can see now is them in fear and death."

"I've got to say that I really don't like to hear you talk like that. You have too much to offer."

"You've said that before. I don't have anything to offer anyone. I can only disgust or make someone sad."

We walked the rest of the way — about fifteen minutes — to Brenda's car without saying a word. I figured she was thinking she did not want to further upset me. I didn't have anything to offer.

"Let me ask you something," I said before she got into her car. "Are you happy with your life?"

"Am I happy? Well, I'm happier than I had been. Why?"

"No one has ever called you on your cell phone when we're together. No one texts you. I have seen people who damn near got hit by cars because they were on their phones walking down the street. I have seen people damn near kill themselves trying to drive and text at the same time. Senior citizens. Kids. Even homeless guys, guys in the shelter have cell phones and get phone calls. But you — no one calls you. *Ever.*"

I did not mean to embarrass Brenda, but I had. I was not going to apologize because I considered apologies worthless. But I was going to try to temper it a little, but she stopped me.

"Sad, right? You said something that was true: We're alike. Maybe that's what drew me to you. I don't know. But I'm OK with not having a lot of people calling me. People are only of good when they are not focused on themselves. And most people most of the time don't give a damn about you."

Suddenly, I knew I liked and cared about Brenda because the roles reversed. I tried to give her advice.

"You're an attractive woman. You should be going on dates, not walking around with a homeless, hopeless man. I told you months ago that your life was shit, but that doesn't apply anymore. I see that you have life in you. It's a waste to waste it with me."

"You don't get it, do you? Rodney, I have life in me, as you put it, because I met you. You were right when we first met. I had nothing going on. But since I began talking to you, which helped me feel better about myself, I've gotten a new job. I've lost weight. And most importantly, I have a new friend.

"Maybe I will meet a guy one day. But it's

not what's going to make me whole."

Her answer again reinforced who she was — a good person. In an indirect way, I was testing Brenda, which was not fair, but I could not help it. I did not want her to find a man. Finding a man would mean she'd likely spend less time with me. And after two years, I could finally admit that even in my pain, I was lonely.

Although I spent most of my time alone, because Brenda cared, *really* cared, I did not feel as lonely anymore.

CHAPTER THIRTEEN:
WHAT HAVE WE HERE?
BRENDA

The new job was in Buckhead, across from Phipps Plaza, which was great for two reasons: one, it was full time and with a salary slightly more than my previous full-time salary and, two, there were two shopping malls one block away.

It was strange how my world opened up when my attitude changed. I almost believed the unfortunate and bad things that happened to me fed off each other because I did not put up a fight. Instead, I just sunk deeper and deeper into a personal abyss.

No way I could have known befriending Rodney would be the jumpstart to rebuilding my self-esteem. Above all, I had been taught by my parents to help people: *And do so unconditionally, without expecting anything in return.*

The nightly walks with Rodney helped me to get closer to my old size, a size in which I felt more comfortable: in my clothes and in my skin. I had called myself "big-boned" or "thick," when the reality was I should have been wearing an 8 or a 10, not a 16 or an 18.

By cutting out fast-foods and processed foods and walking with Rodney, I melted away six sizes, down to a 12. I was so proud of myself. Gaining weight was easy and fast. A couple times I told myself I would go on a cleanse or get a personal trainer or stop eating junk food. But it was all talk. I was addicted to the bad stuff, and it had a stronghold on me.

One night after I had met and then could not find Rodney, I looked at myself in the mirror and I cried. Not just because I was not happy with what I saw, but mostly because I believed I did not have it in me to change it.

Rodney deserved the credit for my change because he challenged me. Not only did he walk me, but he also talked to me about diet and educated me on the value of eating fresh fruits and vegetables instead of Krispy Kreme and Mrs. Smith's. He introduced apple cider vinegar into my life, a health tonic that fought diabetes, suppressed the appetite, lowered blood sugar and so much more.

He said if I followed his plan, I would see

major results in a few weeks. He was right. And he said I would feel better and feel better about myself in the process. He was right about that, too.

It was strange that I did what Rodney suggested. I easily could have found most of what he told me to do on the Internet. I had Googled how to lose weight in a healthy way and the entries were limitless. But I did not act on anything I had read.

I smiled to myself thinking about the irony as I walked out the Tahari boutique at Phipps Plaza during my lunch break. This man, Norman, noticed.

"Must be a good daydream," he said.

Norman was not tall. We were eye-to-eye in my heels, which made me appear about five feet ten inches. But he oozed confidence. And he was so comfortable with himself that he made me comfortable.

"I'm just a happy person. So I smile," I said. That was the best relatively clever thing I could come up with.

"That's a good thing. Most people are burdened by something, and it shows on their faces. It's a good change to see happiness on someone's face."

He then introduced himself and within ten minutes, we were sitting in The Tavern having lunch. Turned out, he was on his break and browsing the mall when our paths crossed.

I felt reinvigorated, much as I did with Rodney, only different. A professional, attractive man had an interest in me. This was another world from where I had been just a few months earlier.

Preventing a perpetual smile from creasing my face during that forty-minute lunch was a chore. My heart danced — not because I was so caught up, but because it was awakened.

Before we departed, Norman said: "Thank you for trusting me enough to have lunch with me. I'm glad we met. I hope it's not the last time I see you."

Too excited to follow protocol, I volunteered my phone number. We hugged and I felt like a woman.

The essence of being a woman was feeling sexy and powerful and in control and smart and tender and tough and caring. Yes, all that. And I had begun, through Rodney's influence, to regain much of that. The sexy part was missing . . . until that moment.

Having not dated in so long, I could have been a little rusty about judging men. And maybe I was wrong, but I left Norman feeling like I had come upon someone good for me.

The remnants, though, of Troy remained, and so I would not dare throw myself into any man, no matter how smooth he was or how horny I was.

Troy did not ruin it for other men, but he definitely made it more difficult for someone to get close to me. Trust was in short supply. *If Troy could walk away from me and we were married, why wouldn't Norman . . . or any man?*

After nearly a month of dating Norman, I made a decision about him: He was not Rodney.

That decision shocked me. I had not planned to compare the two. There was no comparison, I thought. I had no romantic interest or connection to Rodney. But with Norman, I did not have that organic connection that produced hours-long substantive conversations that I had with Rodney. And that was so important to me. Good, mature conversation was sexy.

And one night, Norman sensed something.

"So, can we have a real conversation?" he asked.

"Don't we always?"

"I'm not sure. And I'm not sure because either you don't really like me or you're seeing someone else — or both."

"What? Why would you say that?"

"Because it's almost midnight and it's the first time I'm hearing from you today. And it would be one thing if this was rare, but it's almost every day. I can't reach you until late at night. So, seems to me you're seeing someone when you get off work and then talking to me before you go to bed."

"On weekends, we have gotten together early and gone to dinner," was my feeble comeback. He just looked at me.

"OK, there is someone," I said.

Norman's facial expression changed to disappointment.

"But it's not what you think," I quickly added. "I have a friend that I see on most days after work. His name is Rodney. We walk and talk and he's become my closest friend over the summer."

"So there's no romance?"

"No. We're very close now, though. And here's the thing: He's homeless."

I watched Norman closely. His response was going to determine our friendship. If he acted like a snob, it was over. If he accepted my friendship with Rodney, he had a chance.

"Really?" he said. "That's interesting. How did that happen? How did you meet?"

And with that, he passed. I went on to tell

him about how Rodney and I met and about Rodney and what his friendship meant to me.

"That's really special, Brenda," he said. "That says a lot about you. Have you told him about me?"

"I haven't. Wasn't sure you would still be here."

We laughed.

"But I'm going to tell him tomorrow. And I want you to meet him."

That next Saturday afternoon, I met Rodney on North Avenue behind Ponce City Market. I had bought him a pre-paid cell phone, so we could not lose touch. He was reluctant to take it, but he did. And he improved his appearance on most days. I was so happy that day to see that he looked fresh in "new" clothes and was relatively groomed.

"You got a haircut?"

"A trim. Guy wanted to cut it all the way down, but I didn't want that. Wanted to shave all the hair off my face, but a black man with no facial hair doesn't quite look right to me."

I laughed.

"Can I treat you to lunch? Let's go to Piedmont Park. There's a food truck festival."

And so we walked and talked over the almost three-mile walk to the park. I paid our entry fee and we walked among the thousands of people on the picturesque sunny day.

It was strange that I felt uncomfortable telling Rodney about Norman. Intuitively, I believed he could get jealous. Or was that my ego?

I waited until we had each had a Cuban sandwich and salad. We sat on the grass in the huge open field, watching people toss Frisbees, fly kites and play with dogs.

"So, Rodney, I met this guy and —"

"What? You met a guy? You're dating him?"

That response made me really uncomfortable.

"I met this guy named Norman about a month ago. He's a nice man. I wanted to tell you about him and for you to meet him, so you can give me your thoughts."

Rodney was agitated. *Was he jealous? Or was he about to have an episode?*

"His name is Norman? That's not his real name. Did you tell him about me?"

"I told him I had one friend I wanted him to meet."

"He's a spy. Brenda, don't you get it. People are after me. They won't leave me alone. As soon as I get comfortable or think they're gone, they find another way."

He started looking over his shoulder and all around us. My heart started racing.

"Rodney, you don't have to meet him. Don't worry about it. It's OK."

"It's OK?" he yelled. "How the hell is it OK when you're bringing a spy around me?"

"OK, Rodney, please calm down."

He didn't. It got worse.

"I bet he followed us here. He did, didn't he?"

His voice got louder and people started to notice.

"You told him to meet us here? What's he look like? Did you see him with a gun?"

"Rodney, please —"

Then he jumped up.

"That's him," he yelled, pointing over my shoulder. I turned to look. I saw no one. When I turned back, all I could see was Rodney's back as he sprinted across the field like a track star, looking back occasionally until he disappeared behind the Park Tavern on the corner.

I was devastated. I had set him off. Also, I was disappointed in myself. Rodney had opened up to me that he still experienced episodes, but as long as I did not see them,

172

I did not think much about them. The reality was I should have pressed him on seeking help. If he would not take the medication, maybe he would go to therapy, and maybe there he could be convinced to get the medicine.

People looked at me as if I had a problem after he ran off. I sat there unable to move and uncertain of what to do in that moment. I sipped on my sweet iced tea and decided I would wait a few hours and call Rodney.

I just hoped he would answer.

Chapter Fourteen:
Reality Check
Rodney

"Hello?"

"Rodney? It's Brenda."

"Yeah, I know. No one else calls me."

"Are you OK?"

"Yes. Sure. Why you ask?"

"What? You ran off and left me at the park yesterday. I've been calling you."

"What are you talking about?"

"You telling me you don't remember us sitting down at Piedmont Park, talking? And then I told you I met a guy that I'd like you to meet — and then you got up and ran."

"I don't know what you're talking about."

That scared me. I knew Brenda was speaking the truth. And so was I.

I was scared because there were other times I had been told something happened and I didn't recall.

"You don't remember us walking to the park and —"

"What park?"

"Piedmont Park, for the food truck festival."

"We didn't go to no food truck festival. What are you talking about? We walked the Beltline and then went to the shelter and I introduced you to Tony and Oz. They told you their stories and then the police came. Someone had robbed a couple and they lined all us up to see if we were involved, or knew who was involved.

"You were so nervous. You thought you were going to jail."

"That didn't happen, Rodney. I never met those people. We didn't go to the shelter. We went to the park."

I needed to hear her say it all for me to believe it. I remembered what I remembered. It was perfectly clear to me. But I was certain Brenda was right. Somehow, some way, I conjured up what I thought happened over what really happened.

"I don't understand," I said. "I . . . I just don't understand."

"Me, either."

We held the phones to our ears for several seconds in silence. Brenda finally said: "Well, I'm glad you're all right. I was worried."

"I'm worried now. It doesn't make any sense."

"Has this ever happened before?"

"No . . . I don't know . . . Well, there were a few times I said something to Chester about something and he didn't know what I was talking about. He basically told me I was tripping. I ignored it because I thought his ass was probably drunk. Now, I don't know."

"You know what I'm going to suggest, don't you?"

"What? Going to a doctor?"

"You already know."

That bit of news hit me hard. How anyone could spend time with someone and not remember it? How often did this occur? Maybe I should have seen a doctor.

"Maybe I will. Will you go with me?"

The request came out of my mouth before I realized it. I didn't ask anyone for anything. The fact that my instincts allowed me to ask her was stunning.

"Oh, Rodney, of course, I will go with you. I'm honored that you asked me."

"I don't know when it's going to be. But I will let you know."

"So what are you doing today? How about we walk the Beltline? I've never done it and I've heard how nice it is."

And so a few hours later, we met near the Krog Street Market, not far from Martin

176

Luther King Jr.'s birth home. I could see that Brenda had lost more weight. I could see the confidence in how she walked; it was not the sluggish gait it had been.

Her posture was more upright. Her head was up, not hanging.

"Look at you," I said. "I see some changes in you. You look better all around. Your clothes. Your facial expressions. You don't look down anymore. You look hopeful. I am proud to tell you how . . . how good . . . how I can see changes in you."

It was hard for me to pay anyone a compliment. I had turned off nice emotions. But Brenda turned them back on, slowly but surely.

"You look good, Brenda."

"Why, thank you, Rodney. And so do you."

She stuck out her arm for me to interlock with mine. It was not what I expected. I hadn't really touched anybody — except for during the many fights I got into over two years. Nobody wanted to get close enough for me to touch them and I didn't feel anything that would make me want to do so.

But Brenda forced me to break all my rules. It really was a *friendship,* something I had blocked out of my mind for so long that I literally had forgotten what it felt like to have a connection with someone.

I slipped my arm into hers and we smiled at each other and walked. She noticed.

"It feels good to smile, doesn't it?"

"I can't lie. It does."

"You know what I did last night?" she asked. "I researched homelessness in the United States. It's pretty remarkable that in this country, so rich and so big, that it's such a problem."

"I never really thought about it."

"It's not as bad here as it is in other places, like New York, San Francisco and L.A. First of all, there are more than a half-million people who are homeless in America. That's way too many. Shouldn't be any, actually."

"Well, that may be true, but what about cases like me? I chose to be homeless. There are other people who have been homeless so long, they don't know any other way. And then there are some who make my bipolar look like the sniffles. You mentioned that mental illness piece before and it's real. Trust me, I have seen it."

"This site broke it down. It said thirteen percent of homeless are 'chronically homeless,' meaning they have been homeless for more than a year or three times in four years. It said almost 50,000 of the homeless are veterans, which is just a shame. In fact, several weeks ago, I met a guy who said he was in Desert Storm. He was homeless."

"You met him? How?"

"Just walking in downtown."

"OK, you have to be careful. I guess it's crazy coming from me, but some of these guys are in bad shape mentally. Some of them have been in jail with me. And while I was in there for public disturbance or urinating outside, they were in there for assault and rape. So you have to be really careful."

"I understand. And trust me, there were some scary moments. But it turned out all right. What I learned was that more than 50,000 young people, under twenty-four years old, were homeless in 2016 for at least a week.

"And this one really got to me: half of the homeless population is older than fifty years old. How does this happen? What's going on in this country?"

We got off the Beltline and took Glen Iris Drive through the Old Fourth Ward, to Ralph McGill up across Boulevard and toward the Peachtree-Pine shelter. I wanted Brenda to get a closer view of homelessness in Atlanta. And I wanted to scare her from being too comfortable engaging men on the street.

As we got closer to the shelter, the harsh realities began to unfold. We turned right onto Courtland Street. Behind us, about a quarter of a mile away, was part of the beautiful Atlanta skyline. In front of us about five hundred yards were two blocks before the shelter that looked like something out of a war zone.

Trash piled up on the sidewalk, in the streets, everywhere. Homeless people lay or hung out on the sidewalk as if it were some inviting park. A woman who looked to be a senior was wrapped in a sweater and jacket despite the eighty-degree temperature. She recognized me and turned her attention to Brenda.

"I'm just hungry. Give me something to buy some food."

Before Brenda could react, I told her: "Don't. Unfortunately, she is on drugs. Crack. And that's where any money you give her will go."

"This is so heartbreaking," she said.

Just ahead of us, coming toward us, was a man in a motorized wheelchair. His eyes were glazed over and his body odor was prominent as he rode past. Brenda pretended to not notice.

"Where is he going in a wheelchair?" she wanted to know.

"No telling. Probably up the street to a friend who has something for him to drink. Drugs and alcohol are a big problem."

The closer we got to the shelter, the slower Brenda walked. I turned to look at her and there was complete discomfort on her face. She looked withdrawn.

A man across the street, in front of the Civic Center, which was awaiting renovation, dressed in a vest, shorts and cowboy boots, yelled at no one in particular: "This is what I'm talking about. People think they can steal from you and you won't do anything. I've seen the world. I ain't no fool. Come back over here and steal from me and you're going to get your arm cut off. I done it before and I'll do it again. The devil is real. He's out here. And he's walking among us.

"His name is John Wash, I'm told. He hallucinates really badly. One night at the shelter, it was winter and I was sleeping. It was around three in the morning. And suddenly, John starts screaming at the top of his lungs: 'Raid! Raid! It's a raid! They're coming. They're coming. The devils are coming.'

"One of the staff guys came in and threw

him to the ground. He was bleeding from his head. So it was sad all the way round."

Brenda shook her head when we got one block from Pine Street. Dozens of people milled about.

"What's wrong?" I asked.

"The air. It seems thicker, even though we're outside."

"And it stinks — I know," I told her. She didn't want to say it, so I said it for her. "It's the combination of all these people out here who live on the streets, who haven't taken a shower and who are sitting out in this sun sweating."

There were at least fifty men, women and a few children out there — hanging out and having conversations that were meaningful to them, but surely nonsensical to Brenda.

"Did you hear what they were talking about?" she whispered to me. "They were talking about someone's dog and how it was a better dog than another person's because it ate whatever it was given. Why aren't they talking about how they can get a place for themselves? Those two women, who had children with them, were talking about who could twerk better — and then they started a competition. I mean, this is unbelievable. They act like this is normal."

"Better start believing it because it's real.

And for them, it *is* normal. *Their* normal."

"But what about you? This is normal for you? You're OK with this?"

"OK with it? I don't deal with it. That's why I'm by myself ninety-nine percent of the time. That's why I come in and take a shower and keep it moving."

We stood at the corner of Courtland Street and Pine Street — the heart of the Atlanta homeless community. I nodded or waved to a few guys I had met there. But everyone was focused on Brenda. She stood out.

Immediately, the community could tell she was an outsider. So they stared at her too-clean clothes and in-place hair and aroma of sweet perfume. Her posture showed her fear — or, more accurately, her discomfort.

Outsiders in the homeless' designated areas were OK as long as they brought cigarettes and alcohol at worst, money or drugs at the best. But if an outsider stood there and stared, they would be told — and not so subtly — where to go. And it was not a nice place they wished to send them.

"But these are your peers, I guess. Trust me, I'm not trying to pass judgment, but I don't know. I'm so overwhelmed. All these people just out here on the street. And they seem so content. And the city does nothing? Did you see that man who was camped out on the ground sleeping in front of someone's garage?"

"Yeah. He kind of lives there."

"Outside? Right there in someone's driveway? And what about that woman with those two kids? They can't be more than six years old."

"I don't know her, but I heard she had an abusive husband and ran away. They're from South Georgia somewhere. She's hiding. I think she's at the Atlanta Day Shelter for Women and Children."

Brenda's head spun. She surveyed the people and had questions about most.

"How can this exist here in Atlanta, a half-mile from downtown? It's two blocks of . . . of madness. *Two blocks.* It's amazing. It's sad."

"That's why I don't spend any time here. I'm already sad enough."

"But are they being helped? What programs are set up for them? I know people donate food and clothes. But what's being done to get them *off* the streets? What counseling is offered? Job preparations? And, see, look at that man. He needs help."

Brenda motioned toward a fellow I had seen often who had the trio of troubles:

bipolar, homeless and a drug addict. He would act out on occasion, singing old school R&B songs, entertaining drivers of cars by dancing as they drove past and generally showing that he was hurting.

He would sleep on the streets — literally. He had a small mattress that he would drop on a sidewalk in the middle of the day and crash. For months on Linden Road, just across the parking lot next to Gladys Knight's Chicken & Waffles, he would lie on that mattress on the sidewalk.

"Want to meet him?" It was a joke. A bad joke. Between the smell and the trash and the hopelessness of the people, she was worn out.

"I just want to go," she said, as we walked away from Pine and Courtland Streets. "I feel so helpless. I want to help all these people. But I can't. But I'm going to try. I'm writing the councilman in this area. Look at these streets. How can they let these two blocks be so disgusting?

"And can I ask you something that I hope doesn't offend you?"

"Go ahead."

"Why are they so nasty? I don't mean attitude. I mean why do they throw so much trash on the street? They are hanging out there all day. Why wouldn't they put the trash in a dumpster? Why make the streets look so horrible?"

"Because they are hopeless. They want people to notice. Did you see the guy sitting in the chair with the sign? It read: 'Stop, Look and Help.' Believe it or not, I remember seeing homeless people before I became one. In D.C., right near the White House, among all the tourists. War veterans would be there with legs and arms amputated and living on the streets. I saw a guy one time in Chicago, on Michigan Avenue, who had the most hideous, deep gash on his leg.

"It was an open wound, probably gangrene, and he had it exposed for people to see as they walked by. None of those cases made me feel good. But just like those folks back there — they want people to notice."

"I read where Mayor Reed wants to close the shelter. In fact, one year it almost closed because it couldn't pay the water bill. But someone saved it by paying it. The mayor says it doesn't work, which I tend to agree with him after seeing this. But there has to be a plan. You can't just put a thousand people out on the street like that."

"It could close at any moment. The City Council voted for the city to buy the building and turn it into a first responders and police SWAT headquarters. I went to the meeting. It was ugly. Lots of people want that place to stay open. Black Lives Matter wants it to stay open."

"Should keeping it open be the focus or should the focus be finding a way to get those who need help counseling, doctor care, psychiatric care, job training? My focus would be on helping the people who need help, not kicking them out."

"It's a debate that could go on for a long time. I just wanted you to see up close what it's really like, so you will be aware of who you could come in contact with. I'm not saying those are bad people. But some of them are. Some of them are criminals and thugs who prey on people like you."

"Like me?"

"Yes. Nice and innocent people who want to save the world. For some of them, you're a juicy piece of meat."

CHAPTER FIFTEEN:
ANOTHER LEVEL
BRENDA

I thought about and decided to wait to tell
Rodney about Norman. I was no psycholo-
gist, but I realized that maybe Rodney ran
as a reaction to news he didn't want to hear
from me.

Maybe he felt threatened or territorial
or . . . I didn't know. I just believed I triggered something by telling him that, and I
couldn't take upsetting him again.

I did, since he asked me to go with him,
begin looking for therapists. I had insurance
with my new job and so it would pay for us
to have some sessions. I didn't have to tell
them Rodney would be a part of the sessions. I was hoping to encourage him,
through the sessions, to take medication
that would lead to him getting off the
streets.

I found Dr. Jane Taylor. I wanted a
woman, believing Rodney would be nicer
and more open. Also, Dr. Taylor was black,

had played sports in college and she was from Atlanta.

It wasn't easy to get Rodney to go, however. Although he brought up the idea of me going with him, the reality of it "annoyed" him, he said.

I told him he was "just scared."

We had grown so close and comfortable that I did not have to cushion most things with him. I knew he appreciated my directness that I learned from him.

"Scared of what?"

"Getting better."

"No. No. It's hard to talk about that night. You wouldn't know."

"I've had traumatic things happen to me, too. We never talked about my sister dying, but that was devastating. And it happened at a time when you had disappeared on me, too."

"We didn't know each other then, really. Me being around then wouldn't have helped you."

"Maybe not, but my point is that it was a devastating time for me. I think about my sister every day. It hurts me that she's not here. So, I can relate a little bit about missing someone you love."

"You know the difference, don't you?"

"Yes, I know the difference."

"You didn't —"

"Rodney, you don't have to say it."

"Why not? If we go to the doctor, I'm going to have to say it."

"You know, I talked to this guy the other day, and he told me that most people or many people with bipolar disorder are *very* smart."

"Maybe. That doesn't matter to me. If you don't get . . ."

"Get what? Go ahead and say it."

"Never mind."

"Help," I said. "That's what you were going to say. 'If you don't get help, then it doesn't matter how smart you are.' And you're right. I'm glad to hear you say that. I have read about people killing themselves, acting out and hurting other people."

"I told you months ago that I wish I wasn't here," Rodney said. "I just don't have whatever it is to put a gun to my head and pull the trigger. I guess I'm not crazy enough to do that."

"No, you're smart enough to know that would be pointless."

"You have all the answers, don't you? Well, answer this for me, Senorita Know-It-All. What is a doctor going to tell me that I don't already know?"

"I have never been to therapy — God

190

knows I needed it after my husband left and after my sister died. But you know black folks. We try to pray it away. We think therapy is stuff weak white people do. But I have read up and learned. If you need to talk to someone, I don't care what race you are, you should talk to someone. You learn things about yourself that help you.

"Black folks still thinking not talking to a therapist makes us strong. What it actually does is make us stupid. There was this movie called *Burnt,* with Bradley Cooper. He was a renowned chef at a restaurant in London who wanted to reach the ultimate rating. But he believed he could do it himself. A therapist, played by Emma Thompson, told him, 'There's strength in needing others, not weakness.'

"Church has its benefits and I sho-nuff believe in praying to God. He has carried me through some things. But when you're talking a mental issue, we have to seek therapy, Rodney.

"I want you to get the help you need. Talking to someone might give you a little peace or allow you to sleep better or dream better. Or there's always the electro-shock treatment that lights you up like you've been struck by lightning."

"Yeah, well, we know *that's* not happening."

"I couldn't imagine. But seriously, let me set up an appointment with Dr. Taylor. She takes her last appointment at five on most days, four on Fridays. I will leave work early or we can go on my lunch hour. Whatever you say."

"Let me think about it."

He thought about it for about two weeks, during which time Norman and I got closer. It was strange, though. I felt like I was sneaking behind Rodney's back.

"So when can I meet him?" Norman asked. "If he's your boy, we should meet."

I told Norman my concerns and about the Piedmont Park incident. "You think he has something for you, romantic interest?" he asked.

"No, I don't, not at all."

"Do you have romantic interest in him?"

"No. Of course not. He's my friend. Period. We've built something special. I told you he welcomed me into his world. And I've done the same. Now we're going to counseling."

"Wait," Norman said. "Hold up. You're going to counseling together. What? Couples counseling?"

"I just told you we are just friends. He

asked me to go with him for support, and I am. That's what friends do."

"OK, cool. Don't get offended. I'm just asking. It's sort of a strange friendship. You go home to a nice apartment at night. And he lays down on the street somewhere? Strange."

"Are you making fun of us? It's not funny and it's not nice, Norman."

"Well, it may not be nice, but it's real. I'd rather be authentic with you and tell you the truth over being nice and telling you what you want to hear. The authentic me thinks you're crazy for befriending a homeless man."

"And the authentic me thinks you're insulting me and my friend. We didn't become friends to be judged by you or anyone else. That man has helped me regain my sense of self. I see him struggling with his past, but trying to fight back. I had a little hand in that. I'm trying to help him. He's helping me. He's done more for me than anyone in the last several years. So, I don't really care what you think about me and Rodney."

The more I talked, the angrier I got. And Norman could sense it.

"OK, let's not get into an argument over a homeless guy."

"That's being condescending. It's not an argument over a homeless man. It's an argument over you disrespecting my friendship with Rodney."

"You can't have a real friendship if you're not comfortable with the guy coming to your home. You can't even sit down with him in a restaurant. And if you could, he couldn't buy you a meal."

"You're disappointing me right now, Norman. I'm so disappointed. You think friendship is only about coming to someone's house and buying him dinner? That's how you think?

"Well, here's what I think, Norman. You should leave."

"What? Over this? I thought we agreed we would take the relationship to the next level tonight."

"You think I'm going to have sex with you after you insult me and my friend? I don't think so."

Norman left. I wanted sex with him that night. I needed it. But I was turned off. And when I was turned off, I was turned off. Sending him away also told me that Rodney was more important to me than him.

So, instead of bumping and grinding with Norman, I pulled out my laptop, retrieved a vibrator from the drawer and went to work.

I found a porn site that did not require I give them my credit card information and let it take me there.

I had not watched porn since my husband left me. It was something we did together on occasion — or just about every Saturday night. I wasn't into it at first. It seemed, well, nasty.

But to please my husband, I tried it. My thinking was that I'd rather him watch it with me than by himself or with someone else. Over time, it became less and less nasty. In fact, I came to look forward to those Saturday nights. It meant we'd get passionate and, more importantly, adventurous.

One time, however, I almost had to go to the hospital. I forgot how limber I was *not,* and tried to contort my body as I had seen one of the women in a video. I was on my back, with my head at the foot of the bed.

I slid toward the end until my head was hanging over and almost on the floor. Troy stood over me, and held my legs up and open as he tried to enter me.

It was OK for a few seconds. But soon I got dizzy from being upside down and I caught a cramp in both my legs — a calf on one leg and thigh in the other.

Troy thought he was doing something as I

screamed. He had no idea at first that it was about pain, not pleasure. It took him a few strokes before he realized the sounds I made were not primal — they were agony.

We laughed about it after I got myself together. But we used porn for excitement purposes only from that point on, not to emulate.

That night after Norman left, the porn did the trick: It got me wet and my toy did the rest. In three minutes, I had achieved a release that was long overdue. It was not the same as having a man — the physicality, the smell, the groping — but it served a purpose.

Oddly, I credited Rodney for me being open to pull out a vibrator after so long. Before he and I became close, I had lost my sex drive. That's a sad thing for a woman at forty, when sexual desires reach a crescendo.

But in feeling better about myself, all the things that mattered to me began to matter again. I was not sure if I would have ever gotten to that place if I didn't have Rodney in my life.

CHAPTER SIXTEEN:
A SEAT OF THE COUCH
RODNEY

I was surprised at myself. Instead of walking and sleeping, I spent much of the day using the cell phone Brenda got me. I read about what was going on in the world, something that had been a pastime for me.

Brenda had encouraged me to read and to scan the newspaper websites to learn what was happening in the world. I had not read a newspaper in two years. I kept thinking I'd see my face in the paper as the man who killed his family.

Enough time had passed for that to not be a possibility, and I dug into it as if I were famished. My mind felt open and fresh to process new information. Not all the news I read was good — much of it was disheartening, in fact — but I was reminded how much I used to love to learn.

I spent more than three hours reading about President Obama and his family and his accomplishments. I had proudly voted for him twice and I cried in the voting booth, when he won and at his inauguration.

Often I heard people at the shelter, black people, talking about "He didn't do enough for the African-American community" or "He could have done more."

I was ready for the next person to say something around me. I had read so much about the value of the symbol of a dignified black man as president. I was going to tell that person: "It's OK to try to be fair and even critical about President Obama and what he did or didn't do for black people. But you cannot deny and you cannot put a value on what he represents to all of us.

"I read about old people who said they could die in peace because they saw him serve the country with class and grace. I read people, the toughest people, who melted at his presence because he represented them in such a dignified manner. I understood that because as a black man, every time there was tragic news — someone being raped or killed — I literally prayed it was not a black person who did it. The black man's reputation was a lie, but to white people, it was real, and the more cases of a brother doing something horrific, the worst we looked in the eyes of others. Every bad case was an indictment against us.

"But here was the most popular and important man on earth who, for all his time in office, lifted up black people by his mere presence. No scandals. No angry black man. No indignant comments. He personified elegance and intelligence and strength. And our children got to see that. He had been the best example of a leader and a man and husband and father and a black man.

"So for anyone who said he didn't do enough for black people, I say he did more for black people than anyone on earth. Here I was, a man living on the streets who felt pride knowing he represented me. You can't put a value on that."

Problem was, I hardly talked to anyone but Brenda anymore, and so I told her my feelings.

"I'm so glad you started reading," she said. "And I feel the same as you. And taking it a step further, Michelle Obama was just as powerful and gracious as the president. She rocked it out."

We ate gelato on a bench outside of Paolo's Gelato Italiano in Virginia-Highlands. The guilt still covered me. But I felt more alive than I had in years. Talking politics while sitting outside on a gorgeous evening, enjoying the company of a good woman . . . it all felt so . . . normal.

I told Brenda that, and she said, "I'm so glad. It makes me feel good to hear that. We've come a long way, Rodney. I'm really proud of you. But you know what the next step is, right?"

"Therapy. I know."

"We can go next week. Think of it this way: President Obama would want you to go. You can believe that."

It was a cheap trick, but it sort of worked. I thought: If he could endure all the hate and disrespect he did for eight years — for me and the country — I could take a step to trying to get better.

"All right," I said. "Tell me when."

Four days later, we met at Dr. Taylor's office on Fourteenth Street in Midtown. Brenda was there before me. When I walked into the building, she stood up and smiled. I had gotten a blue blazer from the shelter and a close-to-new pair of jeans and a white shirt. For the first time in a long time, it mattered that I did not look homeless.

"You look so handsome."

Before I could respond, she hugged me. It felt awkward. I did not hug her back.

"Come on, it's this way," she said.

Dr. Taylor was tall and calm. She dressed in a striking pants suit and heels and she wore expensive-looking, wire-rimmed glasses.

After the formalities, she said: "So why are we here?"

I looked at Brenda. She looked at me. I could tell she wanted to speak, but she wanted me to step up. So I did.

"Dr. Taylor," I began. "I'm homeless. I have been living on the streets and in the Peachtree-Pine shelter for just about two years. I have been diagnosed as bipolar and —"

"OK, hold up right there for a second please," Dr. Taylor said. "Are you on any medication?"

"No. Well, I used to take a combination of olanzapine and fluoxetine."

"OK, I see," she said, writing. "How did they make you feel?"

"I felt good for a while. I felt in control. But then I began to feel uncomfortable, like I was being held back. Eventually, I just stopped taking it."

"But you knew if you stopped taking them, you would have the issues you had, which were what? Paranoia? Bouts of depression? Feeling wired?"

"Yeah, all of that."

"Well, first, let me say this: I commend you for being here. I'm guessing Brenda is responsible for getting you to come. That's a good friend. I can say to you that coming here is a great step in the direction of getting you in a better place in your life.

"The reality is that at some point you're going to need to resume medication. When we get to that point, we're going to find the right combination to make sure you feel good all the time — but Rodney, you will have to take the medication every day. No matter how good you feel, you should take it every day, as prescribed.

"That said, what concerns are you now experiencing?"

"Besides feeling so guilty that I want to punish myself and not enjoying life?"

"You feel guilty that your family is dead and you're not? That's not that far-fetched. In the simplest cases, it's called survivor's remorse. Because you've been classified as bipolar, we have to look at it in deeper terms. We can't ignore that you have a condition that reacts to heightened stress."

"There's also, if I might add," Brenda said, "the idea that at times, he believes people are coming for him and he runs off. It happened several weeks ago when we were at Piedmont Park, talking. All of a sudden, he started talking about spies and people after him and he just ran."

"I don't remember it," I said. "I believe her one hundred percent. But I don't remember anything about that. I thought we had done something else."

Dr. Taylor nodded her head and typed something on her iPad.

"How often do you have these periods where you don't remember something you've done?"

"I can't say exactly. Every week or ten days, something like that. It's strange to me because I feel OK most of the time."

"But if you've seen doctors before, I'm sure you've been told that's what bipolar is about — dramatic behavioral ebbs and flows. What we can do here is talk about what triggers your episodes. So, Brenda, what do you remember about that day Rodney ran away?"

I hadn't asked Brenda that question. Didn't think to. So I was curious about her answer.

"Oh, wow," she began. "Let me see. We started the day at Ponce City Market and we walked to Piedmont Park. It was a food truck festival that day. We ate Cuban sandwiches and sat on the grass and watched the people."

"What did we talk about?"

"On the way to the park, we talked about

203

President Obama and what he meant to the black community from a self-esteem standpoint. We talked about how he made us proud, how he showed the world a black man of dignity and intelligence."

"What? We did? Didn't we talk about him today?"

"We did. I thought it was strange you brought him up again, but I went with it. We talked about the greatness of the president for about thirty minutes that day, too."

Dr. Taylor asked: "What was the last thing you were discussing when Rodney had an episode and ran off?"

"I don't know if I should say," Brenda answered.

"Why?"

"Because what if it upsets him again and triggers an episode? I'm here to help him. I don't want to hurt him at all."

I was torn between knowing what triggered that episode, as Dr. Taylor called it, and not knowing for the same reason Brenda shared.

"It was so sudden, Dr. Taylor. We were talking just as calmly as we are now. And then, boom, he changed. And in ten seconds, he was gone."

"Rodney, do you want to know about the conversation?" Dr. Taylor asked.

"Right now, I would say I don't want to know. She can tell you what it was and you can decide whether she should tell me."

Dr. Taylor and Brenda stepped away from me, to the other side of her office. She whispered to her for several seconds. She nodded her head.

When they returned, Dr. Taylor said: "Eventually, we will talk about this; today probably isn't the best day. But we will get to it. Let's move on."

I was relieved. I obviously did not have control over what I would do when something was triggered, and I wasn't willing to risk messing up a good day.

"Let's talk in general about how you got to my office," she said. "How did you and Brenda get to this point?"

I was not eager to talk about how mean I was to her when we first met. Becoming friends hardly was something either of us considered at that point.

"I blew her off and she came back to the McDonald's to talk to me. I blew her off and we ran into each other at Piedmont Hospital. I blew her off and there she was on the West End at eleven o'clock at night, looking for me. That's when I knew she was sincere and I had to at least listen to her."

"And why were you so persistent,

Brenda?"

"I was at a bad place in my life, Dr. Taylor. Down in my luck. My husband had left me. My nephew got locked up. I lost my job. My sister was sick and eventually died. But there was Rodney, who was mean to me, but he made me think — about who I was, what my life was, what I wanted for myself and about him, how I could help him.

"Turned out, he helped me."

"We helped each other," I interjected. "Trust me, before this woman, all I thought about was punishing myself — not helping myself. She's the only friend I have."

"You never know what life has in store for you," Brenda said. "All you have to do is live it and everything will take care of itself. I'm not as close to anyone as I am Rodney. We've spent a lot of time and walked a lot of miles together."

For me, that made the session worthwhile. Sharing my feelings, my emotions about someone, emotions that were pleasant and not filled with anger, illuminated my spirit. It had been dark for so long.

The streets had grown on me and were a part of my makeup, so I did not do a lot of smiling. But I smiled as broadly as I ever had when the session was over and Brenda said: "I'm so proud of you coming today, Rodney. I'm so glad you're my friend."

CHAPTER SEVENTEEN:
EXPLOSION
BRENDA

When I got home from our first session with Dr. Taylor that night, Norman called. It was as if he watched me walk into the house, drop my purse on the table, kick off my shoes, rip off my bra and plop down on my bed. It was then when my phone rang.

"Didn't expect to hear from you again," I said. I didn't believe that and I was not sure why I said it.

"What? You trying to get rid of me? I'm calling to apologize. I had told you it was great that you made friends with the guy, whatever his name is."

"His name is Rodney."

"Right, Rodney. It's great Rodney is your friend. And I shouldn't have tried to diminish it. My bad. I'm sorry."

I couldn't be mad at an apology. I didn't agree with Rodney's position that there was no need for anyone to apologize, that apologies didn't matter.

Norman's apology meant the world to me. I had grown to like him. I wondered about why he was interested in me; that was my self-esteem talking. I had been so down on myself for so long — or right after Troy left — that I had no confidence a man would be interested in me.

But Rodney helped rebuild my confidence.

"You want to come over?" I asked Norman. That was a show of two things: one, that I was becoming more self-assured and not concerned about appearances; and two, I was horny.

Norman had been a gentleman for the most part. He had been patient. I had grown attracted to him. It was time.

I showered as he took the thirty-five-minute drive from Cobb County to my place. I thought about Rodney and how I wanted him to meet Norman and give me his view on him. I wanted them to be friends.

But I couldn't trust that Rodney would not have an episode.

And I wondered what was that about anyway? Did it mean he had romantic interest in me? Did it mean he was jealous? Or did it mean nothing? Maybe it just happened to be time for him to have an episode, and me telling him about Norman had nothing to do with it. I couldn't really know.

Those thoughts were dismissed for another day when Norman knocked on the door. I went into seductive mode, a place I had not been but had become eager to visit. And after a few minutes and kissing and caressing right there near the door, I could tell by the look on his face and bulge in his pants that Norman was just as ready as me.

The buildup to the passionate moment was intense. I knew after a few dates that I would sleep with him. It was just a matter of time and how my feelings for him grew in the interim.

I didn't believe there should be a certain amount of days before you slept with a man. I didn't believe in sleeping with a man so quickly, in the first week or two, either. It sent a wrong message, one I believed and experienced could make the guy believe you were "easy," and therefore not worthy of a relationship.

With Norman, it had been several weeks and I was comfortable we had passed that threshold of time. So, I passed on offering him a seat in my living room. It was go time, and a living room stop would have signaled yield. We went to my bedroom, where I had lit a candle and found the Sade station on

Pandora.

Having to look up at Norman while standing barefoot meant a lot. Most women needed a man they have to crank their necks to see his eyes. There was some security in that.

Norman was smart; he did not mention Rodney's name. Instead, he kissed me with a passion that solidified his earlier apology and confirmed it was our night to consummate the relationship.

I called it a relationship, but we had not set any ground rules. I knew the woman code calls for there to be a stated relationship status before sex, but I discarded it without a second thought. In fact, I thought it was lame at worst and unnecessary at best for women to try to pin a man down on a relationship status, especially just before sex. It was like a ransom.

As a grown person, I believed the decision on sex should come without the pressure of having to answer a useless question to validate whether it would happen or not.

It was a useless question because what was the man going to say with sex on the line? In most cases, he was going to say whatever he needed to say to have sex and deal with the inevitable repercussions later — *after* he got what he wanted.

So I didn't bother. Also, I wasn't sure I wanted a relationship with Norman. It had been about eighteen months since Troy had left. But it had only been about four months since I had gotten over it and began to feel I deserved someone wonderful to share to my body.

I liked Norman enough for that. A lot of women did the same thing — they just were not woman enough to admit it. They preferred to lie to themselves that sex was part of the relationship, when, really, there was no relationship in the sense of a commitment. The relationship was the sex.

For me, Norman delivered. I didn't see the sky open up or birds chirping around my head, but he was patient and tender and unselfish. He was concerned with pleasing me, which was a change. Troy wasn't dismissive of me, but he watched porn and focused on what a woman could do for him.

Norman and I tussled in my bed for about fifteen minutes — fifteen minutes that seemed like two days because I had been denied for so long. I was reminded how wonderful it was to be handled by a man, to be coveted, to be caressed. Norman was not the most skilled lover, but he tried hard and that effort was sexy.

He made it easy for me to appreciate his

passion because he was eager and attentive. He *wanted* me. That alone meant so much.

Our night together restored the sexuality in me. Rodney awakened it by helping rebuild my confidence. Norman confirmed that I still had warm blood running through my veins. I rested on my back afterward in a euphoric state. And I didn't even get an orgasm.

Orgasms mattered, but in that case it mattered more that someone I liked wanted me, found me attractive and treated me as a sexual being. I needed all that. The sex was important and invigorating. But it was more important for me to feel like a woman in a man's presence.

"That was so good," Norman said, lying next to me. Just having a man in my bed felt renewing. "I think we're going to get along well."

"I would have to agree with you," I said. "Not so much because of sex, although I did like the sex. But I especially like that you're a real man and you like me and respected me. I never felt rushed into bed, but I always felt like you wanted me. I appreciate your patience."

He pulled me over into his arms. I rested my head on his chest and dozed off. But my last thoughts were of Rodney. I wondered where he was sleeping.

When we woke up that morning, I wanted some more. I eased closer to Norman and placed my ample, bare breasts on his back. He exhaled.

"Now that's a nice feeling to wake up to," he said.

I reached around him and grabbed his manhood. "Yes, this is," I said.

He laughed, turned over and we hugged. And before long, we were at it again. I needed to climax this time — an orgasm with a man was more intense that a sex toy-generated orgasm.

And so I concentrated and opened my mind and body to Norman's passion, and then it came — an inner explosion that covered my hot body and left me feeling suspended in air. I had almost become unfamiliar with that feeling. But it was cathartic. I felt better about myself.

The release helped me sleep more soundly than I had in years. I was certain I snored . . . and I didn't care.

"Yeah, you were doing your thing," Norman said. "But I wasn't gonna bother you. Obviously, you needed that rest."

"I did, huh? I'm sorry. But I slept like I was in hibernation. I don't recall moving."

Norman laughed as he gathered his

clothes. It was 7:40 a.m.

"I hate to hit-and-run, so to speak," he said, laughing. "But I've got to go."

I was not offended. My body felt too good to feel anything but ecstasy.

"Let's get together around six-thirty this evening. I have a spot I want you to experience," he said. I was so glad Norman was interested in seeing me again. After so long, I wasn't sure how he would react.

"Today? I can't today. I'm meeting Rodney at that time. That's a standing thing with us," I told him.

That did not go over well.

"So, that's how it's going to be? I take a backseat to this guy who does not have a home but has a date with you?"

"Norman, we had a good night and a better morning. I can't cancel on him. I just can't. It's important that we connect. It's like therapy for us."

"I thought you said you went to therapy with him."

"I did. But . . . Why are you being like this? I already have plans. Can't we go another time?"

I needed Norman to back off, and, thankfully, he did.

"OK, it's cool. I'm good. We'll figure out

another day. So, what are you and your boy doing?"

"Rodney and I are meeting at the J.R. Crickets on North Avenue and then going for a walk. We walk in the evenings. And talk."

"OK, cool. I will see what the rest of the week looks like for me, and you can let me know what works for you and we can plan it."

"Thank you. I appreciate you understanding."

CHAPTER EIGHTEEN: FIGHTING MAD RODNEY

The session with Dr. Taylor was not as bad as it could have been. It actually was all right. I left there feeling like talking about what was going on in my head was a good thing.

I still had the same dreams about that night that changed my life, but only one each night, instead of what seemed like a continual loop playing in my head.

A few days later, Brenda met me at J.R. Crickets to go for a walk. I was a little disappointed, though, because I had called her the night before and she did not answer. And I did not hear back from her until the next afternoon.

I had no grounds to be disappointed; she had a life to live. But because I had grown to know her so well, I knew there was not much she had going on in her life. So it made me wonder.

But when she showed up five minutes

early in the restaurant parking lot, I dismissed my issues. They were an overreaction.

She greeted me with a hug, and it felt good and right. She was my friend.

"You're mighty perky," I told her. "Why?"

Brenda seemed like she was hiding something. "Who? Me? I'm, huh, always perky, aren't I?"

"No, not really. You're definitely more energetic. Way more than when I met you."

"I was a different person then. You know that."

"I do."

"OK, which way we walking?"

"We can walk downtown all the way to The Underground and back. I know the parking lot guys here. I'm gonna tell them to leave your car alone."

"I brought some shrimp and veggies for us to eat when we get back."

She always had my back, and I appreciated her for that. I couldn't tell her that, though. It seemed like too much. So I kept it to myself as we walked up to Peachtree Street and turned left, toward the downtown skyline.

To get there, though, we had to pass the Peachtree-Pine shelter, which was only four blocks away. Most of the residents hung out on the Courtland Street side of the building, though.

"What's it like inside that place?" Brenda asked as we passed.

"Not a place you want to visit. I sleep on the streets. That should tell you all you need to know. Oh, and this: There was a story in the paper at some point that said almost ninety percent of the cases of tuberculosis in Atlanta came out of that shelter."

"Damn," she said. I thought she was reacting to what I had told her about TB, but her response was about the guy coming at me from across the street. He went by Skip; didn't know his given name and didn't care.

He was a white dude who looked like he had been through it. He and I got into an argument about President Obama one day. Skip called him "Obama." I told him, "You mean, *President* Obama, don't you?"

And that's when it went bad. He raised his voice, saying, "He doesn't deserve to be called president. What has he done for anybody? Look at us out here on the street. What did he do to get us off the streets?"

"What did you do to get *yourself* off the street?" I told him. "You white people kill me. You want to blame President Obama for everything. He had nothing to do with your wife fucking your coworker and you losing your mind behind it."

Men had to hold him back from attacking me. I stood there waiting and ready for him to break loose, so I could kick his ass. We were about the same size, but I was more coordinated and had boxed until I was fifteen. I was going to beat him down.

"Next time I see you, I'm going to bust your ass," he said.

That day with Brenda was the next time. And her warning prevented me from getting blindsided by that angry white boy. I saw the horror on her face and turned to see where she looked. There was Skip running at me full bore with a knife in his hand.

I turned to face Skip and avoided his lunge with the knife by leaning to my left. He flew by and before he could gather himself and turn around, Brenda hit him over the head with her purse. He stumbled, mostly out of surprise than force. But his imbalance was the opening I needed to attack, and I did, pushing him to the ground.

He held on to the knife, though — until two swift punches to the face knocked it loose. A third punch to the chest and a fourth and fifth to the head opened a wound and alarmed Brenda. She first yelled for me to stop, and when I reared back to deliver another blow, she attempted to grab my arm.

But I was already in motion and ended up hitting her in the face. She fell over and my heart stopped. I jumped off of Skip and over to Brenda, who was conscious but holding her jaw.

"Oh, shit. Are you OK? You know I didn't mean to hit you? Are you OK?"

She nodded her head, but tears rolled down her face as I sat her up. To our left, Skip was moaning in pain and bleeding. And as I got Brenda up on her feet, a police officer arrived on the scene.

Although Skip had the knife, I was grabbed and pushed against the wall by the cop.

"What are you doing?" Brenda asked. "What are you doing?"

"Miss, please back up. I saw what happened here."

"No, you didn't. Why are you harassing him? He was defending himself."

"I saw from across the street that he hit you. Are you all right?"

He handcuffed me, told me "don't move" and turned to Brenda.

"That was an accident, officer. This is my friend. We were going on a walk when this guy came over and attacked him with a knife."

The cop turned to Skip, who tried to conceal his weapon.

"Is that true?"

"No, it's not true," Skip lied. "This guy has had it out for me for a week now. Threatening me every time he sees me."

"Oh, he's lying, officer. I promise you we were walking and I looked over and saw him coming at Rodney."

"Where's the knife you said he had?"

"I knocked it out of his hand, officer," I said. "It's on the ground over there somewhere. Or in his pocket."

"Get over here on the wall," he told Skip. "Where's the knife?"

"I ain't got no knife. I was minding my business and he jumped on me."

"I don't see a knife," the cop said. "Both of you, turn around. What's this about?"

Brenda could not contain herself. "Officer, I swear this man had a knife. I don't know why he came after him, but he did."

"Look at me. Look at my face. Does this look like I came after him?" Skip said.

"Looks like I whipped your ass. But you attacked me," I said.

"Now, both of you shut up. What I saw was you beating on this man and hitting this woman."

"Officer, she's already told you we're friends. We're on a walk. This guy attacked me. What's this about? Because he's white and you're white, you don't believe me and you believe him?"

"Don't start that racist crap with me."

"But you immediately went to Rodney, and didn't even consider that that guy had started it. So it doesn't look like you're being fair. Looks like you're being biased."

"I know what I saw, Miss. I saw him hit you."

"Then you didn't see everything. He came running across the street wielding a knife."

"Where's the knife?" the officer said. "I don't see one. Do you?"

"Check him. He must have picked it up and put it in his pocket," I said. "It was right there on the ground."

"The man said he doesn't have a knife."

"And that's it — you believe him?" Brenda said. "Rodney said the guy attacked him and you didn't believe *him.* But you believe the white guy?"

"Don't make this about race."

"If it's not about race, pat him down like you did me," I said. "If he has a knife, you know the deal."

It was a gamble to say that because he

could have tossed the knife when I turned to attend to Brenda. His certainty that he didn't have a knife made me uneasy.

The officer seemed reluctant to search Skip, which was strange because that was protocol. But he did and found the knife.

"So what's this?"

Skip didn't respond. He turned him around to face the wall and took off the handcuffs from around my wrists.

"Go," the cop said.

I had so much to say to the officer, and Brenda must have known, because she grabbed me by my elbow and pulled me away.

"Let's just go," she said as we walked away. Brenda breathed heavily and kept looking back as we walked on.

"You all right?" I asked. "Your face?"

She put her hand up to her jaw. "Yes. I'm fine. I'm just . . . That guy. Who was he? What's his problem?"

I explained my history with Skip. "And for that," she said, "he was trying to kill you?"

"Not everybody is sane. Not even me."

"But you aren't trying to kill people . . . are you?"

"Only myself. And you see how good a job I have done with that."

"Well, we're about living now, right? Both of us."

I couldn't answer because I was not sure. I had definitely taken some steps I had not expected to take — smiling, enjoying someone's company and going to counseling — but my dreams still haunted me.

Brenda continued to look over her shoulder for the next few blocks — until the cop car came riding past us and we saw Skip in the backseat.

"Good. I don't wish jail on anyone. But he has some issues. He really acted like he wanted to kill you."

"We can't worry about that now. It's over. What's going on with you?"

"What do you mean? Nothing."

"Nothing? I called you yesterday and never heard back from you. That never happened before."

"Yeah, I apologize. I realized today that I had the ringer off by accident. Not sure how I did that. But I noticed I had two missed calls from you when I was on my way to meet you today."

"OK. Still, you seem more upbeat than usual."

"I do? Well, I'm glad. I have to admit, Rodney: I feel better about my life than I have in a long time. Walking with you and taking your diet advice has helped me lose weight. I think a lot of my self-esteem issues centered around just not feeling good about how I looked.

"Now, you have me obsessed with walking and eating right and so the weight is coming off. Probably the biggest thing is that I am proud of myself. I'm doing something to make myself look better and be healthier. And I feel better. It's a big thing for me."

I was proud to have a small role in Brenda's jovial state. It gave me a sense of purpose, which was another feeling I had dismissed.

"This is where I walked a few weeks ago and met some interesting people," she said.

"Yeah, and that's why I took you to the shelter — so you would be scared straight into not taking that walk again at night by yourself."

"Let me ask you something," she said. "What will it take for you to get off the streets?"

That was a good question because I had not pondered it. Once I found myself on the streets, I believed it was where I belonged — considering what had happened — and where I would stay.

"Who said I wanted to get off the streets?" That was the best I could come up with on short notice.

"No one," Brenda said. She knew how to talk to me: She never applied pressure and always projected calmness.

Then she added: "I'm thinking that I see you in a leadership role, working with kids or leading young entrepreneurs or some kind of project manager with people you direct. And that person has a place he calls home."

Words could not formulate in my head. I got where she was going in her first comment. "I am not sure about who I am right now," I said. "I . . . You spend two years living on the streets, and it becomes a way of life. The great author Thomas Wolfe wrote a book, *You Can't Go Home Again.* He's right. The only home I knew is gone."

Brenda did not respond. Instead, she pulled out her cell phone. We walked for a few minutes, and I had to prevent her from strolling into traffic, as her head was glued to her phone.

"What are you doing?" I asked.

"I'm sorry. I'm looking for something. OK, this. This is from Thomas Wolfe's *You Can't Go Home Again:* 'The human mind is a fearful instrument of adaptation, and in nothing is this more clearly shown than in its mysterious powers of resilience, self-protection, and self-healing. Unless an event completely shatters the order of one's life, the mind, if it has youth and health and time enough, accepts the inevitable and gets itself ready for the next happening like a grimly dutiful American tourist who, on arriving at a new town, looks around him, takes his bearings, and says, *Well, where do I go from here?*'

"What do you think of that, Rodney?"

We had stopped to sit on a short wall in front of the SunTrust Building. He looked at the passing traffic.

"It's interesting for sure."

"Interesting?" Brenda said. "It's more than interesting. It's inspiring. You brought up the book, not me. And in it, it is saying you have the 'mysterious powers of resilience, self-protection and self-healing.' That's what you're doing.

"Anyone who lives on the streets when he doesn't have to, and makes it, is resilient. You've done so by defending yourself, just like a few minutes ago is one example, which is self-protection. And slowly, you've healed more and more each day."

I said, "Yeah, that's true. But I focused on the part where he wrote, 'Unless an event completely shatters the order of one's life . . .' "

"My point exactly. It goes on to say, 'It accepts the inevitable and gets itself ready for the next happening . . .' And it ends, with the man looking around, getting his bearings and then he says, 'Well, where do I go from here?'

"You see all this? This passage of the book is about you. Someone who was wrecked by an 'event' in his life and instead of giving in to the grief, stands up, gathers himself, gets his bearings and wonders where he goes — not where he stays.

"This is you. You have to adopt this same position. Where do I go, which is the same as asking what do I do? And I say you get yourself all the way together and live your life."

"That's so easy to say."

"You've been through some things, I've been through some things. But we're still here, Rodney. And since we're here, why not make the best of it?"

She made sense in my rational mind. But my mind was not always rational, and I couldn't control when it wasn't.

"I'm not saying you don't make a good case. I'm just saying I'm not ready to make any dramatic changes right now."

"Well, I understand, I guess. But I think if you continue the therapy sessions, you'll get there. It's just a matter of time."

"These are like therapy sessions, really," I told her. "We talk and walk and talk and walk. And I have opened up to you more than anyone in the last two years. Do you know they used to call me 'Silent Night' at the shelter?"

" 'Silent Night'?"

"Yeah, because I hardly spoke when I got there. I can't really remember how I got there. It's not that clear."

I could see Brenda's mind churning. One thing I liked about her was that she thought about what she wanted to say before saying it. Wasn't sure if she was like that in her everyday life, but that's how she was with me. Too many people I had dealt with said stupid shit and then, instead of saying they were wrong, would try to justify it.

"How did you end up there? I mean, after the funeral, what did you do? How did you go about leaving your home?"

She stumped me. I had been in such a fog, such pain, that I hadn't given that much thought. I only knew I could not go back to my home without my family and that I didn't deserve to have anything but discomfort. Since I didn't have the courage (or weakness, depending on your side on the argument of suicide), I could not kill myself.

So the idea was to suffer.

"I'm not sure. I literally don't recall all that went into me being out here," I told her. "I just knew that life in that house without my family was something I could not bear. The funeral was a blur. I cried the entire time. I don't remember the repast and I don't remember going home afterward.

"I *do* recall telling myself that I didn't deserve to live. Guilt beat me down. I felt so guilty I could hardly breathe. I cried and walked in the light rain until I fell down on the grass, up against a tree.

"I slept there. I wandered the streets for three days and I did not eat. I couldn't eat; didn't have an appetite. A cop woke me up one night and told me I couldn't sleep wherever I was. There was this guy who told me about the shelter. I had seen it before and I knew where it was. But I did not go there for at least three weeks. I just wandered around Downtown and Midtown Atlanta. It was a blur that I don't quite recall. I was under the radar — I didn't want anyone to say a word to me. So I avoided contact with people, except when I finally got hungry and began asking people for money."

"Rodney, this breaks my heart," Brenda

said. "I'm so sorry."

"It is what it is," I said. "I wasn't sure what to do, other than to stay away from family and the few friends I had. I threw away my cell phone — slid it right into a gutter. I was just out there in the world. Had nothing but my pain."

"I wish you had talked to someone — a friend, a doctor, a coworker, someone — who could have helped you."

"I couldn't think straight. And, Brenda, I was humiliated. I fell asleep and my entire family was killed. And I lived. It was the worst-case scenario as far as I was concerned. Living was not a gift. It was a curse that carried a burden I can never escape."

"Well, I'm not going to push it. But I said to you before: Your family would not want this life for you. They know how much you love them. They know it was an accident. They would never want you on the streets."

"That may be true. But I'm the one who has to deal with what happened. Not them. Not you. Not the therapist. Not anyone else."

"OK, Rodney. You know I care about you. You're so smart. You will figure it out. One day."

CHAPTER NINETEEN:
ARE YOU IN OR ARE YOU OUT?
BRENDA

I felt horrible lying to Rodney. But I could not pull myself to tell him about Norman. I was afraid he would react as he had when I told him at the park.

It was a tough position for me because I felt closer to Rodney each day, with each walk and talk. The way we opened up to each other changed our lives.

Norman was the confirmation of my change. After that night together, we saw each other more and more, and the intimacy increased at the same time.

The day after Rodney accidentally hit me during the fight with Skip, Norman noticed a small bruise on my face.

"What happened here?" he asked.

I told him the story and he sat up in bed and turned on the light on the nightstand.

"OK, something has to give here," he started. "It's bad enough that you're spending time with this homeless guy, but now you're telling me he hit you in the face?"

"I told you it was an accident; he was defending himself against someone and I got in the way."

"But what if you hadn't seen that guy coming at him with a knife? What if he had stabbed both of you?"

"But I did see him and he didn't."

"The point is you're putting yourself in harm's way with this guy. I read up on bipolar disorder and it says most are very smart, but that when they have an episode, it could be violent. So why wouldn't he eventually attack you?

"You said he does stuff and doesn't recall he did it. He could hurt you and claim he didn't remember. Who knows what will set him off?"

Norman irritated me with his thoughts, but there was a sincerity and concern in them that prevented me from going off on him and endeared me to him.

"Thank you for being concerned. But Rodney is not violent. He ran away from me. He didn't try to hurt me. But I still haven't told him about us, although I know I need to."

"See, that right there, I don't like. You're hiding our relationship from him because you think he can't handle it? Well, he has to handle it. I don't like being anybody's secret."

"Is that what we have? A relationship?"

"You don't think so?"

"You never asked me. You never said, 'Be my girl, my woman.' You didn't do as we did as kids and ask for 'a chance.' None of that.

"Because we've slept together a few times does not mean we're in a relationship."

"So wait — women are always looking to be in a relationship. Most of the time you can't have sex *unless* you proclaim you're in a relationship. And you're telling me you don't want to be in one?"

I had done exactly what I had intended — to take him off the subject of Rodney and me not telling him about Norman.

"I never said I didn't want to be in a relationship with you, Norman. I said you didn't ask me to be in one with you. You can't assume anything with me. I'm an official kind of woman. I need to be asked if you want me to be in a relationship with you."

"So we're just having sex to be having sex?"

"We had sex because we're grown and made a decision to do so. That's what grown folks do — decide what they want to do.

Sharing my body with you means I like you a lot and care about you. But until we have a conversation about a relationship, there is not a relationship."

"Well, do you want one?"

"Want what?"

"OK, now you're playing."

"You have to say what you mean to me."

"Brenda, I like you and I care about you and would like to know if you'd like to officially be in a relationship with me."

"Now that was nice, Norman. Thank you. But tell me, what does being in a relationship with you mean?"

"Come on now. You're pushing it. You know what being in a relationship means."

"I know what it means to *me*. I need to know what it means to *you*."

Norman was exasperated. I could see it in his face. And he breathed heavily. But he made me smile.

"A relationship means we are dating. We're together. And we're not dating anyone else."

"Monogamous?"

"Yes."

"I would love to be in a relationship with you, Norman. But I have to tell you something."

He gave me a side-eyed look that said,

What now?

I just came out with it.

"I'm married."

"Come on. Stop it. I was just at your place."

"*Technically,* I'm married. I've been separated from my husband for about two years. I just think it's important to be up front."

"So what's the deal? Why aren't you divorced? And why are you telling me this now? Your husband could have rolled up on me and shot me and or confronted me and I wouldn't have known what the hell for."

"No, that would never happen," I said. I did not want to tell him that Troy walked out on me, but I had to. He deserved the truth.

"I haven't seen or talked to him since he left. He walked out on me and never looked back. I haven't been able to find him to serve him divorce papers."

"Oh, wow. That's crazy. What happened? He just left?"

"I don't know what happened, to be honest. He basically said he didn't want to be married anymore. And that was that."

"That's crazy. How did you handle that?"

"I can be honest with you and tell you it hurt my confidence and self-esteem. If you had met me four or five months ago, I wouldn't have looked like this. I was at least forty pounds heavier. I walked with my head down and shoulders slumped. But my relationship with Rodney turned my life around."

"The homeless guy? How did a homeless man turn your life around?"

"You ask that with so much sarcasm, and that's not fair. Rodney is extremely smart. His family — wife and daughters — were killed and it messed him up. Anyway, we met and we walk and discuss our lives. I had gained a lot of weight, trying to eat away my misery. Walking with Rodney helped me lose a lot of weight and talking with him helped me find myself."

"You know what?" Norman asked.

I braced myself.

"I saw you and, uh, Rodney the other day, at J.R. Crickets in the parking lot," he said. "I was driving by on Courtland and there you were. I only saw you all for a quick second, but I can tell he has an interest in you."

"Cut it out. That's not true. And you couldn't tell anything about how he feels in a glimpse."

"I had more than a glimpse. I was at the light. I saw you walk across Courtland and him move to the outside. I think he was trying to avoid being seen by someone."

"What? Norman, he was being a gentleman. He knows the man should walk on the outside and the woman inside, away from the traffic. You don't know that?"

"Never heard that before."

"Oh, my goodness. That's a problem for me, Norman. We're being honest here and just talked about starting a relationship. But I need a gentleman in my life. You think it's OK for the man to walk inside?"

"I didn't say that. I said I didn't know it was some law or rule or —"

"Etiquette. It's etiquette. Pure and simple."

"Well, OK. I don't know everything."

"How old are you?"

"You're not going to stand in judgment of me because I didn't know one thing. Not happening. And haven't I been a gentleman? Haven't I opened the door for you?"

"You have, but I didn't say anything, but it bothered me."

"What?"

"When we got into your car, you just jumped in. You didn't open the door for me. That's an important part of being a gentleman. Troy, my husband, never let me touch the car door handle."

"Well, I ain't Troy and I ain't the homeless guy —"

"Rodney."

"I ain't Rodney, either. I'm Norman. What you see is what you get."

"So you're telling me you're not going to open the car door for me or walk on the outside?"

"No, I'm not telling you that. I'm saying I'm me."

"And I'm asking are you going to be more chivalrous?"

"Seems like you're trying to change me, Brenda."

"You can call it that if you like. I'm trying to receive what I should receive from a man I'm in a relationship with. That's all. If that's too much to ask, we can forget the conversation about being in a relationship. One thing I'm not going to do is accept less than I deserve."

"Well, I don't like ultimatums. They get you nowhere with me."

"I don't like them, either. But this is important to me. And I'm not asking you to change the oil in my car or to cook me breakfast in bed every morning. I'm asking you to be a gentleman. I do not understand why that's such a problem."

"It's not a problem. But —"

"If it's not a problem, then why are we

going back and forth about this?"

"Because I don't do well with people try-ing to control me."

"I can't speak to other women you have dealt with, but I am not controlling. I would like my man to treat me the way I'm sup-posed to be treated."

I had reached my tipping point. I was not going to argue with that man another sec-ond.

"So, that's it? You're not going to be a complete gentleman because you think that's trying to control you? Just tell me yes or no, so we can move on, one way or another."

"I'm saying I am a gentleman."

"And?"

"And I don't have a problem walking on the outside or opening the door for you."

"That's all I wanted to hear. We could have saved the last ten minutes. But be clear about this: I'm not trying to control you. That's not my personality. I actually follow the man's lead. I believe that's the way it should be."

"OK, well, are we good?"

"We're good."

"Well, there is one more thing," Norman said. "A requirement I have is that the woman I'm involved with does not hide me from people close to her. You seem to not want to tell your friend about us and I don't like that."

"You make a good point. This is a different case, though. It's not that I don't want to tell him about us. It's that I already did and he didn't handle it well. He does not remember me telling him. But he ran away from me, talking about you were a spy trying to catch him."

"Oh, this dude has problems."

"I told you that. But we're going to a therapist to —"

"*We?* What do you mean, 'We're going to a therapist'?"

"I told you that already."

"I found a therapist for him to talk through his issues to try to get him right, so he can get off the streets and try to lead a normal life."

"And you think this guy isn't falling for you? You're helping him like this, walking with him almost every day, and he just sees you as another woman?"

"He sees me as his friend. There has not been one questionable comment or act in all these months I have known him. We hugged the other day for the first time, and then only because he has cleaned himself up much better lately."

"Yeah, he didn't really look homeless to me when I saw him."

"Well, you didn't see him at the McDonald's on Ponce when I first met him. That's where he spent a lot of his time. It was obvious he was homeless then. But I have helped him and he has helped me."

"Bottom line: Are you going to tell him about us?"

"Yes, Norman. I am. I'm going to talk to the therapist first and see what she says about how I should do it. I'm going to see her by myself. But why are you jealous of a homeless man who has been a blessing in my life?"

"He's a man, right? Homeless or not, you apparently have really strong feelings for him. Maybe I shouldn't be concerned — well, I'm not concerned — maybe it shouldn't matter. But it does."

"I will tell Rodney. I just have to figure it out with the therapist because I don't want to upset him again. Seeing him have an episode like that was scary."

"But are you missing the point? Why would he have an episode when you told him about me if he didn't care about you?"

I had thought about that long and hard. I didn't have a concrete answer. But I had a theory. "This is a man who for two years has been crushed by the death of his wife and children. He went to the streets. He didn't have anyone to turn to. No one talked to him and he talked to no one.

"And then here I come along and convince him — and it wasn't easy — that I was interested in his well-being. So he and I eventually formed a connection. And maybe he felt that threatened that the connection we created, which had become important to him, could be broken. I don't know. It's a theory."

"Well, the guy is obviously very sick, so there's no telling what the deal is with him. But I will say to be careful. Because he's so out there, bipolar, living on the streets, you never know what could trigger him to turn on you."

"He's not a dog, Norman. He's not a pit bull. He's a human and a nice man who had his world turned upside down. There are so many people with bipolar that it's not even funny. And there are ways to manage it. That's what we're working on.

"And doing that with him does not mean anything to our relationship. So I'd appreciate your support as I try to help this man get his life back in order. He deserves that from me because, really, if it were not for him, you would not have said a word to me at the mall when we met. I would not have been at the mall and I would not have looked like I do now. Rodney changed my world."

Chapter Twenty:
Haters Gonna Hate Rodney

I rested on a bench, my jacket serving as a mattress, by the tennis courts at Central Park. It felt like it was about midnight. For the first time in a long time, I could not sleep.

I wondered about Brenda. Each of the previous three nights, she either did not answer the phone or rushed me off it. Was she trying to distance herself from me? That was the only thought that flooded my brain.

When I finally dozed off — after watching two dogs fight on the softball field — I dreamed of my family. The same dream. Only I was awakened before the crash by the sound of thunder. Rain was coming, and I did not have the energy to seek shelter.

Plus, I liked the rain. It was like a natural shower. At night especially, the rain was like sleeping music. That night, though, I could sense it was going to be heaving, so I pulled myself up and took up a spot in the back of

Publix grocery store on Piedmont Avenue.

The storm was aggressive and loud, with bolts of lightning brightening the sky. I had no idea why, but I cried for a time. I think it was the confusion in my head that had me twisted.

I heard so much chatter: my wife asking what I was doing; the devil telling me to punish myself; Brenda insisting I had something to offer the world; Skip telling me he was going to kill me. I felt hopeless.

When the sun came up, though, I felt hopeful in that it was a new day and Brenda and I had an appointment with the therapist. That was new for me. I had no optimism about anything. The next day had been like the last — full of nothing good.

I used the Publix bathroom to relieve myself and rinse my face. I had a small bottle of mouthwash, and so I gargled with that. My clothes were damp and rank. And it seemed like everyone I passed stared at me.

Out of habit, I walked over to McDonald's. A part of me hoped I would see Brenda, although I knew she had given up on fast-foods. Chester was already there. I hadn't seen him in a week.

"Where you been, man?" I asked.

"Hospital. Had pneumonia."

"Damn. How you feeling?"

"Like I just have the flu now."

"Why you leave the hospital then?"

"I don't know. Didn't want to be there anymore."

"Stay away from me. I don't need to be sick."

I pulled out a copy of *The Atlanta Journal-Constitution* to read when a guy came over.

"Hey man, here." He held out what looked like a few dollars. "Get yourself something to eat."

I hadn't asked him for anything. I did not see him. Countless times I received money from people, but never when I hadn't asked for any.

"Why are you giving me money?" I asked him. I did not take the cash. Something about him didn't feel right. He was neatly dressed and I smelled cologne.

"You don't want it? Don't you need it?"

"Man, thanks, but no thanks."

"Aren't you Brenda's friend?"

That jolted me. How did he know that? Who the hell was he?

"Who are you?"

"You're Rodney, right?"

"Who are you?"

"I'm Brenda's friend, too. She didn't tell you about me?"

"What's there to tell? And how do you know who I am?"

"I'm Brenda's man. We're in a relationship. She didn't tell you?"

I was taken aback. Brenda and I had become so close — she was my only friend. Who was this guy who knew my name, what I looked like, where to find me? And yet I'd never heard of him.

"No. Never heard of you."

"Interesting. Well, I'm Norman. We've been dating about a month now. She's my woman. She's told me a lot about you. That's strange if you all are supposed to be so close that she hasn't told you about us."

Something about the way this man spoke to me made me feel like he was trying to get me angry. Or jealous. Or something. I couldn't pinpoint what it was. But I attacked right back.

"Norton, I don't —"

"Norman. My name is Norman."

"Oh, my bad. Nellie, Brenda never said a word about you, so maybe you're not that important to her."

"Why can't you call me by my name? Brenda told me you're crazy, but I thought you could hear."

"Crazy? She told you I'm crazy? Then you should know that you're putting your health at risk being here. Did you hear that?"

"Relax, man. I was just here to meet you and to help you get something to eat. Wanted to meet the man my woman has spent so much time with."

"Why? You threatened?"

"If you had something to give her, maybe I would be. But you ain't got a car, a house and probably don't have a wallet. Damn sure know you ain't got no money in it, if you do have one. So threatened? I'm more threatened by the weather than you."

"Nancy, you should get the hell out of here."

"Nancy? You're being really disrespectful right now."

I was not into fighting, but I could fight, as Skip learned. I was about to show this guy that I could, too. I walked closer to him and leaned into his ear.

"What you gonna do about it, Nana?"

And just like that, I took his heart. He backed away.

"Don't get on edge," he said. "I just wanted to meet you and help you out."

"You came here to talk shit, which means you came here to get your ass whipped. Take that two dollars and buy yourself some courage."

He turned and damn near ran away. I

turned to Chester.

"He's the kind of guy that gets you sent to jail for beating him down," Chester said.

"You got that right. Punk ass."

But I was just as mad at Brenda. Well, maybe more disappointed than mad. Her not answering her phone some evenings finally made sense. She was dealing with that guy. So did she really trust me as her friend? If she had, she would have told me about him.

In the moment he left, the bit of optimism I had about life left with him. I felt worthless, used, inadequate. I could hear Chester calling my name, but I couldn't stop. I walked toward Ponce City Market but with no destination.

My first inclination was to call Brenda. But I was afraid that if she lied to me, I would not be able to take it. I already was on the brink. I could feel something in me not right. We had a meeting with Dr. Taylor scheduled for 5 o'clock that day, and I was not sure if I would go.

For the first time that I could remember, the day went by slowly. I walked all the way to the Virginia-Highlands area of Atlanta, but I didn't remember getting there. All of a sudden, when my head became clear, I was in front of Yeah! Burger. But I remembered that I had issues with Brenda.

It was a bad place. I already was mentally fragile. I didn't want to be disappointed in the one person who made me smile, who made me think, who gave me hope that I didn't seek.

I thought about that guy and something came to me: Why was he threatened by me? Did he think I had a romantic interest in Brenda?

Before my late wife, Darlene, and I got married, there was this guy who was interested in her. Instead of appealing to her, he came to me because she had shown an interest in me; he had seen us together at a party and at a concert.

He said to me then: "What's up with you and D?"

I said, "Who's D? And who are *you*?"

"Darlene. That's the pet name I have given her. I'm David."

"Really? OK, Dick. What do you mean what's up with me and Darlene?"

"I said my name is David. You trying to date her or what?"

"I'm not trying to do *anything*. We're dating, Doug. Why do you care?"

"You need to get my name right. I'm just asking. Seems like she's interested in me, but I don't want to step on anyone's toes."

"Man, you coming at me the wrong way. If Darlene had an interest in you, you'd know it and wouldn't be coming to me, Donnie."

"So you think you're funny? You can't remember my name? David. But you can call me King David."

"I'm going to call you an ambulance if you don't get out of my face."

The guy then backed off. Recalling that made me smile. That was where I came up with the tactic of calling Norman anything other than his name. It frustrated them big time.

The difference in this case was I did not have a romantic interest in Brenda. I had a romantic interest in no one. I had lost that part of my being when I lost Darlene.

Still, it shook me that Brenda did not tell me about this guy, Norman or whatever his name was. Was my idea of the kind of friends we were off base? Why *wouldn't* she tell me about him?

I felt betrayed, something that was hard to handle. All my life, I needed to be trusted and to trust those that mattered to me. When I didn't, my emotions ranged from disappointment to anger to fear. The fear was the worst part, because it prevented me from trusting anyone else.

Before I met and later married Darlene, there was Janet, a beautiful woman whom I coveted. It was not love at first sight, but the first time I saw her, I loved her look, which was polished but sexy, not sleazy. She was tall and fit and was comfortable with her height. I knew that because despite being five feet nine inches, she wore tall heels.

We met at a car wash waiting room. I could not stop staring at her. I stepped out of my box and approached her, telling her that she had distracted me.

"Huh? How?" she asked.

"I can't stop looking at you. It's not a line. I don't know any other way to approach you than with the truth."

Janet smiled and we talked and eventually dated for more than a year. It was a beautiful relationship . . . when it was right. When it was not right, which was every fourth or fifth day, it was ugly. And it all centered on not being able to trust her.

Other men apparently were taken by Janet's lovely presence, and I learned that she was unable or unwilling to shun outside interests. The lack of trust drove me . . . well, I won't say it drove me crazy. But it shaped how I would deal with other women moving forward.

Eventually, I left Janet. There had been

many breakups and reconnections — so many that I had lost track. But as much as I wanted it to work, I needed it to be right. Needing it to be right didn't make it right. When that came into focus, I walked.

With Darlene, I had no such concerns. We met at a Meals on Wheels, the organization that delivered food to the elderly around Atlanta. We both had volunteered. During the brief orientation, she caught my eye and I introduced myself to her.

When she smiled, I felt light cover my body. I had to get to know her. She worked as a greeter that Christmas Eve and I worked in the kitchen, fetching boxes out of the walk-in freezer, setting them up to be placed in cars and delivered.

During a short break, I wandered over to the entrance to see her. She smiled again. "You're done?" she asked.

"Not for another hour or so, it looks like. But when I am, we should go to breakfast."

"We should?"

"Yep. You can follow me. I know a good place."

Then I turned and walked away. Didn't give her a chance to reject me.

That was our beginning. We were married for two years before the first of our two daughters came. At forty-five, we had twenty-two years of marriage before the accident — and I never had a doubt about her commitment to me.

The third woman I cared for in my life was Brenda. We had a much briefer history, but it was important to me. It scared me to think I had misjudged her.

Where at one point I had considered not showing up for the session with Dr. Taylor, I became eager to get there. I wasn't sure if I was going to talk about that guy coming to me or if I was going to wait for Brenda to bring it up. But I knew I needed to have it addressed.

So I got my bearings and headed for the shelter. I had worked hard to not look like a homeless man in the past few weeks — or to look less like one. But the rain soaked out my clothes, so I needed to clean up before therapy.

I had a pep in my stride, a purpose. That made me marvel at Brenda. I walked the streets of Atlanta for two years with no real destination and no purpose. Having somewhere to be at a particular time made me feel . . . made me feel purposeful.

It was amazing how far removed I was from things that were a normal part of my life. Like the idea of getting clean clothes and trying to look my best — things I had dismissed long ago.

I even solicited — OK, bummed — enough money to get a haircut. I decided I would get one before I got to the shelter. Showing up looking better would make me feel better, I hoped.

The barbers knew I was homeless; they had seen me walk past their shop for years. I made sure to not be repugnant when I went. My clothes had dried out, but they were not stinky. As carefree as I was about what life I had left, I didn't want to offend anyone with body odor that would burn nose hair.

"Man, you've been up and down this street for years and now you finally come in here," one of the barbers said.

"Yeah, I'm making changes in my life," I told them.

"Good for you. I can tell. I see a difference in you. Come on. Sit down."

I did and I was satisfied with my new, less-wild look.

When it was time to pay, the barber refused my money and told me: "I'll make a deal with you. You continue to clean yourself up, leave the drugs alone, and I will give you a free cut once a month. Deal?"

"It's a deal. But I don't do drugs. I don't

even drink. I'm just going through some things."

"OK, my bad. I didn't mean to offend you. I just assumed. But we have a deal. And you look good, man."

I looked into the mirror and I looked like myself from two years before taking to the streets. It was stunning how much a haircut could give you back some years.

My hair had been a mess. Only a few times did I have it trimmed, and I did it myself with clippers I either found or borrowed from someone.

At the shelter, I answered questions about my fight with Skip — apparently, a few people saw it and they told everyone else. I tried to dismiss it, but a guy named Dong pressed me. Dong was short for "Ding Dong." It was a name he got from being a bully.

He would knock out guys so frequently, the story goes, that they heard doorbell chimes before going unconscious. Hence, the nickname. It could have been King Kong, he was so big and strong.

"Buddy, you know I like a good fight story," he said in a way that I had no choice but to give him the details — or suffer a doorbell chime moment.

On another day, I might have challenged

Dong. We had more than one run-in over the previous several months because I was not scared to die, much less afraid of him. So I did not back down. I got the feeling he appreciated that.

On that day, I gave him the blow-by-blow of my clash with Skip. "I'm glad you kicked his ass. He's a little racist bastard."

The word was that Dong was bipolar like me and Chester told me he saw Dong have an episode where he threw a shelter worker over a desk and beat up a police officer. Thankfully, they used a stun gun to get him under control and not a revolver.

I was able to get a pair of khaki pants and a brown polo shirt. They were not new, but they felt and looked new.

"Look at you," a counselor at the shelter said as I left. "You must have a hot date."

I turned and pointed at him and kept going. But in a sense, he was right. That therapy session was important. A lot rode on it. And so I got there early and felt nervous as I saw Brenda walk into the lobby.

CHAPTER TWENTY-ONE:
CHOICES
BRENDA

My smile must have covered my face when I walked into Dr. Taylor's lobby and saw Rodney. He looked anything but homeless. He was put together and handsome.

"Somebody got a haircut," I said. It was not the best way to compliment him, but it was all I could come up with at the time. And he did not respond. My compliment made him uncomfortable.

"Remember what you told me when we first met?"

"What? That your life was shit?"

"Not that part. You said, 'Blushing is healthy.' Then you gave me all the reasons why."

"Oh, yeah. I remember."

"Good. So I say to you: Blushing is healthy. It's OK to acknowledge a compliment."

"Well, actually, a compliment is to say something nice or to praise someone. You just said, 'Somebody got a haircut.' Not a compliment."

"You know, you're too smart for your own good. OK, Rodney, I love your haircut. I can see so much more of your face. You're a handsome man."

He still did not respond.

"You can react now with words or a blush."

He blushed.

A minute later, Dr. Taylor invited us into her office.

"You both look great. So good to see you," she said.

"So, does either of you have anything you'd like to discuss today?"

I wanted so badly to speak about Norman, but I did not get a chance to ask Dr. Taylor's opinion on if I should bring it up to Rodney. So I said, "I'm going to let Rodney decide."

"Let's talk about trust and honesty," he said.

"OK, I like that," Dr. Taylor said. "Why trust and honesty?"

"Because that's what's important to me in people."

"Do you trust Brenda?"

"I don't know."

That surprised and hurt me. "You don't

261

know?" I asked.

"I want to. I would like to," he said.

"Why aren't you sure about Brenda?"

I wanted to hear this.

"She's changed my life. I should trust her. But, I don't know. I called her a few times and she didn't answer."

"Is that enough reason to not trust her?"

"It is. And it is because she told me she had turned the ringer off by accident. That didn't sound right, but I believed it because I believed in Brenda. But that didn't add up."

I tried to say something, but Dr. Taylor stepped in.

"Do you know that trust is believing in someone, what they say, what they do? And if you are on the fence about trusting someone you care about, you should really be careful. Trust is like a broken vase. You can fix it, but it will never be the same."

"I know that," Rodney said. "I read, when I used to read books, that trust was the easiest thing in the world to lose, but the hardest thing to regain. That's why I'm not jumping the gun."

"Sounds like you're talking around something, Rodney," I said. "What is it that makes you not sure you should trust me?"

Rodney rose from his seat and walked

behind the couch we shared. I looked at Dr. Taylor and she motioned for me to remain calm and to let Rodney make his point. I obeyed.

"I haven't trusted anyone because I don't like being disappointed. Ask Brenda: When we first met, I was not interested in getting to know her or letting her help me because I didn't trust people and I didn't want her help. Trust is earned, not given.

"But she was persistent and she broke through and earned my trust. One doctor said I might be paranoid schizophrenic, that I had tendencies because I didn't believe anybody really had my best interests at heart — except my wife. Not even other family members.

"But I trusted Brenda —"

"Trusted? So you *don't* trust me?"

Rodney walked around to the front of the couch and looked at me.

"Who is Norman?"

My heart stopped. How could he know about Norman? Did he remember that I told him at the park?

"Norman? He's my friend," I said. "How do you know about him?"

"Not from you."

Dr. Taylor sat up in her seat.

"Well, actually, I did tell you about him."

"No, *he* told me about *him.*"

I was confused. He hadn't met Norman. Was he having an episode?

"Huh?"

"Today, this morning, at McDonald's, this guy comes up to me and offers me money," Rodney explained. "I've never had anyone just offer money without me asking, so I was like, *What's up with this guy?*

"I wouldn't take his money. He then starts telling me he knows who I am and that you're his woman. He tells me I can't do anything for you, that I don't have a car or house or money, so I need to forget about wanting you."

I became furious. How could Norman do that? *Why* would he do that?

"Rodney . . ."

"I had to threaten him for him to leave," Rodney continued. "And all day I wondered why you hadn't told me about him. I asked you why you didn't return my calls and you told me you turned off the ringer. But you were with him, weren't you?"

My heart pounded. I was so angry at Norman that I could hardly contain myself.

"Rodney, do you want to hear Brenda's explanation? Maybe there is a reason she didn't tell you that will help you to continue to trust her."

"I don't know if I can trust her. I could tell that guy was telling the truth, which means she was lying to me. Lying is the quickest way for me to lose trust."

I had so much to say and was not sure how to say it.

"Rodney, I'm sorry. Here's what I think of trust: To earn trust you have to be trust-worthy. And I have been trustworthy with you."

"So why didn't you tell me you were dating someone? Why did you lie about where you were when I tried to call you? You in love with this guy?"

There was an inflection in Rodney's voice and a look in his eyes that sent me a clear message: I had some "splaining" to do — and I'd better get it right.

"Rodney, I wanted to talk to Dr. Taylor about this alone, but did not have the chance," I began.

"Why?"

"Yes, why, Brenda?" Dr. Taylor asked.

"Because I wanted to make sure I would be doing the right thing by telling Rodney about Norman."

"You said earlier that you had told him already."

"That's right. You did say that," Rodney interjected.

"I did. Apparently, you don't remember. It was the day we walked to Piedmont Park for the food truck festival. I know you said you don't remember that, but we did.

"We walked and had a great conversation. We sat on the grass and ate salad and sandwiches. And then I told you I had met a guy during my lunch break.

"You stood up and then pointed and said Norman was following you and after you, that he was a spy. I looked behind me to see where you were pointing, and no one was there. And when I turned around, you had started to run away from me, across the field toward the Park Tavern. I sat there with my mouth open. I looked again behind me and saw nothing, no one. And you kept running, looking back, but never stopping.

"I called you that evening and the next day. When we finally talked, you were confused about the day of the week, and you said you didn't remember anything about our walk to the park. You said we had done something else."

Rodney looked at me with a confused expression. "I remember talking to you about it the next day," he said.

I looked at Dr. Taylor, who instead of interjecting, sat back and listened.

"I promise you, Rodney, that's exactly

what happened," I said.

"I don't remember any of it. I don't. The biggest problem I have with this bipolar thing is there is no telling what will set it off. It frustrates me because I remember dreams — the bad ones — and I have no memory of some things that happen."

"Dr. Taylor, what could it have been that triggered his response?"

"That's always hard to say, but in this case, it's pretty clear: Hearing you had another man in your life was borderline traumatic for Rodney, and an onset of an episode ensued. The fact that he has no cognitive recollection of it says he viewed the information as a threat to him or to his relationship with you.

"Being friends with you has been enormous for Rodney. He let you in — welcomed you into his world, as you put it, Brenda — and hearing about someone else threatened something he not only had come to appreciate, but something he had come to need."

"If that's the case, why didn't I react the same way just now?" Rodney asked.

"Because," Dr. Taylor answered, "Norman had already told you the information. And the way he told you and when he told you and the fact that he told you and not Brenda cushioned the magnitude of it because you didn't trust him. Even though you heard what he said and came to believe it, you had your doubts, which allowed you to receive it with less the direct hit it was coming from Brenda."

"Rodney, I did tell you and would not lie to you. You can always trust me."

"So why didn't you tell me again?"

"Because I didn't want to upset you again. That's why I wanted some time alone with Dr. Taylor. I wanted her to advise me on telling you again and how I should tell you — and if I should tell you. I don't like keeping secrets. But I was there. I saw the fear in your eyes when you pointed and said someone was coming. I saw you run with a panic that I had not seen in my life. I was left there hoping and praying for you.

"There was no way I was going to bring that back up without talking to Dr. Taylor first. But, it turns out, Norman approached you, which I just cannot believe."

"Rodney, what do you think of Brenda seeing Norman?"

"I mean, it's her life," he said. "I care about her, so I will say I don't think that guy is the right guy. Just by the way he approached me, it shows he's insecure. I have dated insecure women in my life. It's no fun. You end up resenting them."

I listened carefully to Rodney. It amazed me that he was bipolar because he made so much sense. That was when the disorder was dormant. I saw it when it rose up, and that freaked me out.

"I can't disagree with you, Rodney," I said. "I was hopeful because — and I'm not just saying this — I have found myself in these months hanging out with you. You rebuilt my confidence. I lost weight and gained my self-esteem. But bigger than that was that I began to love myself again and appreciate the fact that I deserve to be happy.

"As for men, I had lost all faith in ever getting one. I really didn't think about a man because I knew no man would be interested in a depressed woman. But Norman only approached me because I had become a different person than before we met. So, it was important to me that you like him because you made it possible for a man to look at me like a woman again."

"But why did I run when you told me? Dr. Taylor, what's that about? I understand I don't remember it because that's how it has been with me. When something really bothers me, I'm told I run from it . . . and then don't recall the incident. But this? Why would I run?"

"I'm so glad you're asking these kinds of questions, Rodney," she said, "because that means you care. You care about yourself. You care about what you do. You care about how Brenda sees you, how the world sees you. And that's not where you were several months ago, I'm hearing."

"No, he's leap years from the mean, negative, angry Rodney when I first encountered him," I said. "It's been amazing to see the transformation."

"I'm sure it has been," Dr. Taylor said. "But to answer Rodney's very good question, you ran because of something said earlier: Hearing from Brenda that another man liked her pushed you to a feeling of unworthiness. Why would Brenda need me now that she has a man? You didn't want to hear that, and you run when you hear or see something you don't want.

"Her dating someone exaggerates your shortcomings. You may not have a love interest in Brenda, but you do feel threatened by the idea of another man becoming more important to her than you or the focal point of her life, partly because they have the requisite amenities: car, house, money.

"Being territorial, in other words," Rodney said. "Maybe it was about being threatened. In my mind, I would think it was about making sure what we started isn't lost . . . especially not over that joker."

Dr. Taylor asked Rodney: "Couldn't she have both of you as friends? Could all three of you have dinner or drinks together? Would that be awkward? Or fine?"

"I don't drink. And I don't spend time with people I don't like. I don't trust that guy. And if Brenda trusts him, then she can't trust me."

"What? Why does it have to be a line drawn?" I said. "I don't know what I'm going to do about Norman. I cannot believe he would go and find you and then be so disrespectful, so childish. I'm so angry about that."

"Yeah, for him to find me means you told him all about me. He didn't need to know about me."

"I'm sorry, Rodney. I only shared with him because I thought I could trust him, but most importantly because I'm so proud of our friendship. But I won't say another word about you to him."

I had the feeling I was on the brink of having to make a choice: Rodney or Norman. It was a position I did not want to face. Both men meant something to me in different ways.

Norman confirmed I was a woman. Rodney confirmed I was a full person.

And before I could attempt to switch the focus of our session, Dr. Taylor asked a fateful question: "So, Rodney, are you OK with Brenda dating Norman? Not that you have a say in it. I'm asking because when she first told you, there was this reaction that none of us want to happen again. And it won't happen if you accept that she will have other men in her life. If you understand no one would come between you two, who she dates should not matter."

I turned to my left, to Rodney. He looked at the floor for several seconds. When he raised his head, he turned to me.

"For someone else, it might not be as hard to trust. I'm different, as we know. I don't like that guy and so I don't think he's good for her."

"Are you saying it's you or him, Rodney?"

"I don't think that's fair," I jumped in. "It's *not* fair."

"You're right, Brenda. It's not fair. But it is what it is."

I felt like I was pushed in a corner, and I did not like it. But it was not a difficult choice for me.

"If you're saying I have to choose, then I won't hesitate and say it's Rodney," I said.

"My friendship with you has changed my life."

Rodney's facial expression did not change. Dr. Taylor's did. She offered a slight smile.

"How does this make you feel, Rodney?"

"I feel the same way I felt when I woke up on the steps of St. Paul's Presbyterian this morning. Nothing different."

"But you didn't feel that way when you walked into this office today? You had questions about trusting Brenda?"

"Hard to say what I felt."

"Why are you shutting down now? You were much more talkative."

"I don't have anything to say. Brenda said it all."

Then he looked at me and smiled. I smiled back.

"And how do you feel, Brenda? You came in here not expecting to have to make a tough decision, I'm sure."

"It wasn't a tough decision. It wasn't. In the last two years or so, I lost all the people important to me. In the last two years or so, Rodney lost his family. We have that common pain that, once we came together, we have been able to help each other get through — without trying. It just came natural.

"So now he's the most important person

in my life. You're the most important person in my life, Rodney."

He looked away. Unless my vision was out of focus, Rodney looked to be tearing up.

"Ditto," he said softly.

"You guys are something else," Dr. Taylor said. "I'm proud to be in this room right now."

CHAPTER TWENTY-TWO:
FRIENDS, INDEED
RODNEY

We did not bring up medication at the last session, but I wanted to. I had the chance. But trusting Brenda was more important, so we focused on that.

And was glad we did. I was not sure what not believing in her would have done to me. She had made me feel positive, made me seriously consider taking medication, something I vowed to never resume.

It was strange to feel positive about my life. You do something long enough — live on the streets, beg people for money, eliminate ambition — and it becomes a part of you. Being homeless had become a part of me.

As much as Brenda helped me, it remained hard for me to shake the mental prison I was in. Between being bipolar and immersed in homeless life, I had lost a lot of the characteristics that made my wife and family love me.

Violence and mental health issues were so much a part of the homeless culture that I had become paranoid about being in large crowds or tight spaces. I had read about ex-cons feeling trapped or unsafe around a lot of people because they had seen so much violence in prison and believed it could creep up on them.

It was that same reason I refused to sleep in the shelter unless it was below freezing outside. I saw too much. I saw enough violence and rage and chaos that I could not stomach any more of it.

One night, about two months after the accident that took my family, I hung out on the corner with some of the guys from the shelter. Most were lying about what they had or had done. They were funny, but I could not bring myself to laugh. Laughing made you feel good, and I did not want that.

All was fine until three white guys tried to join in on what they considered fun and threw in a joke about Trayvon Martin, the teenager who was shot to death by a punk community security guard, George Zimmerman.

Apparently, those guys, from south Georgia, near Florida, did not realize how sensitive a case it was, or they didn't care.

"Look at him over there wearing a hoodie,

talking shit," the first white guy said to Banks, a shit-talking homeless guy from Jackson, Mississippi. Banks had talked about how sick he was of the racism he experienced in his hometown and bolted for Atlanta. He said he expected to have a job in the coming weeks that would allow him to get an apartment.

"Looks like that Trayvon Martin fellow who was breaking into houses and got killed. Probably his long-lost daddy."

He and the other two white guys laughed.

They did not notice that none of the six or seven black men were amused. Another white guy said, "Yeah, he probably got some Skittles in his pocket, too."

The third guy realized we did not laugh. "What? That's not funny. You talk about each other's mother, but that's not funny? Don't be so sensitive."

Banks was the first of all of us to step forward. And he was livid.

"You think some punk killing an innocent black kid is a joke? You think that's funny?"

"Wait, man. Back up. It's just a joke."

"You don't joke about a kid being killed for no reason," Banks yelled. Spit flew out of his mouth, onto the first white guy's face. He backed up. "Listen, man, get outta my face. It was just a joke."

And on cue, as if all the black men had practiced a gang assault, Banks punched the first white guy in the face — and the other men attacked and beat down the other two white men.

I knocked the third guy to the ground as he tried to get away, and kicked him in the stomach. Before I could do anything else, the other men knocked me aside and executed brutal assaults that made me fearful that they were going to kill them.

Someone alerted shelter staff, which came out and stopped the beatdown. But it was an ugly scene. We all ran from it, too, scattered.

That was just one case. There were times when I heard men across the room getting stabbed. Fights broke out over petty concerns. With so much anguish and despair dominating the residents' existence — no home, no money, no job, mental illness, alcoholism, drug abuse — it was a powder keg that often exploded.

Even the staffers were so disconnected and desensitized that they were mean to the homeless residents. It was routine to hear them belittle the men instead of being a positive, encouraging force. Once, on a Sunday, when people would come from around Atlanta, park their cars on Court-

land Street and donate food and clothes —
like some big, homeless flea market — the
shelter workers would berate the residents,
boss them around and generally make them
feel worse than they already did.

When the guy they called Cunningham
told me, "Get to the back of the line. And
don't let me tell you again," I lost it. "Who
the fuck you think you talking to? Get the
fuck outta my face."

I was not that vulgar in my previous everyday life. But the streets had already changed
me. Cunningham was a bully, and just like
a bully, when I stood up to him, he backed
down, slinked away. It was then that I
decided I'd be better off on church steps or
a park bench or under a highway overpass.

About a year and a half later, after
Brenda's influence, I thought about leaving
that life. It was ridiculous that the conditions didn't move me off my mission of
defiling myself. But I came to a realization
that was hard to accept: I was sick.

Ever since I was diagnosed at twenty-
eight, I accepted what the doctors said, but
not really. There always was something in
me that doubted it. It was a burden most
people could not bear — to believe you were
not *normal.* To accept something was wrong
with you.

People wondered why a person with bipolar disorder — or high blood pressure, for that matter — many times did not stay on the prescribed medication. I would say because it was hard to accept you were sick, especially when you didn't feel sick.

My wife, Darlene, told me about instances when I had an "episode" and fell into a depression and would not leave our room. Somehow, I did not thoroughly recall most of them. There were dreams that seemed so real . . . until Darlene made me realize they were only dreams.

The cases when the disorder took over were plentiful, and still, I could not admit, fully admit, to being sick. It went against everything I thought about myself.

Seventeen years later, I dismissed the façade and stopped lying to myself. It happened after we left that meeting with Dr. Taylor. Brenda and I stood in the building's lobby and just looked at each other. I felt her heart and caring and trust in that moment more than ever.

She offered me a ride and I did as I always had — refused. But we hugged like real people, real friends, hugged at her car.

"I have a gift for you," she said.

I was shocked.

"I don't know how to accept a gift."

"Just open your hands. That's all you have to do."

Then she popped her trunk and pulled out a gift bag. It reminded me of the gifts my wife used to give me, with all the colorful tissue paper sticking out of it.

I wanted to say something clever, but I couldn't think of anything.

It was difficult to not seem excited, but I calmly pulled back the paper and reached into the bag. There were multiple presents in there. The first thing I pulled out was a bottle of cologne, Viktor & Rolf Spicebomb.

"It's not a hint," she cracked. "Women, people, love a good-smelling man. You have really committed yourself the last month or so to focusing on your appearance, which I respect. I love the haircut you got today. Now we've got to trim that mustache and beard and you'll be a looker."

I opened the box and took a whiff of the cologne. It was refreshing but manly. But wearing cologne was not a priority for me, so I put it back in the box. And reached in for the other gift and pulled out an iPod with earphones.

"You said you loved music and used to dance a lot.

"We've never talked about music, but I was sure you liked music. Music can take you places, beautiful places. I loaded at least fifty songs, all kinds of songs from different decades. They are categorized. I just wanted you to have something when you walked during the day or at night to listen to instead of being trapped by your own thoughts all the time. That can't be healthy or help you find a new reality."

"Wow, thank you. And thank you for the cologne. I love it. I do love music. And you know what? I haven't really *thought* about music since I've been out here. I hear it when people drive by with it blasting in their cars. But I'm not aware of any new music, so I will definitely put this to use. Tonight."

Brenda flashed a broad smile. "There's one more thing in there."

I put my hand in the bag again, and I felt a small book. It was *What It Feels Like,* a compilation of stories provided by *Esquire* magazines from people who told personal tales about dramatic events in their lives.

"Interesting," I said, as I found and read the "Table of Contents." *'What It Feels Like To Be Shot In the Head. What It Feels Like To Walk On The Moon. What It Feels Like To Be Bitten By a Snake. What It Feels Like To Participate in an Orgy. What It Feels Like To Have Amnesia. What It Feels Like To Perform an Exorcism.'* Wow. This is pretty cool."

I told Rodney: "Men don't like to read novels, but these true stories are about some pretty wild stuff. In the end, for me, it's about how we have the capacity to overcome anything. There is a story in there called 'What It Feels Like To Die.' Now that's something, right? And the stories aren't long. They are straight to the point.

"I got you a book because you're a smart man and smart people read. *Something.*"

"I love the book. That's something else I did not think much about over the years. I loved the written word. I even thought about writing a novel at one point."

"Now you can write your story."

"My story?"

"Yes. The story you're going to be able to tell when you finish therapy and find the right medication and create a new life for yourself. It will be a best-seller."

"See, that's why I like you. You're a dreamer. You believe in good stuff. I let all that stuff go and built this wall to block me from dreaming. And yet somehow, you've penetrated the wall I took two years to build."

"We were destined to meet, Rodney, and to be friends," Brenda said. "This is bigger than us."

I could not argue with her, but I was not sure whom to give the credit to, either. I had my issues with God. *Why did he let my family die? Why did He allow me to live? Why were so many people homeless across America? Why was I bipolar?*

But I also submitted that God had protected me on many nights I was vulnerable while sleeping on the streets, from disease and, ultimately, from myself.

"You're right," I responded. "You're right. But you know, I feel bad because I don't have anything for you."

"Trust me, you being here is more than enough for me."

I actually felt a little emotional about that moment, so I told her: "Gotta go. Thanks again for the gifts. They are right on time."

We hugged briefly because it was about all I could stand without getting emotional. And then I walked away, without looking back. But when I turned the corner on Juniper Street, and ducked into a parking garage, tears streamed down my face. They were tears I had not shed in . . . I could not remember the last time I had been overcome with emotion from joy and relief.

That's what I felt that day. Becoming emotional in that way had left my spirit. But the tears represented that I was connected to something or someone, which was something I had tried to avoid.

And all that suppressed emotion came gushing out like a New York City fire hydrant. The release was significant. For about three minutes, I sobbed — from joy, from the memory of my wife and kids, from having a true friend in Brenda, from believing there could be a life out there for me to live.

Guilt had been such a heavy burden. I had no idea how heavy until I opened my mind to release it. When I finally composed myself, I was physically drained. I gathered myself, pulling out a bottle of water from my backpack and sipping on it.

I filled my lungs with the warm, humid air and began a slow walk through Midtown Atlanta. My destination was Central Park, where I could claim a bench and sleep. I was not hungry, but I had chicken strips from Publix and chips in my backpack if I needed something.

The walk was torturous in eighty-eight-degree heat that accounted for the sweat that poured down my back. The walk, though, was a haze. I was consumed with where I was in my life and worried about how I would or could rejoin society.

Homelessness was a different world in and of itself. It fed off of itself and bred contempt for others, sadness, hopelessness, depression. Listening to the stories of those without a place to call their own was heartbreaking and toxic. If America was the home of the free, why would there be such disparity in how people lived? I hadn't thought about that until I was on the streets.

I heard the story of a man who had been without a home as a ten-year-old and found himself back in that position forty-two years later — and had no apparent recourse to overcome his plight. I heard stories, countless stories, where losing a job meant eviction . . . and a place in the shelter. I heard stories of alcoholism that moved me to shake my head over men who could not go two hours without a drink, starting during the morning-rush hour.

I heard stories of drug addiction that crippled the strongest of men: cocaine, crack, methamphetamines, painkillers, heroin and the sort. They were walking zombies.

I heard stories of war veterans who survived, who were still of the earth, but whose minds and coping mechanisms had been killed on the battlefields. They saw so much up-close-and-personal death and brutality that their minds were blown. Worse was the lack of care for those who fought for the country and had no place to go when they returned home.

And there were many like me, with bipolar or some other mental disorder that impacted how they functioned in everyday society. I saw it in men and women on the corners or walking the street yelling at no one, screaming nonsensical gibberish. It was hard to witness.

I saw enough to know I did not belong on the streets. It astonished me that it took two years to come to that realization.

On the park bench, finally I rested on my back with my backpack serving as my pillow and looked up at the stars. It seemed like the first time I noticed stars in two years. And that simple thought made me cry.

I thought about how much I had missed while trying to punish myself. The simple things like the stars, television, music, books. What had I done?

I pulled out the iPod and attached the earphones. It was unusually busy in that area that quieted after 10 p.m. But the music took me away from it all — and my jacked-up life. Brenda had programmed Anita Baker and Incognito, Earth, Wind & Fire and Luther Vandross, Beyoncé and the Notorious B.I.G. and so much more.

I texted Brenda: "Thank you again for the gifts. I'm listening to the music and it is awesome. You made some great selections."

All night, I listened to music. I was reminded how it could take you to a place and time in your life, moments you may have forgotten but remember through the song. The songs made emotions resurface, too, made me cry because it filled my heart with memories of my family.

When I heard Will Downing's "There's No Living Without You," instantly, I was taken back to 1993. Darlene and I both were twenty-three, and while our friends were heavily into hip-hop, we loved soulful R&B and romantic songs with meaning. And we talked about how important we were to each other and that living apart would never work.

We were young, but it was not puppy love. We connected because we were serious about family and commitment and travel and work and love.

Listening to music helped me come to the realization that I did not want to be sick anymore — at least not sick in the way I had been, without medication. I could not bring back my family. But Brenda was right: I had tortured myself enough. I was alive, so I should *live.* Or at least try to live.

There was one big question, though: How?

Chapter Twenty-Three:
The New Me
Brenda

Rodney's text message came just as I was beginning to lay in to Norman. But it startled me because he had never used the text messaging feature on the phone. Until I met Norman, no one texted me. But since he was sitting in the chair across from me at my apartment, I knew the text did not come from him.

"Excuse me," I told him as I read the text and responded. "Hold on a second."

After I hit "Send," Norman asked, "Who was that?"

That was not the question to ask me in that moment.

"Nunyah," I said.

"Who?" Rodney asked.

"None of your business."

"Hold up. Why you talking crazy to me?"

"My husband used to say, 'Meet crazy with crazy.' "

"Oh, so I'm crazy now?"

"Crazy and something else, too."

My body was rounding back into form and my hair had grown and I looked good. And so I made sure I stood up and strutted around as I shared my anger and disappointment with Norman.

Standing over him, I placed both hands on my hips.

"I cannot believe you went and found Rodney and said the things you said to him."

He slowly shook his head and looked up at me. "That was him you were texting just now, wasn't it?"

"Why do you care? And you do not get to ask me that."

"What difference does it make that I went and met the guy?"

"If you had met him and was kind to him, it would have been fine. Wonderful. But to go there and insult him and tell him what he doesn't have, like he's not good enough for someone; that was inappropriate, out of like and, I have to add, a bitch move. Real men do not go to a man who is downtrodden, homeless and insult him."

"Bitch? You're way outta the box calling me a bitch. I did what anyone would do: I checked out the competition."

"That's so silly, Norman. What's wrong

with you? I told you Rodney and I are friends. That's it. And you even said to him that he didn't have the tools or whatever to have a relationship. So why do Rodney and I think we would have a relationship?"

"I saw how he looked at you that day. I saw how you looked at him. Even when I said your name at McDonald's, he lit up."

"The man is homeless and I'm his only friend. So our relationship means something to him. It's important to him. And it's important to me."

I walked around Norman and crossed my legs after sitting down on the couch. He stared at my legs, which were shining from coconut oil.

"Well, my woman has to be about me and me only. She doesn't have time to be seeing other men, even if it's totally innocent. It's not jealousy. It's being proactive. I know because women who I've dated had friends who ended up coming on to me because I was friendly to them. That's how it starts, as friends who are cool and overly friendly. Then it escalates."

"You just called me a hoe," I shot back.

"No. No I didn't."

"You used code, but you surely called me a hoe. And that I don't appreciate."

"And you think I'm OK with you calling

me a bitch?"

"You're off subject, now, Norman."

"The subject is this: If we're going to do this, we have to figure out how to deal with that homeless guy. And by deal, I mean get rid of him. No woman would want to be in a relationship with a bum anyway."

"That man you call a 'bum' is smarter than you and kinder than you and would never be mean to a person who is struggling.

"At the same time, I agree with you that we have to deal with this situation. I actually dealt with it before you ever arrived here. I just wanted to tell you to your face that I'm done. I had to make a choice and I chose the homeless man with bipolar disorder over you."

He looked at me with disgust and anger. And before he could respond, I hit him again: "And for those friends of your ex-girlfriend who tried to come on to you? What charms you had that would make them put their pride on the line and risk their relationship, I'm *sure* I don't know."

That last line infuriated him because it was a variation of a line of his favorite actor, Samuel L. Jackson, had recited in the movie, *The Hateful Eight,* which we had watched together a few nights earlier.

He stood up and pointed at me. "There's a lot I can say, but I won't."

"You said all you needed to say this morning to Rodney. When he told me what you said, I knew you were not for me. I don't deal with mean, hateful people. And you're paranoid and you clearly don't trust. I don't know what happened in your previous relationships, but for sure something happened to make you so untrusting. But I am glad I learned now."

"You're going to miss me one day," he said, heading for the door.

"Yeah, when I need a laugh."

I was proud that I had a comeback so quickly. Norman did not have a retort, although I knew he wanted to call me what I had called him: a bitch.

Even though it was sad that I had to end it with Norman, the way I did it was confirmation that I had found much of myself that had slithered away in self-pity, pain and fat.

So I did not feel that badly about ending it. Truth be told, I felt reinvigorated that I could stand up to a man, that I could say the things I needed and wanted to say.

I was so tempted to call Rodney and tell him how the conversation with Norman went, how I felt as strong and as confident in myself as I had in years. I felt like myself before my world spun out of whack, only better because I knew I would never go back to that dark, unfulfilling place.

In a very real way, I wanted to see Troy. I wanted to tell him how badly I wanted a divorce and to thank him for leaving me. I hated the cowardly way he had walked out on me, offering no true explanation and basically disappearing.

There were plenty of names I wanted to call him, names that would have been insulting and hurtful. Mostly they would have made me feel better about myself. Troy walked out because I gave in to an age-old idea of allowing the husband to lead, to be the man and to play a secondary role. A responsible man would have appreciated that, not take advantage of it. All that did was grant him the freedom to do as he pleased, and that hardly ever included me.

So I sat at home and watched TV as Troy used work as an excuse to find love elsewhere. For years I knew he ran the streets as if he were a single man, but I did not have the strength to stop it or walk away. And even though I stayed, he *still* left me.

I was humiliated. I felt like an idiot. I was close to hating myself. I surely did not like who I had become: a weak, sniveling patsy. I would have walked away from myself if I could have.

Still, it would have given me so much joy to tell Troy about himself. And to thank him, for if he had stayed, I never would have met and become friends with Rodney, and I never would have found myself.

I would have remained a dummy in a marriage that benefitted me not at all. I would have been miserable, lazy, unfulfilled. And I would have deserved it. Not because I was a bad wife or bad person, but because I had stayed and I knew my husband had no respect for me.

Troy did me a favor. He allowed me the chance to save my life, and with Rodney's influence, I did. It was strange how the dominos had to fall in order for me to grow stronger as a person and as a woman.

Pushing aside Norman did not cause me anxiety. I did what I had to do. I loved having that power over myself. What dating him for that short time did was reawaken my need for male companionship, though. And it helped me feel a need to reconnect with people.

So, I joined Facebook. I heard people talk about it and would see people at work, on the elevator, pretty much everywhere posting photos and information. Maybe I could find my girlfriend, Gail, who moved to

Australia, and some of my high school and college friends. I was not sure how I would find anyone, but it was exciting to experience something new.

I put in names of people I was friendly with and found a few profiles and sent friend requests. I had taken a selfie with Rodney before I gave him his gifts after the meeting and used that as my profile photo.

The whole time I reviewed friends' and strangers' Facebook profiles, I smiled. Some of my old friends looked fabulous, better than they had when I had last been in contact with them. Two of the classmates from college, women who were stylish and petite, hardly resembled their younger selves. The extra weight made them seem a little older than they were.

It was familiar because I saw it in myself. I guessed those women were burdened by something that charged them to not maintain their weight. Or it was just a slowing of metabolism. Or sometimes it happened so gradually that you didn't really notice until one day, it hit like a hammer to the head.

Actually, it was unfair for society to require a woman to remain her weight from her youth when so many elements take over: metabolism slows, eating habits change, desire to work out diminishes. And suddenly you go from a size 6 to an 8, and 8 to a 10, a 10 to a 12 and on and on.

I hoped they could find an inspiration, a Rodney, or find it in themselves to get healthy. Physical health improvement would improve their mental health. I knew all about it.

Still, Rodney was all I had in my life, and that was just fine with me. I was excited about myself. And I was excited that I could sense Rodney was coming around, too — and that I had played a role in his development.

But I would not be as I was with Troy. And even though there was no romantic connection with Rodney, I would not put so much into him that I ignored myself. The new me understood the value of being happy with myself in order to embrace anything good in life.

CHAPTER TWENTY-FOUR:
READY FOR RECOVERY
RODNEY

With the earphones on, I slept as well as I had when I was in the hospital on heavy medication. But this was better because although I was asleep, I could hear the music playing. And maybe that's why I did not recall any dreams for the only time I could remember.

I told Brenda that as we walked down Monroe Drive the next day.

"The music probably made you think about good things," she offered. "Music can do that."

"Could be," I answered. Really, I did not care to figure it out. I knew one thing: I would not sleep again without the music playing in my earphones.

"So what happened with that guy?" Rodney asked about Norman.

"I ended it. He seemed to think it was OK to talk to you and be mean to you. The bottom line is that he was jealous of our friend-

299

ship. He said if I wanted to be his woman, that I couldn't have any male friends."

"I knew insecure fools like that," I told her. "They are dangerous because you would never know what would set them off."

"The only thing worse than an insecure woman is an insecure man," Brenda said. "It's worse because a man's ego drives him."

"You think that? Well, I had a girlfriend once. This chick would get upset if I missed her call. She was so insecure that she took my car to the grocery store one day and got a duplicate key made to my apartment. And one day, when cell phones first came out, I had one. And I get this call on my cell. I'm confused because the number looks so familiar. Then it hit me — *that's my home number.*

"I answered and she had no shame, talking about 'Where are you? Who you with?'

"I knew then I had to walk away. As they used to say, *Who does that?*"

"Wow. I guess women can be just as bad," Brenda said. "Soon as you told me he found you and was talking crazy, I knew something wasn't right. It was crazy how he could act normal and then be so insecure that . . ."

"Go ahead. You can say it."

"You get the point."

"Be so insecure to think a homeless man

would be a threat. That's what you were going to say. Listen, I understand. It's OK."

"I didn't get him. We were just getting started. But he literally asked me to make a choice between you and him."

"I didn't want that. I told you he came to me because I thought you should know and because of the way he came at me. I hope you don't feel bad about ending it. He was not good enough for you."

"You know what? About five months ago, I wouldn't have agreed with you. But now, I know who I am and what I'm worth and I know who is worthy of me."

I was proud of Brenda. I had seen her for months looking meek and disconnected from the world. But she had become a new person, almost unrecognizable from her physical appearance and mental outlook.

And in our friendship, I saw the growth, too. Where she was hesitant to ask questions when we first got together, she now tossed them at me regularly and with ease.

"You know what you've never talked about," Brenda said, "is your children, your daughters. Is it too painful to talk about them?"

I looked away as we approached Amsterdam Avenue, where we took a left turn toward restaurants and shops at the bottom of the hill.

"It's not easy, that's for sure. But Diana and Joy were tough kids, but they worried about me a lot — and I worried about them. Would they be bipolar, too, when they got older? They worried about me being able to stay on the meds to let them help control me.

"We were close. Diana was older by two years over her sister, Joy. It's so interesting how they could grow up in the same household, have the same parents, get treated the same way, but be two totally different people. I guess they have their own personalities."

"Who was more like you?"

"Diana, definitely. She was inquisitive and outgoing. She could be friendly and she could get along with anyone in any circle. Versatile. But tough. And she would make hasty decisions based on her feelings in that moment. She was emotional.

"Joy was more reserved and quiet. She said only enough to get her point across. She wasn't like me or her mother in that regard. She was tough, probably tougher than her sister. She grew to be taller than her sister, so people couldn't tell who was older because Joy always carried herself like an old soul. And there were no rash decisions with her. She'd dissect people and she'd think things through before making a decision. That's why she was a better golfer than Diana. Diana had more talent, but Joy was more patient and played the percentages, didn't take unnecessary risks."

"Wow, you taught them how to play golf? That's great. I wanted to play about five years ago. Troy told me that was the only time he had to himself, so I should pick another hobby."

"That was pretty cold. But yeah, we played a lot of golf. My wife played, too. It was a family outing to drive to Stone Mountain and play a round of golf on a Saturday morning and then take the trolley to the top of the mountain after lunch and enjoy the view."

Apparently, Brenda could tell I was getting lost in the reminiscing, so she changed the subject before it became too much and sparked an episode. She could not have handled that — and I did not want that.

"You know, I never wanted children," she said. "Let me take that back: I never wanted children with Troy. I didn't always feel that way. There was a time I considered him my ideal man. But after a few years of marriage, I knew I would be raising that child alone. And I knew that child would not feel love in the house the way it's supposed to be. So I stayed on the pill."

"That's smart," I said. "But I will tell you this: You'd make a great mother. I see a lot of Darlene in you: nurturing, genuine nature, caring, smart. True. That's what a child needs. So don't give up on being a mom. That kid would be lucky to have you."

"Awww, Rodney. That means so much. Thank you for that. I can tell you were a good parent . . . You hungry?"

We stood outside of Loca Luna, a Mexican restaurant with a good reputation. I had not sat inside a restaurant and dined in a long time.

"I don't go inside restaurants," I told Brenda.

"What? Why not?"

"Because I don't want to upset people's meals. I usually smell and don't look so put together. And nobody —"

"But that was then. Look at you now. You look great. You wouldn't upset anyone's meal. Come on, let's eat."

It was not a comfortable feeling. I had entered restaurants in the past to use the bathroom, but I could feel the stares at me. And the reservationists treated me badly because I would sneak by them when they left the front station.

"What if we ate right here, outside on their patio? I can go in through this gate and not the restaurant."

Brenda agreed to my condition. I entered through the outside gate and she went inside to the hostess stand. We met at a table with an obstructed view of Piedmont Park. We sat outside in the sun and sipped water with lemon before the food came. "So, your wife — what was she like? Wait, before you answer, I have another gift for you."

"Brenda, no. I have taken charity from people long enough."

"No, really, this is small. You need this."

She dug into her purse and pulled out a pair of sunglasses.

"You need these. And sitting out here, in this sun, these will help you. And you'll look cool."

She was right. Wasn't sure how cool I looked, but the blocking of the sun directly in my eyes cooled me. It probably was psychological, but I felt better with them on. Brenda grabbed her phone and asked me to pose for a photo. I looked at her. She clicked.

"Nice," she said of the photo. "I'm going to text it to you."

"Why? I know what I look like."

"You need to see how you look."

Her Samsung 8 took a clear image of me. "Blushing is healthy," Brenda said. "You can blush. Heard those words before?"

"Touché," I said before smiling. Brenda took a second photo.

"So now," she said, "tell me about Darlene, the love of your life."

I was glad to have on the dark sunglasses because my eyes were on the verge of tearing up. "We met in a strange situation," I began. "Along Camp Creek Parkway in Southwest Atlanta, not far from the airport, there is the place marked with a cross and stuffed animals, flowers, etc. It's where a friend of mine died in a car accident. Belinda.

"I stopped there one Saturday afternoon to put flowers on the memorial of flowers and cards people created. Before I left, Darlene pulled up. I wiped my tears and spoke to her. She was crying before she actually got to the site.

"Instead of getting into my car, I waited for her to pay her respects. I cannot say why I waited. It wasn't that I was interested in her. It was not a place to pick up a woman, you know? But she came toward me when she was done and I asked her, 'How did you know Belinda?'

"She told me they were coworkers at the

Delta Airlines corporate offices. I told her she and I took golf lessons at Charlie Yates Golf Course together. We stood there and talked about Belinda for at least twenty minutes.

"When we finally left, I said: 'I hate that we're meeting like this and in this situation. But I'm glad I met you.' I handed her my card. I was working at IBM then. 'Please stay in touch,' I told her and went on.

"About two weeks passed before I got this call from a strange number. It was Darlene. She said, 'I feel kind of guilty calling you. But maybe it was meant to be for us to meet as we did. I talked to my mother about it. I told her, 'I didn't go there to meet a man.' She said, 'But you did.' That's how her mom was — direct and no-nonsense.

"We went bowling that night. I liked that she was athletic and would try anything. She liked to swim and bowl and golf and dance. Anything that required movement. I knew then I had gotten lucky."

"How?"

"Because it was all so easy and natural. We did not have a quiet or awkward moment. We had fun. We had serious conversation about the plight of the country and young black men. We laughed at ourselves and told stories about our lives. We talked about rap music and debated between Biggie and Tupac. We looked up and the bowling alley was almost empty. We didn't even notice. That's how into each other we were.

"That was in the early 1990s. We got married the next year and our kids came soon after. We enjoyed the Summer Olympics in Atlanta and built our family."

"Somewhere in there, you got the bipolar diagnosis, right?"

"You do pay attention. That's a good thing. Yeah, a few years later is when it started to show up. But Darlene was there for me. She was scared, but she loved me, and that's what got us through. I fought her about taking the meds and getting second opinions and talking to a therapist.

"I wish I could tell her now how much she meant to me. *Means* to me because she's still in my heart."

Our food came.

"I can tell, Rodney. And Darlene, Joy and Diana are the reasons I say let's get you fully together, so you can live the life they'd want you to live."

I did not have an inclination to refute Brenda. It was like a fog was lifted from my eyes and allowed me to see into who I was: a heartbroken man overcome with so much grief and guilt that I felt unworthy to live a good life. Knowing my wife, Darlene would have said, "Let it go. Live your life."

"Brenda, I don't know how to live my life. I can't just go get an apartment and take a shower and wash off two years of living on the streets. Living on the streets is a part of me. I'm more that than anything."

I leaned across the table and looked to see if anyone was close enough to hear me.

"I'm sitting here at this restaurant, and I'm uncomfortable. I'm used to eating while sitting on a park bench or on a curb. This isn't me."

"But it *was* you," Brenda shot back. "I'm not saying it will be easy."

"I want to battle for my family. I want them to be proud of me."

Brenda nodded her head. Then she motioned for me to come closer.

"That's great and I agree. But you mostly have to do this for yourself. You have to want this for you. That's what you taught me. And trust me, when you accomplish your mission, you will have a pride about yourself you never had before."

I believed her — but still was unsure of the steps to take to make it happen.

"I need to see Dr. Taylor next week," I said. "I need to talk to her about a process to get where I want to go."

"You're not going without me," Brenda said. I smiled at her — it was amazing to smile freely and to embrace the feeling it gave — and we tapped water glasses.

CHAPTER TWENTY-FIVE:
GROWING PAINS
BRENDA

In two days, I became a Facebook junkie. It was fascinating to find friends and to be found — and to see what was going on in other people's worlds. It was a snapshot that we did not get before social media was invented.

I got comfortable enough to post photos of my family and two of Rodney. I posted pictures of my late sister, and they drew a reaction from friends of hers I had never met.

From all over the country, her college classmates and coworkers sent messages expressing their condolences. It made me feel good to learn how many people liked and respected her.

It was interesting to receive a message from a man named Rick who asked me in a private message: "Nice to see you on Facebook. So that guy in the photo with you. Is that your man?"

Before I responded, I checked out his profile. He was a handsome man, with a nicely groomed beard and pretty teeth. Teeth always mattered to me.

According to his profile, he was a partner at a marketing firm in Washington, D.C., but originally from Atlanta. He did not wear a wedding ring. Some photos on his page showed him with women, but none looked like they could claim him.

I thought: This Facebook thing may be all right.

After about fifteen minutes of reviewing as much as I could about him, I responded to his message: "Hi. Thank you for contacting me. To answer your question, no, that's not my man. I don't have one, in fact."

For the next hour, I waited for a response, but got nothing from Rick. I received a few friend requests from men I did not know. And I thought: This Facebook thing was a less direct version of a dating website.

I accepted two of the friend requests because the men seemed interesting and did not look creepy. The third one I ignored. His profile photo was of him with jeans hanging off his butt holding up two fingers for the peace sign. Turnoff.

My interest in hearing back from Rick was another indication that I had come full circle. I wanted a man. I didn't *need* one, but I was sure that having one in my life would or *could* be a good thing.

I had been married to Troy for eight years — long enough to get used to having someone in my everyday life, but also dysfunctional enough to know I would not accept just anyone.

Since I felt so much better about myself — better than I ever had because I had more self-awareness and confidence — it made sense for me to get back into the things in life that I had enjoyed but abandoned when Troy walked out on me.

One of them was a cigar. There were a few things about my marriage that I could consider positive, and enjoying a cigar on occasion was one of them. Troy got me into them. I resisted at first, because of the health factors and I could not stand the smoke in my hair and clothes.

Over time, I found cigars that were light and tasty like the Java or Tatiana, which were smaller in size and infused with chocolate or vanilla or some other flavor to make it appealing. I went to Leaf, a cigar bar, with Troy and was amazed that I had such a nice time with smokers. There was a cigar culture that I did not know existed. And the smoke did not bother me.

It got to a point when Troy did not come home or was missing in action, I entertained myself by going to Leaf and enjoying a cigar and the nice people.

So imagine how disappointed I was when I learned that Leaf had closed. But my search located countless cigar lounges in the Atlanta area. In my two years struggling with who I was, Atlanta became a popular cigar destination.

I met Rodney after work for our daily walk and I pulled out two Tabak cigars.

"How did you know I liked cigars?" he said.

"What?"

I was so excited.

"I didn't know. But I like them, too. I don't smoke the bold ones. I like these that have flavor."

"I used to sneak and have mine because my wife hated the smoke and my daughters got on me, saying they were no good for my health."

"Well, you probably haven't had one since I had one," I said. "I got these from Highland Cigar in Inman Park. This really nice and knowledgeable woman who worked there, Amber, suggested these after I told her I wanted something with flavor and not too strong. They are coffee-infused, although they smell like chocolate."

I had Amber cut them and she sold me a nice torch. We stopped in front of the Bank of America building downtown. Rodney took the torch. "You should not have to light your own cigar when you're with a man," he said.

"I appreciate the chivalry. Trust me, a woman needs that in her life." He lit us up and we walked to Spring Street and turned toward downtown.

"Do you know cigars are like a thing now," I said. "I lost myself on the Internet for about an hour. There are black-owned cigar lounges in Atlanta like Cigar City Club, Trilogy, Habanos and 617. I was stunned. And check this out: There is a popular women's cigar organization called Stixx & Stilettos in New York that I read about on the *Ebony* magazine website. Also, there is a woman here named Octavia, who calls herself 'HERficionado'; she has a monthly woman's cigar event called She Smokes Too."

"You sound excited."

"I am. There are options and there are so many more women enjoying cigars than when I was as long as five years ago. I'm going to check out all those places."

"You should."

"Anyway, so, I was thinking, Rodney, one

of the best ways to get back to your life is to do the things you used to do — or new things that you'd like to do. That's what I'm doing with smoking cigars."

Rodney puffed on his. "Thank you for this. This is a nice, *very* nice, cigar."

"Yes, it is. But what do you think about what I said?"

"I . . . I think it's a good idea. But I have to work up to that."

"OK, let me think of some things you might want to do that will make you feel — I don't know — feel right."

"Like what?"

"Like church. I know you said you had a problem with God for allowing you to live and not your family. But you're here because He wanted you to be here. And He has a purpose for you."

"Listen to the young preacher," Rodney cracked. "Didn't know you were of the cloth."

"Very funny. But I'm serious. Don't you think He would not have spared you if He didn't have a purpose for you?"

"I have no idea."

"Well, we know going to church can't hurt. Maybe you would get a word that will touch you, move you."

"I doubt that. I'm cynical about preachers, especially in this town. I'm sure there are some who are on the up-and-up. But most of them are running a scam."

"Rodney."

"You don't think so? What church do you go to?"

"I was going to Ebenezer, but after Troy left, I was embarrassed to go back there because many of the members knew us as a married couple. I didn't want to get the questions."

"And you didn't find another church?"

"I wanted to. But a few days after he left, I got depressed. I couldn't do anything but work and go home — and see my sister in the hospital. Once I fell into that pattern, that was my life."

"Until you met me."

"Until I met you. How great is that?"

"Look, don't feel like you owe me anything or have to keep walking with me every day. You've gotten yourself together. Go on with your life."

"Walking with you is a big part of my life. Period. Please don't bring that up again."

We worked our way to Suite Food Lounge at the corner of Luckie Street and Ivan Allen Jr. Boulevard. On the side of the building was Trilogy.

"This is one of the cigar bars I told you

about. How ironic. *I just told you about this place. Let's go inside.*"

"Brenda, I don't know. I don't go into people's businesses — unless I have to go to the bathroom."

"OK. Go to the bathroom. We're right here. We don't have to stay long. *Please. For me.*"

Rodney gave in. The place was quaint and inviting. We were greeted at the door. "Welcome to Trilogy. I'm Gary, one of the owners. This is Henry, the other owner."

They were fashionable young black men who looked to have themselves together. They extended their hands for us to shake, but Rodney acted as if he didn't see them. He had told me he did not shake hands.

"Love your place," I said to distract them from Rodney's slight. "We were walking by and I wanted to check it out. But we will be back."

"You guys did a good job with this space," Rodney said. "I've been here before, years ago. It was called Luckie Lounge then."

"Yes, we've been open over here about three months," Gary said. "We have a full food menu and a nice selection of cigars."

"Cuba being open through President Obama gives you entrée into the most respected place for cigars," Rodney said.

"But I will tell you this: They are making some high-quality cigars in Honduras, Nicaragua and the Dominican Republic that rival Cuba. Plus, the huge inventory of fake Cuban cigars hurts more than it helps right now because people are skeptical about paying the money for something that might not be authentic."

Gary and Henry nodded their heads.

Two other men came over. "This is Tory, one of the owners of Suite and Al Williams, the manager," Henry said.

Again Rodney acknowledged the men, but did not shake their hands. "It's great to see young black men doing something so big. I'm proud of you," I said.

"Me, too," Rodney chipped in. "I wish you the best."

And then we left.

Rodney was quiet as we walked toward downtown. "What's wrong?" I asked.

"Nothing. I just hadn't had any real dialogue with anyone — other than you — in a long time. I don't count the guys in the shelter or on the streets . . . It felt good."

"Great. See, that's a step right there toward doing things you used to do."

Rodney didn't respond.

"You OK?"

"I'm all right. But . . . I'm scared."

"Scared? Of what?"

"I had a cousin — *have* a cousin — who was in prison. I went to visit him about three years ago. He had close to a year left on a seven-year sentence. I told him: 'Hang on, man. That's not long. You have to be excited about getting out.' And he said, 'Man, to be honest, I want to get out, but I'm scared. I don't know if I can fit back into the world.'

"I had no idea what he was talking about. But I do now. It's like I've been in prison for two years. To be pretty much disconnected for that long makes me question how I can fit in. The world kept on moving. Look at those young guys with their own businesses. I'm forty-five. How can I get a job now? I worked in human resources. I would have two years with no work experience on my resume. I have no connections. That's hard to overcome."

"Yes, but people have done it. Many, many people have been in prison, been out of work for a long time and recovered. You are too smart to *not* make it.

"Plus, I saw a light come on when you were talking to those young guys who own the cigar bar. You enjoyed it. And that thing about Cuban cigars and Honduras and the D.R., where did that come from?"

"I started reading the newspaper more. See, that's another thing. I have these emotions conflicting with my actions. I'm scared of being back in society, so to speak, but at the same time, I'm reading the paper. That's a sign, in my mind, that I want to know what's going on. I want to start over and be up on the important stuff in the world.

"But then my mind tells me I'm not ready."

"And that's OK, if you're not ready. Don't pressure yourself. Take your time. You'll get there. Go at a pace that works for you. I think enjoying a cigar was a good start. And talking to the guys. And listening to music. That's good stuff."

"There's something else," Rodney said.

I did not respond. I waited.

"This disorder I have. I'm afraid of it. I'm scared something will happen and I will do something or run away and don't even remember what happened."

It saddened me to hear my friend speak like he did. It reminded me of me when I was down. It was all dark and stormy. So I had to be encouraging.

"That's where we're going to let Dr. Taylor take over," I said. "What we did today — walking, talking, having a cigar, meeting people — that's all therapy in a sense that's going to get you right. And medication. I'm not worried."

Like it mattered if I was worried. It was my attempt to show confidence in him.

"And there's one more thing: I'm scared that I am or will be too reliant on you and run you away. I know you said to not bring it up again, but it's important. I need you to tell me when I'm doing or asking too much because one thing I'm sure of is that I can't make it without you."

"You have to dismiss that," she said. "We need each other. Don't think that dating Norman for that short time meant anything to our relationship. We're tied together now. Unbreakable."

CHAPTER TWENTY-SIX:
EPISODES
RODNEY

My days were different after I decided I wanted to live like people live. Instead of walking aimlessly and asking for money, I was consumed with thoughts of a relatively normal existence, meaning a house or an apartment, a social life that included friends and doing fun and interesting things.

Getting there was another story altogether. And it depressed me. Three days after having the cigar with Brenda, I was overwhelmed with negative feelings about almost anything I saw or thought of.

I found a shaded place on a bench in Piedmont Park and I curled up. I was petrified. I felt like everyone walking toward or past me was out to get me. But I was so dark inside that I could not run.

So, I pulled a jacket out of my backpack, covered my head with it, curled up on that bench and lay there almost all day, quivering I was so scared.

I knew it was the bipolar disorder; Darlene had read some of the characteristics of it to me when I was first diagnosed. One said something like: life changes can trigger a manic or depressive episode.

I felt the disorder claim my body, the way a demon would an unsuspecting child. It was aggressive and decisive and dominating. I had been there before, many times, and there was nothing I could do until it passed.

I got there because I told myself that I was all right. That arrogance showed me who was in charge — and it was not I.

The remarkable part about those episodes was that I could feel them ending. It would usually last much of a day, two days on a few occasions.

When I came out of it on that occasion, I sat on the bench with my head in my hands — and an Atlanta police officer standing in front of me.

"Sir, you can't sleep here. You've got to go," he said.

"What time is it?"

"Time for you to go."

I was discombobulated and attempted to get my bearings when the cop grabbed me by my arm and tried to pull me up. I yanked away from him.

"You don't have to touch me," I told him. "I'm getting up. Was just trying to get myself together. I wasn't feeling well."

"Listen, you're about to get arrested for resisting."

Before my life on the streets, I had at least a modicum of respect for law enforcement. But seeing how they had beaten down black men for no reason other than sport, how they bullied and often judged their attitude on class and race, I hardly trusted any of them.

But I did not make an assessment until I had enough to judge. That cop incited me to let out some pent-up anger.

"Don't threaten me with arrest. Nothing happened for you to go there. I'm not resisting. I'm *insisting.* I'm insisting that you look at me as a man and not a black man who is homeless. I have chosen to be homeless. And even if I hadn't, you have no right to put your hands on me. I have done nothing to make you want to use force on me.

"This is why there is a breakdown in the relationship between the police and the citizenry. You want us to respect you, but you respect only your badge. You think that gives you license to shoot us, beat us, intimidate us, threaten us and arrest us for no good cause. I ain't afraid to die. I'm already in pain. I'm not scared and I've been to jail. So, the power you *think* you have over me, you don't."

The officer was taken aback for a second.

"OK, you obviously are an intelligent man. Why don't you go on home? OK? You can't spend the night at the park on a bench."

I had picked up a new — well, not new, but new to me — pair of shoes at the shelter. I needed them because I had worn down the previous pair.

"I'm leaving. I just have to get my shoes out of my bag."

I had taken them off because someone, probably some silly teenager, once had taken off my shoes as I slept and ran with them. They were not expensive, so they had to do it as a prank. They were laughing as they ran off. I was not going to let that happen again.

As I gathered myself and walked past the officer, he stopped me. "Hey, man, look: Between you and me, I understand your issues. I do. But all of us aren't like that. I'm not like that. So, while you don't want us to judge you based on other people, we don't want you judging us on other officers. That's fair, right?"

"Fair enough," I said. And I turned and

walked away.

I found a covered parking lot on Juniper Street and slept there. When I woke up, that depressed state had completely subsided. But I felt melancholy. Nothing fazed me. It was like I was high on acid or something. I had never taken acid, so I wasn't sure about what it felt like to be on it.

But I felt so mellow. I had more energy than when I was younger. On that day, I made my way to Caribou Coffee on Tenth and Piedmont. Wasn't a coffee drinker, but I wanted something that would take the sluggishness off me.

Against the objection of her husband, a woman had given me five dollars the day before. They got into an argument about it before she shut him down. "This is my money, not yours. I can do what I please with it."

And Brenda slipped a twenty in my backpack when I wasn't looking. I would not have known if she hadn't texted me about it.

The coffee worked . . . to a degree. I had not eaten the previous day, so my stomach was empty and all that caffeine went straight to my head. Suddenly, I felt jittery.

Other than being bipolar, I seldom had been sick or even felt badly. But I quickly surmised I needed to put something on my stomach, so I went back into the coffee shop and ordered a breakfast sandwich and a bagel.

After not exactly looking like a homeless person for quite a while, that morning was a relapse in appearance. I was frumpy and smelly. My hair had not been combed. I hadn't brushed my teeth. I hadn't wiped my face.

I felt so out of sorts that I had not thought about those things until I noticed how women backed up when I walked into the coffee shop. And the person at the counter rolled her eyes when I came back in.

"I will make this quick: a breakfast sandwich and bagel," I said. "I'm sorry to interrupt your business like this."

The woman's position softened. "I'm fine. We're fine," she said. "I just want you to be fine."

"I will one day. I promise. And I will come back here to see you."

"Please do," the young lady said with a smile.

The food helped. The uneasiness subsided. I got myself together and made my way back to the park bench. We had another meeting with Dr. Taylor. It was then that I hoped to get the biggest thing that could help me: medication.

I slept on that bench all day — until Brenda came to get me. I sent her a text message to let her know where I was and how I felt. She told me to "stay put."

Within an hour, she was there. I sat up on the bench and she looked down at me.

"What happened?"

"I don't know. Episode, I guess."

"Oh, no. What happened? Are you OK?"

"I'm, you know . . . I'm gonna be OK."

"You're right. But you don't look OK."

She reached in her bag and handed me a bottled water. "Drink this."

I did.

"We have a session in an hour. Do you want to cancel it?"

"No. I'm ready for Dr. Taylor to get me some meds. I can't keep up like this. Forgetting what happened. Dreaming bad dreams. Feeling depressed. Feeling out of control. I need something to change."

"I'm glad to hear you say that. The office is up the street, but you need to clean up."

"I have some more clothes in my bag. I'll change in the bathroom at the pool."

"I'll wait for you here," Brenda said. "You gonna be OK?"

"Yeah. I feel better. Yesterday was rough. I was just depressed about everything. It was so strong. It's part of the disorder. It's happened before. Plenty of times."

When I returned from changing and cleaning myself up — I brushed my teeth and washed my face — Brenda was on the bench, looking the other way. And for the first time, I noticed something about her: She was beautiful.

Maybe it was the way she sat and the way the sunlight hit her face. I was not sure. But she was almost a different person from the one I insulted many months before.

I could see then that she had an attractive face. But she was overweight and so lacking in self-esteem that her shoulders slumped. She was a shell of who she was or who she could be. I could see that in her posture.

"You look really good today," I told her. "Looking like a movie star."

"Ha. That's what losing weight can do."

"No, that's what gaining your sense of self can do. That's what it did."

Brenda nodded her head. "*You* look a lot better. I don't see you for three days and you fall apart. We have to do something about that."

"Yeah, I agree. We need Dr. Taylor's help."

At the session, Dr. Taylor noticed I did not look as comfortable as I had the previous meeting.

"Rodney, you don't seem as upbeat today."

"I need medication, Dr. Taylor."

"OK. What makes you feel that way?"

"I'm not myself. Actually, I don't know who I am often enough. And often enough should be every day."

"And only medication will get him there, right?" Brenda asked.

Dr. Taylor looked over her notes for several seconds before looking up at Rodney. "You said you have taken olanzapine and fluoxetine, which is an antidepressant. Correct?"

I nodded. "Yes."

"From my observation, it feels like that combination is the right combination to keep you consistently where you'd like to be. But, Rodney, you have to take the medicine. Every day.

"At some point, you're going to feel so good that you don't need the dosage or need it as much. You cannot give in to that. You already told me you had stopped taking the meds in the past. I cannot stress enough how important it is to stay consistent. OK?"

"I got it."

"But I have an important question," Brenda said. "This medication has to cost a lot of money when you don't have insurance. How we gonna pay for it?"

I was more moved by Brenda's use of "we" more than I was of her concerns about payment.

Dr. Taylor flipped to an empty page on her notepad and started writing. "You can try NeedyMeds, which helps those who can't afford medicine or healthcare costs. There is also The Medicine Program, which has free services or medicine and many other healthcare needs. The Medicine Program's benefits are subsidized by running Google ads on its site.

"Those are the two best places to start. I know doctors and administrators at both, so if you hit any roadblocks, I probably can help."

"This is exciting," Brenda said.

"There remains the issue of where you're going to live," Dr. Taylor said. "Quite frankly, the medication is going to help you a lot, and you're going to likely see being homeless as something unacceptable."

"I'm already beginning to see it that way," I told her. "But for a while, I feel like that and then I feel differently. Really, I told Brenda, I'm scared."

"That's natural. It's akin to being incarcerated for a time and then attempting to reenter society."

"That's exactly what I told Brenda. I even used a prison analogy."

"That's good. That means you're aware of how you feel, which is a gift because you'd be surprised how many people have an emotion but have no real understanding of it. They are unable to articulate what they feel."

"Dr. Taylor, I just want to make sure something I suggested to Rodney that I thought would help is OK. My idea to help him get comfortable with advancing his life was to do some of the things he did before, like cigars, listening to music, reading books, going to the movies. I thought that could be a way to transition into the life he wants."

"Should I show you my notes for today?" Dr. Taylor said. "That's an excellent idea. It literally was something I had planned to suggest. And the reason why this is such a strong idea is that regenerating a way of life can be traumatic. As a doctor, I wouldn't recommend smoking anything, including cigars. But the life you have lived for two years is drastically opposite of your previous life. In that time, the life you have lived becomes 'normal' to you, and so leaving it, even though you want to, can be a challenge.

"Doing little things that you used to do creates a feeling of familiarity and creates a desire for more. There is a buildup over time that prepares you. Someone coming out of prison does not have a chance for such a transition. It's *You're in this world today. Tomorrow enter a new world.* That's extremely difficult and a major reason we have so much recidivism among former inmates. They just are not prepared for the onslaught of change.

"The other thing I would strongly suggest is that we continue to meet and talk after you make your transition and are taking the meds. It's healthy to talk about what you're feeling. And while the medication will definitely help, PPD and bipolar are best tackled in multiple ways."

She added that it would take up to two weeks before we could get the medication through the options she had given.

We finished the session with me talking about what it felt like to listen to music and smoke a cigar and talk to the young cigar lounge owners.

"I'm excited for you, Rodney. I believe you're on a solid path to a comfortable transition," she said.

"I hope so," I said. "I hope so."

CHAPTER TWENTY-SEVEN:
WAIT. WHAT???
BRENDA

The idea of Rodney getting his life together made me feel better about my life. There was no denying it: Our lives were connected.

After the session with Dr. Taylor, he walked me to my car.

"One thing that really makes me want to get myself together is seeing how you have done it," Rodney said. "It makes me feel good to see where you are from where you were."

"That's because we will forever be linked," I told him. "We're taking these journeys together."

We hugged and he walked off. And for all the wonderful feelings I had about building our friendship, it always pained me to leave him in the evening to God knew what while I went home to my comfortable apartment. It was beyond awkward. It was not right.

I wanted to offer him the couch in my

apartment, but I knew he would not accept it. It was important to me to not insult Rodney as I tried to help him. He was a proud man and he was intent on doing what he had to do his way. I respected that.

Before leaving, though, I gave Rodney a container of roasted chicken, broccoli and sliced tomatoes. "If you don't take this, you're insulting me," I said. "A friend should be able to cook for a friend."

He reluctantly accepted it. "But this is the last time, Brenda," he said. "I appreciate you. You know that. But I don't want you doing more than you need. I will be fine."

I went home that evening and changed into more comfortable clothes and ate a salad with a piece of baked salmon I had bought from Whole Foods.

Nothing was that compelling on television, so I decided to scan Facebook for entertainment before going to bed. I was surprised and glad to get a notification that I had a direct message from Rick, the guy in D.C.

"I apologize for just getting back to you. It's been hectic with work. But I was glad to learn that guy was not your man. I'd like to talk to you and get to know you better. I know this is a strange way to meet someone. And you could be a serial killer, for all I know now. But you'd be the prettiest serial killer I have ever seen."

I wrote back: "This is awkward. You saw my photo on this site and now you want to get to know me? I'm skeptical. Why should I engage you?"

"You shouldn't," he wrote back. "And if you end this back-and-forth now, I would understand."

"Why would you want to get to know me? Don't think I'm some fool you can run game on."

"I could be wrong about you. But what I got from your FB posts and photos is that you're kind, confident and caring. You posted about your sister that she was your beacon of hope. Anyway, through observing your FB page has made me want to see you. If you don't think we should meet for a cup of coffee, I will understand."

He played it the right way. I was willing to take a chance, but only in a public place. Rick had said he was coming to Atlanta the next day. I arranged for us to meet at Live Edge, a new restaurant I read about that opened in Southwest Atlanta.

This time, though, I told Rodney what was about to happen before it happened.

"I'm glad you're smart enough to meet the man in a public place where lots of people will be," he said.

"I don't expect anything to really come of it."

"You may not expect anything, but you hope something comes of it. If not, why bother?"

"Well, I guess that's true. I want to call you after I see him to tell you about it. So please keep your phone on."

My fitness and eating habit changes were put to the test for this meeting of this attractive but mysterious man. One of my favorite dresses was a pale-blue number that gripped my body like Saran Wrap, with a deep V-cut in the front. I could not get into the dress the previous two years.

On that night, I slipped into it with ease, confirmation that I had lost all the weight I had gained. The scale told one story about my weight; how my clothes fit me told the most accurate story. Wearing that dress with ease again made me smile.

So I showed up at Live Edge intentionally about ten minutes late, so I could make an entrance and he could see all of me. If I didn't do that, then I would have been wasting the dress.

I could tell it had the desired impact. Rick stood up as I approached the bar and greeted me with a smile. I smiled back and extended my hand to shake. He ignored it and hugged me.

I smelled his cologne and was lost in it for a second. I knew then with that man, I had to be careful. I was a sucker for pretty white teeth and a good-smelling man.

"You look great. Beautiful dress," he said. "Would you like to get a table?"

"You look nice, too. Very nice. I like sitting at the bar, but tonight, I think we should get a table. It's easier to talk and fewer distractions at a table. And I can look into your eyes to see if you're lying."

He laughed. "You know that goes both ways, don't you?"

I smiled as we walked to the hostess, who seated us. At the table, the conversation flowed without effort.

"So you picked a public place because you don't trust me?" he asked.

"I picked this place because it's black-owned, first and foremost. And, yes, I wasn't gonna meet you in a private place where there would be no one to verify you attacked me before I shot you."

He laughed.

"So what's your full name, Rick? You go by 'Rick The Ruler' on Facebook. And ruler of what?"

"Myself. We have to own who we are and control who we are before we can do anything else. My name is Rick Morris, though."

I nodded my head. The server came over and Rick suggested a bottle of wine. I liked wine but was hardly a connoisseur, so I went with his choice.

"You live in Washington, D.C. You're a handsome man. You seem to be successful. So why are you down here with me? You want me to believe you don't have someone up there calling you her man?"

"You're funny. First, I appreciate the compliments. But I ended a three-year relationship about six weeks ago. So, no one has claims on me."

"Why did you end it?"

"It wasn't going anywhere. Good woman, no doubt. But we, as it turned out, did not have the same ideals about life or how to live it. She was more centered on herself and career. But to be honest — and I still can't believe it — she said she was going to vote for Trump in the upcoming election."

"Oh, my God. Good for you to let her go. How could she justify it?"

"The same way any of his surrogates do — with crazy talk about changing America and we need a businessman to run the country. I'll be honest. It pains me to think about it. I never saw this coming.

"I told her: 'If you wanted to vote for Bush or Daddy Bush or Reagan, I wouldn't understand, but it wouldn't be a deal-breaker. But this guy? It's a deal-breaker. I love you, but I'm sorry. I cannot be involved with someone who supports this . . . this . . . ingrate. I will never be able to look at you the same. He has done nothing but discriminate and preach hate about black people. If you can trust him, I can't trust you.

"We were at her home in Old Town Alexandria, Virginia. I was tired. It was almost three in the morning. I got up, put on my clothes and left."

"Wow. I understand. But do you think you really loved her? You seemed to walk away so easily. There are many couples that have one side Democrat, the other side Republican. They may disagree, but they stay together."

"This is not about political parties. It's about that guy. He's a shit-for-brains narcissist who loves money and hearing himself talk more than anything. I don't even think he wants to be president. But to not see him for what he is — a con man, a white privileged stain — I can't get past that."

Rick impressed me with his position. I felt the same way. Trump was a unique case that shifted the paradigm.

"I could go on and on about that, but I'd rather know more about you. Why don't you have a man?"

"Well, actually, I'm married."

Rick froze. He looked around.

"Well, we shouldn't be here. You told me you didn't have a man. I asked you."

"I don't have a man. I have someone I'm technically still married to, but he has been gone for two years and I haven't heard from him. He just left. His family wouldn't share any information with me. So I'm filing the divorce papers, and I will tell the judge that he has vanished. I'm told that will make it quick and easy."

Our food came. Before we partook, Rick offered to say grace — another bonus point for him.

In the time it took to eat, I envisioned myself traveling with that man, enjoying walks in the park, cooking for him and even making love to him. I was not going to share that with him, but that's how fast romance and a future together can play out in a woman's head.

He probably was sitting across from me thinking about hot sex with me. Meanwhile, I had his life figured out in my mind. The combination of my fantasy and the wine made me flirty.

"So, how do you keep that beard together?" I said, tilting my head, pursing my lips, anything to show I was interested in him.

"Pretty easy. I use this handmade, all-natural pomade called Shwaxx. It's made by a brother who lives here in Atlanta, Kevin Rodgers. I love it. His shop, The Tilted Crown, isn't far from here. And I should have told you earlier that you made a good restaurant choice. I love supporting black business, too."

And a third Brownie point for Rick.

I had not been on a lot of dates in a long time, but that one flowed so effortlessly. I was comfortable with Norman. But Rick had a stronger presence and a self-assuredness that made me feel safe.

"So, how long you in town?"

"Just the weekend. My parents are here. Just came in to see them. Hadn't been home in about eight months."

"You're a good son," I said. "I wish my parents were still alive. And I lost my sister earlier this year. She was in a coma. I used to visit her every day, talk to her. Don't know why I did. She couldn't hear me."

"Well," Rick said, "that may not be true. There are countless studies that indicate those who have come out of a coma said they recall hearing specific things from people.

"In fact, there's this book called *What It Feels Like* and —"

"Wait. I have that book. I mean, I recently bought that book for a friend. How crazy is that that you would bring up that book?"

"I'm talking about the small book put together by *Esquire.*"

"Yes, me, too."

"Wow. You're the first person I know who has heard of the book," he said. "I have not read all the stories, but there's one about 'What It Feels Like To Come Out of a Coma,' and this guy tells the story of being hit by a car as a kid. He was in a coma for several days. When he came out of it, he asked, 'How's Francis?'

"Francis was a kid in the bed next to him in the hospital that he had never met, but died the day before he came out of the coma."

"Wooowww. That's so crazy. OK, I gave mine to a friend, but I need to get one for myself. I saw the subjects the book covers and it's pretty interesting."

At that point, Rick was trippin' me out.

"I think I'd better go home."

He looked puzzled. "Why?"

"This has just been an interesting dinner."

"I hope 'interesting' is code word for fun."

"It has been fun *and* interesting," I reiterated. "I'm just blown away by this book thing."

"I know how you feel. I had something similar happen to me."

"Really? What?"

"A friend of mine went to South Africa and brought me back this wine, Pinotage, which I had never heard of. About a month later, I met this flight attendant. We hit it off and sometime later, she came to visit me. On the way to my house, I told her I had some wine at home.

"She said she only drinks Pinotage from South Africa. She had been there recently. I told her, 'I think that's what I have at home.' She said, 'There's no way you have Pinotage. Most people have never heard of it.'

"Well, we get to my place. She gets comfortable on the couch and I get two wineglasses and the bottle. Didn't say a word. Just opened it and brought it to her. She was like you were just now: stunned. 'How can this be? I can't believe this.' I just smiled because I couldn't believe the only wine she liked was a wine I had but had never heard of. Crazy."

"That *is* crazy. I'm finding you more and more interesting."

"Really, well, this will flip your wig then," Rick said.

What more irony could come forward in one night, I thought. I braced myself.

"That guy in the picture that I asked you about? The picture on Facebook?"

"Yeah, what about him?"

"What's his name?"

My heart rate increased, but I was not sure why.

"His name is Rodney."

"Bridges? Rodney Bridges?"

"Yeah."

"Thought so. Haven't seen him in years. But I know that guy. Thought he was dead."

"You thought he was dead? Why? How do you know him?"

"He's my cousin."

I almost lost my breath. I was conflicted. I was happy to know someone who knew Rodney, but ultimately not sure what to think.

"His cousin. You're right: This is crazy."

"How well do you know him?"

"Well, it's a rare story, I would say. We met outside McDonald's at the very start of summer. We got into sort of a disagreement and then, somehow, came together and became the closest of friends.

"I was going through something and he

obviously was going through something and he —"

"Excuse me, but what do you mean he was going through something?" Rick wanted to know.

"I mean, he was — he is — homeless."

Rick sat back in his seat. He looked down and shook his head. It was obvious he was unaware of Rodney's life.

"Homeless? I can't believe it."

"I'm sorry, but it's true."

Rick sipped on his wine and cleared his throat.

"What do you mean you thought he was dead?" I asked.

"No one has seen or heard from him in years. Not his wife, not his family. No one."

"You don't know?"

"Know what?"

"His wife and kids are dead. They died in a car accident. Rodney was driving."

Horror took over Rick's handsome face. Tears formed in his eyes. "What? When did this happen?"

"I don't know exactly, but Rodney said about two years ago."

Rick looked at me sideways. He grabbed his cloth napkin and wiped his eyes. He had anger in his voice when he said: "You think that was funny?"

I was confused. "Funny? What are you talking about?"

"Why would you say his family is dead?"

"That's what he told me. Wait, you're saying they aren't dead? They're alive?"

"Yeah, they're alive."

"Wait a minute, wait a minute, wait a minute," I said. My head spun. "Please, let's slow this down. You're telling me Rodney did not kill his family in a car accident."

"Brenda, Rodney left home for the airport one morning in 2014 and never came home. Two days later, they found his car badly damaged off of Camp Creek Parkway, near the airport, in a ditch. No one has seen or heard from him since."

"I'm blown away right now. He's been living on the streets of Atlanta since then — *fifteen miles away*. In plain sight. And no one knew this? I can't believe this."

"*You* can't believe it? I cannot believe it, either. When he never called from wherever he was supposed to go, Darlene, his wife, and his kids were panicked. They checked all the hospitals in the area. His story was on the news: *Local man's car is found crashed, but he's missing*. It's been something that really damaged his family."

"You know Rodney has issues, right?

Mental issues. Something called PPD. Bipolar."

"Of course. It didn't really show up that much, but then I wasn't around a lot, so I don't know. But I know he had his challenges."

"I have been going to therapy with Rodney. In his head, he believes he killed his family in this car accident. He told me many times. That's why he ended up on the streets. He said he didn't deserve to live but was afraid to die. Said he didn't deserve to live comfortably after he caused their deaths. So he's lived on the street, mostly sleeping on a park bench or church steps or the Peachtree-Pine shelter during the winter."

Tears flowed down my face. Rick held back his. We waited several seconds to continue. We had to compose ourselves.

"This is a miracle, something that I never would have expected," Rick said. "I thought the guy got killed by some thugs who carjacked him and no one ever found the body. After several months, that's what everyone thought. It was easier to accept than him leaving and not returning."

"How can a man people are looking for live in plain sight, not trying to hide, and not be found?"

"Well, think about it? It happened with kidnapped kids. What's the girl's name who had been kidnapped and was finally found nine months later about fifteen or so miles from her home?"

"Yes, Elizabeth Smart. Her parents even wrote a book called *In Plain Sight.* It was in Utah."

"And the family ripped the police department because she was so close and out in public, but not found," Rick recalled.

I was dazzled. I had one question for Rick: "What do we do now?"

CHAPTER TWENTY-EIGHT: LIFE'S TWISTS AND TURNS RODNEY

Sleeping on the streets felt different when I did not want to be there. Before, in the beginning, I didn't think about it. I just did it. I believed I *had* to do it. And then it pretty quickly became a way of life.

With the idea of trying to make a transition, I found it almost difficult because I finally understood it was not normal. It was not normal for me to punish myself in that way.

Until change happened, though, that's where I was. So I was again in a conflict with my emotions: excited about the potential of leaving the streets, sad to be on them.

But I changed. I became more paranoid about my surroundings. I spent my days working for people. I stood with dozens of men on the corner between the CVS and Starbucks on Ponce de Leon Avenue, where people seeking help with odd jobs, moving furniture, etc., would come to get muscle for a fraction of the cost of hiring a company.

I usually got two jobs a day, either moving someone from one place to another or moving around furniture in a home for some old lady. I didn't mind the work. It gave me something to do, some money, and it killed time.

At that point, it was like watching the big hand on the clock click another space: slow and boring. I did not like having something to look forward to. And I was not sure about what I was looking forward to.

"You should relax," Brenda said. I texted her and she called me during her lunch break. "What's something you can do to help in your transition?"

I had no answer. I had been trying to forget that, so I wouldn't look forward to it. Didn't work.

"I know. Read that book I got you. The stories are short and interesting. Skim through the table of contents and pick three stories and text me what they are. I have a copy of the book, too. We can read the same stories and discuss them when we go walking later."

I wasn't excited about the idea, but I went with it because it was something to occupy my mind. I read the story "What It Feels

Like To Be a Hostage." I skimmed the many stories and stopped there. The word "hostage" resonated with me.

Barry Rosen, who was taken hostage for 443 days spanning 1979 and 1980 in Iran, told the story. It resonated with me because I had felt like a hostage all my time on the streets.

My disease held me hostage. My emotions held me hostage. My pain held me hostage. My sorrow held me hostage. And unlike Mr. Rosen, who was finally released, I was not sure I could ever feel free, no matter how slowly and easily I transitioned back into society.

It made me say "Wow," to read that Mr. Rosen, who had been held mostly in total darkness or blindfolded, said when he finally was released, he "couldn't focus well for weeks" because it was too bright outside. That registered with me because I had envisioned that the light would be too bright on the other side of my transition.

I could relate because as sunny as a day was while on the streets, it always felt gloomy. When I was with Brenda, I had momentary breaks from the dreary nature of my life. I wore those sunglasses Brenda purchased for me, but they were good mostly because no one could see the discomfort in my eyes than for blocking the sun. In my mind, the sun was hot, but not bright.

I refused to read the story "What It Feels Like To Have Multiple Personalities." I didn't need to read it. I had seen it.

The first time startled and scared me. The guy's name was J.C., for James Carlton. J.C. was a muscle-bound man, reserved and nice, smiling all the time, which made me wonder about his state of mind. There was nothing about being homeless that merited a smile. But that's who he was and that's what he did.

Well, one day, a car came to a sliding halt in the crosswalk, and avoided hitting J.C. by about two feet. And that's when it happened. Like clicking a mouse on a computer, he flipped, banging the hood of the car so hard that he dented it while screaming at the same time.

"You trying to kill Zeus? You can't kill me. I'll kill you first. Get this car outta here. You see Zeus, you run the other way."

He turned to the people who were on the street and yelled: "You see what I did to that car? I'll do it to you, too. Don't mess with me."

No one moved. The man in the car knew better than to get out. I prayed he would not. I believed "Zeus" would have killed him. When he finally moved from in front of the car, the man sped off.

That same night, I had gone to the shelter to shower. When I came out, I noticed this woman with a long wig in front of me. "She" turned around and it was J.C. — or "Zeus." I took a step back.

"Honey, is it raining outside now?"

I didn't answer.

"Honey, don't you hear Crystal talking to you? Is it raining outside?"

"Oh, no. No. I don't think so."

"It better not be because I can't get my hair wet. I just got it done."

"Crystal" wore tight jeans and a chiffon shirt that exposed "her" chest and a colorful scarf around "her" neck.

It scared me. I heard from other homeless men at the shelter — homeless men at the shelter loved to talk — about four or five others with multiple personalities. I didn't see those guys act out and I didn't want to see them. Seeing J.C. was enough.

I read the story "What It Feels Like To Have Amnesia" because too often I had been told about something I did, but had no recollection of it. That had to be a form of amnesia.

It wasn't like drinking alcohol. When I was

young and in college, I drank so much at times that a part of the night was lost. Couldn't remember. The episodes when I lost time after being diagnosed bipolar were deeper, stronger.

Like the day I ran from Brenda. Not only did I not recall that, I did not recall any of that day. It was like none of it had happened. But I had walked and talked with her, had eaten with her — and then gone. It was like I had been sleepwalking.

The story in the book was different from mine. The person telling it had a skiing accident and could not remember details of the day. He was rightfully scared, but in less than an hour, he regained his mental coordination.

I shared that with Brenda during our nightly walk. "Well, with medication, you're going to feel better all the time. I'm sure of that."

It was another good night for us. But I sensed something was not quite right with her. "What's wrong? You met a man and don't want to tell me?"

She laughed. "I'm not going down that road again."

That did not answer my question. Brenda chimed in.

"Can I ask you something personal?"

"Don't you always?"

"This one is *really* personal?"

"Go ahead."

"You ever think about sex? I know you had been in so much pain and did not want to think about pleasurable things. But you can't control sexual desires."

I smiled. I had expected that question from her long before then.

"Definitely think about sex. And this might be weird to men, but I only think about it with my wife. And since we're so close — my only friend, you are — I will tell you that I have masturbated more in the last year than I had in my entire life.

"And I'll tell you something I won't tell anyone else. One night, the urge hit me hard, and I was sitting against a building in Midtown. It was late and quiet. No one was around — or so I thought. There was a light rain, sort of misty, so I didn't expect anyone on the streets.

"I'm a pluviophile — a person who loves rain. So, I start doing my thing. I got lost in the moment and closed my eyes. I've got my stuff out, in my hand, and this woman walks by, turns to her left and sees me, uh, holding the goods, so to speak.

"She screamed and ran. I jumped back and hit my head on the wall. She called the police. Within three minutes, they arrived, shining a bright light on my face. I wasn't exposed any more, but they arrested me anyway. It was thrown out of court because there was no proof — her word against mine — and she didn't show up for the hearing. But it was not a good night."

"Oh, my goodness. You've always got a story," Brenda said. "I was thinking about your cousin you said you visited in prison. Did he ever get out? What's his name?"

"Yeah, he got out. Rick. He moved to D.C. and tried to rebuild his life. Didn't want to do it down here, where he wrecked it. Don't know what happened to him, though. Hope he found a way. If he could do it after eight years in prison for drug possession, then maybe I could make it, too."

"That's what I was thinking. Maybe I should try to find him."

"You don't have to do all that. Like you said, there are plenty of stories of people overcoming obstacles. I'll read about them. That's another thing the book did for me: Made me realize how much I miss reading."

"I was also thinking about how your life is going to change," Brenda said. "We can talk about it with Dr. Taylor in three days, but I wanted to know if something really big or exciting happens to you, if the medication will prevent an episode from occurring."

"Big and exciting like what?"

"I don't know. I'm just looking at all the possibilities. I don't want anything to derail this train. And this is a train now, Rodney. It's moving in the right direction."

"You're more excited than me. I'm still kind of just trying to figure it all out, figure what I'm going to do and how I'm going to do it."

"Do you believe in miracles? Do you believe in things that seem impossible?"

"What are you talking about? Do I believe in angels and unicorns and leprechauns? Are you talking mythical stuff? Or do you mean a miracle like falling like ten floors and surviving?"

"I mean all that."

"Do you?"

"I didn't necessarily believe in miracles, but I do now," she said.

"Why now?"

"Every day I learn to open my mind a little bit more, because what we believe are boundaries really are just paper curtains that can be torn down at any moment. And we can keep going beyond that line we thought was the limit."

"You're not the one who has to take the steps," I told Brenda. "It's easy to say what

360

should be done. It's easy to talk about boundaries can be torn down. To keep going sounds great. But when you're in it, when you're scared and not sure of yourself, the boundaries are safe and comfortable. 'Keep going' rings hollow."

Her silence made me feel like she didn't get it. Then she, like always, turned things.

"Remember one thing: Everything you want is just one step outside your comfort zone," she said. "But I apologize — see, an apology can have meaning. I got carried away. I want this so badly for you. I need to slow down and let this take its natural course. I just want you to have the life you want, the ultimate life you want and deserve."

I looked at her with a wry smile. She was not sure what it meant. I could see the guessing game going on in her head through her facial expressions.

"You are right about one thing. There's not only nothing wrong with saying you're sorry, but there is power in it. But don't take this the wrong way: I'm sorry that I was mean to you when we first met, when I said —"

"Trust me, I know what you said. You don't have to repeat it."

"OK. Good. At the same time, while I'm

really sorry, I can't be *completely* sorry because if I hadn't said the mean things to you, you wouldn't have gotten offended and confronted me and you wouldn't be the center of my world now. See what I'm saying?"

"You'll say anything and pull something out of your ass to make yourself sound right," she said.

I burst into laughter like she had not heard.

"Pull something out of my ass? Really? Now that's funny. But, really, I was just trying to make an important point."

"Trust me, I understand. We have no idea how things will turn out. I never would have expected this connection between us. So, I guess I'm actually glad you were mean to me."

CHAPTER TWENTY-NINE: MOVING PIECES AROUND BRENDA

I had so much to do. Rodney's world was about to change, but I had no idea how to make it happen. So I called Dr. Taylor's office and asked for an emergency one-on-one session.

She moved some things around and accommodated me. On my way to her office, I called Rick.

"So, you didn't tell me completely about your past, huh?" I had no interest in playing coy.

"You mean prison? You must have talked to Rodney?"

"I told you: We talk almost every day. Why did you leave that pretty big part out? We did a lot of talking that night."

"I'm not comfortable sharing that part of my life with just anyone. We met, I like you, but I don't know you. So what's the point of telling someone I wasn't sure I would ever see again."

"OK, I understand. It's none of my business. We can get back to that later. We have some serious business to figure out with Rodney."

"Yes, we need to do it fast, too," Rick said. "I spoke to Darlene earlier today. Of course, I didn't tell her Rodney is alive. But I sure wanted to."

"I'm sure you did. I want to be there to see her face when she learns about this. But I'm headed to the therapist we have been seeing to have her help me figure the best way to handle this. I will let you know what she says."

"OK, please do."

"Rick, one more thing: Did you reach out to me because you knew that was Rodney in the picture or because you were interested in me?"

"Both, actually. You popped up as a 'Suggested Friend' and I liked your profile photo. And I saw you were in Atlanta. So I scanned your photos and posts. And there he was. I was pretty sure it was Rodney, but I had to be sure. He looked slightly different with the beard and he has more hair, thicker hair, and skinnier.

"I stared at that photo for at least ten minutes. What convinced me was that expression on his face. We can disguise ourselves — not saying he was trying to do that — but the essence who we are shows in our mannerisms. He always had that same sort of smirk when he took pictures."

Sounded like it was more about Rodney, but I got it. "Would you have emailed me if you didn't think you saw your cousin?"

"I have to be honest and say I'm not sure. I don't troll Facebook to meet women. But the picture with Rodney gave me the opening I needed to message you. And if that was not Rodney in the photo, I still would have been glad to have met you."

I thought to myself: *Good friggin' answer.*

But I said to him: "Things have a funny way of working, someone once said."

"They do, right? Please call me after you talk to the doctor."

I was more anxious than Rick to see Dr. Taylor. When she came out to greet me and lead me into her office, she could see the emotion on my face. But she could not determine if it represented something good or bad.

"How's Rodney?" she said. "How are you?"

"Dr. Taylor, we have a situation," I said. It was the best I could do at that moment. She remained calm. Did not say a word.

"There's only one way to say it: Rodney's

family is not dead."

"Go on," she said. I was waiting for her to say, *Girl, what? Are you kidding me? What the hell?*

"OK, I'm gonna front-load the story. A guy emailed me on Facebook. We eventually met. Had a nice time talking and getting to know each other. Then, late in the date, he asks me about a photo of me and Rodney I had posted. I tell him and he tells me Rodney is his cousin.

"Tells me he has been missing for two years. Left home for the airport one morning and they never heard from him again. Found his car crashed near the airport."

"This is pretty astonishing," Dr. Taylor said, finally. "Have you told Rodney?"

"No. That's why I'm here. I need you to guide me through how to do this. I'm thinking he may have a heart attack or something. Or an episode."

"Thank you for being so thoughtful about this, Brenda. It is a delicate thing. I see in Rodney that he's a passionate person, and that means he's emotional. Before we look ahead, let's look back.

"Something happened that morning that caused him to disappear. With the crash, he could have been trying to kill himself. But something happened, likely at home, to trigger that episode.

"And during the accident, he may have been injured, but he definitely had a dream or illusion that they were killed or more likely, a visual hallucination, which is one type of sensory misperception. Although visual hallucinations are not pathognomonic of a primary psychiatric illness, they are symptomatic in patients with bipolar disorder."

I had a simple response to that.

"What?"

Dr. Taylor broke it down: "Rodney had what's called a visual hallucination, which simply means he saw something that was not there. It does not fit the clinical definition of insane. It's not a psychiatric illness. It's what can happen with bipolar patients.

"With visual hallucinations, there is a disturbance of brain structure, which is psychophysiological. There also is a disturbance of neurotransmitters, which is psychobiochemical. And there is an emergence of the unconscious into consciousness, which is psychodynamic. Given the interplay with all three processes, visual hallucinations occur."

My mind was blown. "Dr. Taylor, first, let me say this: You know your stuff. You make me proud to be a black woman. Secondly,

367

can the medication you prescribed prevent this from happening again?"

"Yes and no," she answered. "Rodney, as I stressed, has to stay on the medication. He cannot miss a day or a dosage, no matter how good he feels. The prescription is an antipsychotic and antidepressant. The two together should keep him balanced. So, whatever happened that morning that precipitated the episode would not trigger the same reaction if he takes his medication. And so, it would, in effect, prevent a visual hallucination."

"OK, I get it. Bottom line: He must stay on point with his meds. Next big thing: How do we tell him he hallucinated his family dying in a car crash? How do we tell his family that he's alive? They thought he was dead when he was living right here, not twenty miles from his home, on the streets."

"Because of his bipolar disorder, he was perfectly fine immersing himself in a new world, even on the streets because he had nowhere else to go. Or that's what he believed. But he was certain he could not go back home. I would guess that he has not talked about a gravesite to visit.

"He might have, through a dream or in his own head, seen or attended their funerals. His brain took over to confirm with him things he was convinced had happened because he saw it in the hallucination."

"This is too much. I feel like I'm in school."

"Just wait until you talk to his family."

We spent the next forty minutes outlining a plan, which was for me to talk to his family and then, bring Rodney into our session. His family was to arrive fifteen minutes after our session started. We would break the news to Rodney if Dr. Taylor believed he was up to receiving it. Then we would bring in his family.

I shared the plan with Rick, who arranged for me to come to Rodney's old home to meet his wife, Darlene, and two daughters, Joy and Diana, who were home from college.

That next day, I made the drive to Southwest Atlanta. Rick greeted me at the door. Immediately, I could tell he positioned me as someone he was dating.

Rodney's family was beautiful. I had already seen them based on his spot-on description.

"Darlene, can we sit in the family room?"

"Sure," she said. "What's going on?"

I observed the photos on the fireplace mantel. There was Rodney — with that same smirk that Rick noticed in my Facebook picture. It made me smile.

"Mom," Joy said, "we're about to go to meet some friends at Medu Bookstore at Greenbriar Mall."

"Trust me," Rick said, "this is important."

I went to my gallery on my phone and found the photo of me and Rodney.

Rick went on: "I met Brenda on Facebook. I wasn't stalking her or anything — I see how you girls are looking at me. But I noticed her photo and clicked on her profile. Then I looked at other photos and one of them stopped me. Brenda, you can take it from there."

"OK, well, thank you for welcoming me into your lovely home," I began. "As Rick said, we met on Facebook and eventually met in person over dinner. During our talk, he asked about one particular photo he had seen on my page.

"He asked me the name of the man in the photo with me. I told him his name was . . . Rodney."

The mood of the room instantly changed.

"Daddy?" Diana asked. "You knew my father?"

This was the moment that had kept me up all the previous night.

"I *know* your father," I said.

"What do you mean, *know*?" Darlene asked.

"Rick told me everyone assumed he was dead after his car was found, that he was carjacked and kidnapped and murdered. That was the only thing that made sense because, otherwise, where was he?

"Well, the photo Rick saw had been taken a few weeks ago."

Darlene put her hand up to her mouth. Joy stood up.

"Are you saying Daddy is alive?" Diana asked.

"Yes. Rodney Bridges is alive."

Without hearing details, Darlene wept. His daughters hugged and cried. I looked up at Rick, through my tears, and he wiped his eyes.

After several seconds, Darlene wanted details. "Well, here's the thing: He's fine. Of course, his bipolar condition has really impacted him because he hasn't been on medication."

"Where has he been for almost two years?" Joy asked.

"On the streets. He's been living as a homeless man on the streets of downtown Atlanta."

"Oh, my God," Darlene said. Rick went over and comforted her.

371

I continued to hopefully end their dismay and pain as quickly as possible.

"But he's OK. I met him in May. We ended up forming a friendship. I was in bad shape. My husband had left me. My sister was sick and eventually died. I was over-weight. I had no self-esteem. Through walking and talking to your husband, your father, I lost weight and found myself. And I also found a new friend."

"So why didn't you try to find us when you met him?" Joy asked.

"I assumed what he told me was real," I said. "I had no reason not to. The therapist said he had a visual hallucination about the accident. It was one hundred percent real to him. So, he told me he had to punish himself because he was driving the car and felt guilty. He said he'd wish he had died and not you all. He's been deeply depressed thinking he had killed his family. He didn't believe he deserved to live comfortably. So he punished himself."

I gave Darlene my phone with the photo and passed it around to her daughters. "I can't believe this. Daddy is alive," Diana said. "So where is he? We need to go see him and bring him home."

"This is the plan that I set up with Dr. Taylor, his therapist."

"He has a therapist?" Darlene asked.

"Yes. I set it up. When I started getting myself together, I wanted him to seek help. He was reluctant, but we have been to several sessions. There has been a breakthrough in that he wants to finally try to move on. But the pain is still there. Seeing you will remove it all.

"But, the doctor said we have to go about it delicately because it's going to be a huge shock to him to see you. He's on medication, and he's promised to not get off of it again. So, the plan is to go to her office this afternoon. I will give you the address in Midtown.

"We have a four o'clock appointment. You all should get there at four-fifteen, so Rodney does not see you. Dr. Taylor will talk to him and assess where his head is and give him the news. He will be excited like you all are, and Dr. Taylor will come to the waiting area and bring you in for the reunion."

"This is a miracle. I'm so stunned," Darlene said. "It's been two years of . . . I don't know how to describe it."

"Hell," Joy said. "Pure hell. But I'm not surprised. I accepted what the police said. But I never believed my daddy was dead. I didn't."

"Me, either," Diana said.

"I didn't either," Darlene added. "I know I told you we had to accept that he was gone because nothing else made sense. But in my heart, I felt he was still with us."

"It's like the girl who had been kidnapped by people who lived right in their neighborhood. Kidnapped for years," Joy said. "And no one noticed her."

"We could have driven right by Dad and not even noticed him because I know I don't make any eye contact with the homeless," Diana said.

"I'm going to leave you all, so you can have your private time to discuss all this," I told them. "My heart is so full right now, knowing your family will be put back together in a few hours. I'm so happy for you and I'm so happy for Rodney. That man loves you all very much."

The daughters, Rick and Darlene hugged me. "I'll walk you to the door," Darlene said.

When we got there, I asked her to step outside.

"I hate to ask this; the doctor was pretty sure something really traumatic happened the morning Rodney had the accident while heading to the airport. Do you know what it was? You remember anything? And Rodney definitely doesn't remember."

Darlene reached back and closed the front door. The joy on her face turned to anguish. She could not look me in the eyes. I knew what that meant.

"You don't have to say," I told her. "It's OK. He doesn't remember. But are you still with that man? Are you in a relationship?"

"It's over. That morning, Rodney — and I'm only telling you this because I haven't told a soul, and it's been eating at me for two years — was excited about a work trip to Chicago. It was a Thursday and the girls had already headed to school.

"I was working from home that day. Around nine-thirty, the doorbell rang. Rodney answered. It was a package for me. He opened it. He opened it because the person had drawn hearts on the box. In it was a bottle of perfume and a note that basically said, 'Wear this the next time we're together.' It was from our accountant. He thought Rod would be gone early as usual. But he had a late-morning flight.

"When he confronted me with it, I was stunned. I had no idea the package was coming. I told him we should talk. He was hurt. I could see it on his face. He knocked over a table. He threw a glass at me. Finally, he got in his car and sped off. I called and called him on his cell phone. He wouldn't answer. The next day, I learned about the car crash.

"I have prayed and prayed for a chance to hug Rod and apologize to him. But I never got that chance."

"Well, it may be hard to believe, but now you do," I said.

CHAPTER THIRTY:
WELCOME TO MY NEW WORLD
RODNEY

"Why are you so happy?" I asked Brenda when I saw her in Dr. Taylor's lobby.

"I'm happy to see you. And look at you. Cut down that beard even more. Look nice. Distinguished."

I had looked at it once in the mirror and kept it moving. But I felt better. My thoughts were more clear and my dreams were so nondescript that I hadn't remembered any of them lately. I had been on the medication for a week and things were on an even keel.

"I'm ready for the next step," I told Dr. Taylor. "I'm ready to look for a job, find a place to live. Maybe I will renew my license and drive Uber and find a room for rent."

"I'm so happy to hear you say that," Brenda said. "Didn't even know you knew about Uber."

"That's great progress," Dr. Taylor said. "This is a monumental day, Rodney. You've grown so much and it's wonderful to see. But I want to talk to you about some things before we talk about a life-changing thing, OK?"

I nodded my head.

"Do you know what visual hallucinations are?"

"I know a hallucination is seeing something that's not there. People who use acid have hallucinations."

"That's right. But you don't use acid, do you?"

"No."

"Right. But you have seen people chasing you, wearing black hats and coats. I think that's what Darlene said you said."

"That's true."

"If she's seen you react to hallucinations in the past several months, others probably have, too. Agree?"

"Yes, but where is this going? I'm not hallucinating now. Am I? Are you really here?"

I laughed and the doctor and Brenda did, too.

"I asked you that because something significant, life-changing happened to you about two years ago, and I'm pretty certain you had a visual hallucination that led you to the streets."

She had me confused. I had no idea where

she was going, so I just kept quiet. But I noticed Brenda slid closer to me.

"What's going on?" I asked.

Dr. Taylor took off her glasses and looked into my eyes. "Rodney, you seem quite in control of your emotions, so I feel comfortable telling you this."

I was scared then. Was I sick? Did I have a brain tumor? That thought didn't make any sense — I hadn't had a CT scan. But that's how jumbled my mind was.

"What? What is it?"

"Rodney," she said, "you did not kill your family."

I literally shook my head, as if to say, "Huh?"

I turned to Brenda, who put her arm around me. "It's true. Your family is alive. You had a . . ."

"Visual hallucination," Dr. Taylor said. "There is a lot of clinical stuff I can and will explain later about it, but —"

"How do you know this, that they are not dead?"

Brenda pulled out her cell phone and handed it to me. It was a photo of her with Darlene, Diana and Joy. I stood up.

"We took that photo today, at your house," Brenda said. I was crying. "I met your family. Everyone is fine and —"

"How did this happen? Where are they?"

I didn't realize I had been crying until I tasted the salt of my tears.

"Short version," Brenda said, "I met this man on Facebook who had seen a picture of you and me. Turned out, he was your cousin, Rick."

"No way. Come on, this is crazy."

"Rick lives in D.C. but he came down here and we went to dinner. He asked about the photo again and I told him your name. He said, 'That's my cousin.' That's how it started. Today, I went to your house in Guilford Forest in Southwest Atlanta."

That was beyond anything I had imagined.

"So, are they mad at me? What do they think? They're OK? How could this happen?"

I thought of the magnitude of what I was told. "Oh, my God."

Brenda looked at Dr. Taylor, who nodded. "Hold on a second," she said as she headed to the door to her waiting area. I looked down because Brenda grabbed my hand.

When I looked up, my daughters came practically running through the door. I believed I was dreaming. They were taller and had longer hair. But it was a beautiful sight to see them.

They practically tackled me in unison.

They were crying. I hugged them like I had never hugged anything before, just in case it was a dream that I tried to clutch it and not let it go.

They were saying, "Daddy, Daddy" and other stuff that I could not make out. I sobbed uncontrollably. It was so remarkable that it felt like a fantasy . . . finally, a *good* dream. Standing a few feet away was Darlene, with her hands covering her mouth and tears streaming down onto her hands. Our eyes met and we were in love again, just like that.

She slowly, tentatively came over and the girls parted so we could embrace. "Rod. Oh, God, my Rodney. I never believed you were dead. I always believed we'd have this moment."

"I wish I could say the same," I said.

"I believed it enough for both of us," Darlene said.

Dr. Taylor passed out a tissue box, but not before pulling out several sheets for herself. Darlene wiped my face, the way she used to when I had sweat covering me from cutting the grass.

Rick came over and we hugged. "You remember the last time we saw each other?" he said. "You visited me and told me to hang in there, that I could make it. Well,

I'm saying that to you now, cousin."

After several minutes of touching and feeling each other to make sure the most remarkable and improbable reunion was real, Dr. Taylor settled us down.

"OK, we should spend these last thirty minutes or so as a family session," she said. "We have to talk about how you all will move forward as a family. This is first of many sessions, I'm sure."

Brenda backed toward the door, wiping her eyes, saying, "OK, I'm going to go. I can honestly say this is one of the happiest days of my life. To see you all so excited to be back together as a family is a blessing. It's amazing. Thank God."

She reached for the doorknob.

"Brenda," I said. "We're about to have a family session."

"I know," she said.

"So why are you leaving?"

She had a confused expression on her face.

Darlene got up and went to her. "What he's saying — what we're all saying — is that you're family now, girl. You ain't getting away that easy. You stuck with us now."

Brenda's eyes seeped tears.

Rick pulled up a chair for her and they embraced. Before she took a seat, I went over and hugged Brenda for a long time.

"Thank you," I said. It was the best I could do. But it was as heartfelt as I could muster. "Thank you."

"Thank *you,*" Brenda responded. She turned to everyone.

"There was a time in my life I had lost pretty much everything, when I thought the world owed me *something.* But this man helped me realize that I owed myself *everything.* He helped me find whatever I had lost. I *guess* I helped Rodney. But I *know* he changed my world by welcoming me into his."

"And here we all are now," I said. "One big happy family."

THE CRAFT

My wife and I live in the heart of Atlanta, between downtown and Midtown. During my semi-regular, two-mile evening walks, I have seen homelessness up close and personal. It is quite disturbing.

Disturbing because it exists. Disturbing because not enough is being done to get 565,000 people shelter. Disturbing because it does not have to be this way.

As an author — and this is my tenth novel — I am keenly aware of my surroundings. I go about my life observing people and places, reactions and behaviors, all with the idea that what I see can spark an idea for a book or add layers to characters or storylines.

Witnessing homelessness in Atlanta, New York, Chicago and my hometown of Washington, D.C., among other cities in the past year — and being troubled by it — charged me to tackle it in a way that, hopefully, provides insight and significant concern that impacts us all. And maybe we will work together to impact change.

Welcome To My World is no one's story. I made it up, but made it as authentic as possible through research and more research. I spoke with homeless people, mostly men, who shared some of their story of how and why they ended up on the streets. I fed the homeless with my Alpha Phi Alpha chapter, Omicron Phi Lambda of metro Atlanta. The stories were heart-breaking . . . and an indictment on the United States. I left each conversation feeling it should not be like it is.

Ultimately, this is a story of humanity, which surely is lacking in how the government and the public treat the homeless. Many of us are afraid of the homeless, embarrassed by them or are disinterested in having any contact with them.

It was not comfortable for me to address these men, to delve into their troubles. But it was hardly what I expected. They were, overall, welcoming because I cared enough to want to hear from them. They were angry and scared and compassionate and hopeful and disenchanted and troubled.

Drug and alcohol abuse could be easily detected. Mental illness was rampant, derived from an inherent condition or from the stress of having endured war and seeing unfathomable pain and death.

On the other side, depression among African-American women is more common than most might think. Depression comes in many levels, and often it is taken on not by therapy, but by eating. And eating causes weight gain. And that causes one to fall into the doldrums.

Pitting a mentally challenged homeless man opposite a depressed woman who eats to feel comforted felt like a juicy starting point to not only tackle two national concerns, but to show the potential for good that can come when we stretch ourselves and welcome new people into our world.

Of course, we cannot just invite anyone in. But it might be OK to at least give consideration to being more welcoming. That is the underlying theme to this story: You never know how your words or actions can change someone's life.

— CURTIS BUNN

ABOUT THE AUTHOR

Curtis Bunn is the former *Essence* No. 1 best-selling author of ten novels, including *The Secret Lives of Cheating Wives, Seize the Day, The Old Man in the Club* and *Baggage Check,* among others. The Washington, D.C. native also is founder of the National Book Club Conference. Find Curtis on Facebook, Instagram, Twitter and LinkedIn as @curtisbunn or at *www.curtisbunn.com.*